ECLIPSING THE FERAL
Through the Glass

By R.W.Wilson

Copyright © 2025 R.W. Wilson
All rights reserved. No part of this book may be reproduced, distributed, or transmitted in any form or by any means, including photocopying, recording, or other electronic or mechanical methods, without the prior written permission of the author, except in the case of brief quotations used in critical reviews or certain other noncommercial purposes permitted by copyright law.

Disclaimer:

This is a work of fiction. All names, characters, places, and incidents are products of the author's imagination or are used fictitiously. Any resemblance to actual persons, living or deceased, or real events is purely coincidental.

Acknowledgments and Creative Contributions:

I only used GPT. Special thanks to OpenAI's ChatGPT for serving as a ghostwriter, providing invaluable assistance in brainstorming, structuring, and crafting dialogue, descriptions, and other narrative elements throughout the writing process. Additionally, ChatGPT contributed to generating custom images that enhanced the visual storytelling.

First Edition: 2024
Published by R.W. Wilson

TABLET OF CONTENTS

Chapter 1 1
Chapter 2 13
Chapter 3 22
Chapter 4 28
Chapter 5 37
Chapter 6 51
Chapter 7 68
Chapter 8 82
Chapter 9 90
Chapter 10 100
Chapter 11 115
Chapter 12 122
Chapter 13 135
Chapter 14 150
Chapter 15 160
Chapter 16 181
Chapter 17 192
Chapter 18 204
Chapter 19 220
Chapter 20 233
Chapter 21 245
Chapter 22 258
Chapter 23 270
Chapter 24 281
Chapter 25 291
Chapter 26 300
Chapter 27 311

CHAPTER 1

Rick snapped the lighter open with a practiced flick, the small flame casting fleeting shadows across his face as it caught the cigarette dangling from his lips. He took a slow, deep drag, the sharp bite of smoke mingling with the faint, lingering mustiness of the truck's cab. Outside, the rain pattered relentlessly against the windshield, turning the dark stretch of road ahead into a hazy blur of shimmering light and shadow.

The radio crackled to life, static ebbing and flowing as he twisted the knob, searching for a clear station.

"...another feral sighting reported just outside the city limits. Authorities are urging residents to stay vigilant—"

Rick switched the dial, his brow furrowing as he took another drag from his cigarette.

"...a family narrowly escaped what officials are calling an unusually aggressive attack. Witnesses described the feral as—"

The next station was clearer, the voice clipped and professional.

"...two fatalities confirmed in last night's incident. Spearhead agents arrived on scene shortly after the—"

Rick turned the knob again, the cigarette glowing faintly in the corner of his mouth as the static shifted to an older, scratchier channel.

"...some residents claim ferals are becoming bolder, but experts say there's no evidence to support this trend. More after the break—"

He snorted softly, shaking his head. The reporter's calm dismissal didn't match what he saw on the job day after day.

One more twist of the dial brought a burst of static, followed by a frantic voice.

"...we heard the glass shatter, and then it was chaos. It just—"

The words cut out, replaced by an old rock song mid-chorus. Rick let it play for a moment, the familiar tune doing little to ease the knot in his chest.

He finally turned the dial down, silencing the radio altogether. The cab settled into quiet again, save for the soft hum of the engine and the steady rhythm of rain against the glass. He exhaled a plume of smoke, the faint glow of the dashboard light catching the edges of his expression. He didn't need to hear the rest of the reports. He already knew how they ended. Blood, fear, chaos—it was always the same. The pattern never changed.

Rick's eyes flicked to the clock on the dashboard—4:12 AM. Most people were still curled up in their beds, blissfully unaware of the things that prowled the edges of the night. But Rick had never been *most people*. His job didn't come with a clock-out time.

Through the rain-smeared windshield, Spearhead's lab emerged from the gloom, its sharp, angular silhouette looming against the backdrop of fog and drizzle. The outer security lights pulsed faintly, their glow struggling to cut through the mist as his truck rolled into the lot, tires hissing through shallow puddles.

He parked, killed the engine, and sat in the sudden silence for a moment. The faint glow of his cigarette punctuated the darkness as he took another drag, steeling himself for what waited inside.

"Teenager, they said," Rick muttered to himself, snuffing out the cigarette in the ashtray. The feral had been brought in late last night, right before his shift ended. He hadn't even seen it yet.

Swinging the truck door open, Rick pulled his coat tight against the rain and jogged toward the lab entrance. The scanner by the door blinked red until he swiped his badge, the sound of the lock disengaging sharp against the backdrop of the storm.

Inside, the familiar hum of fluorescent lights greeted him. The air was sterile, with just a hint of antiseptic. The hallways were quiet, save for the occasional murmur of security staff. He nodded to one of the guards stationed near the observation wing, who gave him a curt nod in return.

"She's in holding room three," the guard said, glancing at his clipboard. "Tranquilized, but... well, you'll see."

Rick sighed, the weight of the task settling onto his shoulders. He pushed through the double doors and down the sterile corridor toward holding. Each step echoed faintly, the sound growing louder as he neared the reinforced glass window of room three.

The feral was curled in the corner, half-hidden in the shadows. Her lanky frame hinted at recent growth, her movements sluggish yet restless, like a caged animal waiting to strike. Her eyes glinted faintly in the low light, unblinking as they fixed on him.

Rick stared for a moment, the familiar tension building in his chest. Another one to try to reach, to fix. But deep down, he already knew how this would end. It always did.

Still, he placed his hand on the scanner by the door, the lock disengaging with a metallic click. "Alright," he muttered under his breath as he stepped inside. The room was cold, sterile, and silent except for the faint hum of the overhead lights.

Rick rolled a nearby wheeled chair toward the center of the room and sat down, the soft creak of the casters breaking the stillness. He leaned forward slightly, resting his arms on his knees as his eyes adjusted to the faint glow of the observation light.

The girl was huddled in the corner, her lanky frame covered in scratches and bite marks. Some wounds had scabbed over, while others were fresher, red against her pale, battered skin. They were the unmistakable signs of a feral accustomed to survival—fights for territory, food, or just to stay alive.

Her eyes followed his every move, unblinking and sharp. She didn't growl or hiss, just watched, her chest rising and falling in slow, steady breaths. The tension in her body was subtle but unmistakable, like a spring coiled too tightly.

Behind him, the door hissed open, and an assistant stepped inside, clipboard in hand. "Morning, Rick," the young man said, his voice low. He glanced at the feral briefly before focusing on his notes. "She came in around two this morning. Patrol picked her up about five miles outside Sector 6. Gave them a bit of trouble, but nothing they couldn't handle."

Rick grunted in acknowledgment, not taking his eyes off the girl. "Got a name for her?"

The assistant shook his head. "Nothing. Just a feral with no tags, no records, nothing."

"Figures." Rick shifted in his seat, rolling a little closer. The girl's muscles tensed slightly, but she didn't move.

The assistant continued, flipping a page on his clipboard. "Age estimate: late teens, probably around sixteen or seventeen.

Female. Weight's on the lower side—probably malnourished. Height, five-six. A few old fractures that healed on their own. Bloodwork's pending, but vitals are stable. No immediate infections."

Rick nodded absently, his gaze tracing the scars on her arms. "And the scratches? The bites?"

"From other ferals, most likely. Her behavior matches up with pack instincts—if she was in a group, she didn't get along well with them." The assistant glanced at Rick, hesitating before adding, "We're marking her as a mid-level risk. She hasn't acted out since arriving, but... you know how it goes."

Rick sighed, rubbing the back of his neck. "Yeah. I know how it goes."

He leaned back in the chair, folding his arms as he continued to observe her. The feral still hadn't moved, but her eyes betrayed a constant, calculating awareness. She was waiting for something—an opening, a threat, a reason to lash out. Rick had seen that look a hundred times before.

"Alright," Rick said finally, standing up. "Let's start simple. Get her records in order, see if we can get her to eat something. I'll take it from here."

The assistant nodded, scribbling a note on his clipboard before heading for the door. "Good luck," he said over his shoulder. "You're gonna need it."

Rick chuckled dryly, his eyes never leaving the feral. "Yeah, I usually do."

The door hissed shut behind him, sealing Rick inside the room with the girl. The faint echo lingered for a moment before fading into silence. He dragged the chair a little closer, the legs scraping softly against the floor, his movements deliberate and unhurried.

"Alright, kid," he muttered under his breath, his voice low and steady. "Let's see what we can do."

Minutes later, the assistant returned, balancing a small tray that held a piece of raw meat and a blood bag. The instant the scent hit the stale air, the girl's head snapped up like a spring wound too tight. Her entire body tensed, muscles coiled beneath her pale skin as her glowing eyes locked onto the tray. A low, guttural growl vibrated from her chest, primal and menacing, as she shifted her weight, every movement sharp and animalistic—ready to strike.

Rick didn't flinch. He stayed where he was, leaning back slightly in the chair with an unsettling calm that seemed almost deliberate. His eyes stayed fixed on her, cool and unreadable, as if he were observing a storm from behind thick glass.

"Yeah," he murmured, his tone just as steady. "Figured that'd get your attention."

The girl lunged forward, stopping just short of the invisible boundary she seemed to sense. Her hands curled into claws, and her growling grew louder, her hunger overriding any other instinct. The assistant hesitated, glancing nervously at Rick.

"She's a feisty one," the assistant said, his voice wavering slightly.

Rick smirked faintly, his eyes never leaving the girl. "They always are."

Rick took the tray from the assistant, his movements slow and deliberate. The girl's growling deepened, her eyes narrowing as she tracked every motion. He knelt slightly, lowering himself to her level while keeping a careful distance, holding the tray in front of him.

"Easy," he muttered under his breath, though he knew the words were meaningless to her. She wouldn't understand—not yet. Ferals didn't respond to language; they responded to intent.

He placed the tray on the floor between them and slid it toward her, keeping his body language neutral, non-threatening. She flinched at the sound of the metal tray scraping against the floor, her sharp eyes flicking between Rick and the food.

"Go on," he said softly, gesturing toward the food with an open palm. He stayed still, his other hand resting loosely on his knee, showing no signs of aggression.

The girl hesitated, her hunger battling with her instincts. She edged forward cautiously, her movements quick and jerky, like a cornered predator. When she reached the tray, she lunged for the meat with both hands, her claws digging into the raw flesh.

Rick raised a hand sharply, palm outward, and made a low, deliberate sound—a soft hum meant to catch her attention. The girl froze, her grip on the meat tightening as her eyes darted to him.

He moved his hand slowly, gesturing toward her claws, then mimicked a gentler motion by pantomiming holding something delicately. "Gentle," he said, his tone even and calm.

She snarled, her teeth bared in defiance, but he didn't back down. Instead, he repeated the motion, exaggerating it this time —open hands, a careful grip, then setting the invisible object down softly. He waited, his eyes steady on hers, willing her to understand.

After a long, tense moment, she lowered the meat slightly, her movements less frantic. It wasn't perfect—far from it—but it was progress.

Rick leaned back, giving her space as she tore into the food with slightly more control. "Good enough for now," he muttered, glancing toward the observation window where the assistant was watching. "It's not about words. It's about showing them what you want."

The assistant raised an eyebrow, scribbling notes on his clipboard, but Rick didn't care. His focus remained on the girl, who had already devoured half the meat.

Rick knelt down again, tray in hand, his posture calm and unthreatening. He carefully held the blood bag in one hand and the piece of meat in the other, his motions slow enough for the girl to track every detail.

"Alright," he murmured softly, keeping his voice low and even. "Let's try this again."

She crouched, her body tense like a spring ready to snap, her gaze fixed on the food. The hunger was evident, overpowering her caution, but Rick didn't flinch. He'd seen that desperation countless times before, and reacting too quickly now would only send the wrong message.

Holding the meat out first, Rick kept it steady, just out of her reach. As expected, she lunged forward, claws outstretched, her movements sharp and frantic. He pulled the meat back slightly, tilting his head and narrowing his eyes in a deliberate show of disapproval.

"Uh-uh," he said firmly but gently. He raised his free hand, palm out, making a halting gesture. Then, exaggerating his movements, he mimicked a slower reach with his hand, pretending to grasp the air carefully.

The girl froze, her growl deepening. Her eyes darted between his hand and the food, clearly confused but hesitating. He repeated the gesture, this time holding the meat out a little closer, his posture calm and patient.

When she darted forward again, he pulled it back once more,

his expression neutral but unyielding. "Slow," he said, the word not for her understanding but to reinforce his tone. He demonstrated the motion again, his hand open and gentle.

This time, her approach was marginally slower, her claws still extended but less frantic. She didn't grab it right away, her head tilting as if testing what he wanted. Rick allowed her to take it when her movements softened, though her grip was still firm, her sharp claws grazing his glove.

"Good," he muttered, leaning back slightly to give her space. She retreated immediately, clutching the meat close as she tore into it. It wasn't perfect, but it was a start.

Rick watched silently, his hand resting on his knee, observing her every move. He didn't rush her, didn't break the moment. He just let her eat. The blood bag remained on the tray for now; one step at a time was all he could ask for.

Behind the observation glass, the assistant leaned closer, his eyebrows raised. "She's actually... responding," the man muttered, half to himself, jotting down notes on his clipboard.

Rick smirked faintly but didn't take his eyes off the girl. "It's not about force," he said quietly, more for himself than anyone else. "It's about showing them what to do... and hoping they figure out the rest."

When the last shred of meat was gone, the girl's demeanor shifted. Her eyes darted to the tray, then to Rick, and back again. The hunger hadn't been satisfied—it never was, not with ferals. A low, guttural growl rumbled from her throat, growing louder with each passing second, a simmering warning on the edge of eruption.

Her attention snapped to the glass separating the room from the observation area. Rising to her full height, she moved cautiously at first, testing the boundary. Then, with a sudden burst of aggression, she slammed her hand against the glass, the force of it making the assistant flinch. The sharp, jarring sound echoed through the small room.

The growl evolved into a piercing screech as she clawed at the glass, her demands unmistakable. She wanted more, and she was going to make sure everyone in the room knew it.

Rick remained in his chair, utterly unfazed. He leaned back slightly, crossing his arms over his chest, his calm, unblinking gaze fixed on the girl. When her predatory stare turned back to him, frustration flickered in her sharp, glowing eyes, but Rick didn't so much as flinch.

"She's got a temper," the assistant murmured from the other side of the glass, his voice laced with a mix of fascination and unease.

"Most of them do," Rick replied evenly, never breaking eye contact.

The room held its breath as Rick rose to his feet, slow and deliberate. The soft scrape of the chair rolling back punctuated the silence, and the girl froze mid-swipe, her narrowed eyes following his every move with predatory precision. Without a word, Rick walked to the tray, his motions steady and measured, every step designed to hold her attention without provoking her further.

Rick gave her a measured look, his expression as steady as his tone. "You got what you wanted on your terms this time," he said quietly, knowing full well she wouldn't understand the words. "Now you'll wait."

The girl snarled, her frustration boiling over, but Rick didn't flinch. He turned his back on her without hesitation and walked to the door. The lock disengaged with a sharp click, and he stepped through, leaving her alone in the room.

"She'll figure it out," he said to the assistant, placing the tray on the counter. "They always do."

The assistant gave him a skeptical glance but didn't argue. Rick had dealt with more ferals than anyone else in Spearhead, and he always operated on his own terms—just like the ferals did.

CHAPTER 2

A few hours later, the situation had only deteriorated. The girl's aggression had grown more erratic, her frustration boiling over into a frenzied storm. She clawed at the glass relentlessly, the screeching sound grating like nails on a chalkboard. Deep gouges scarred the surface—jagged lines that caught the flickering overhead light, glinting like fractures in steel.

The assistant winced with every rake of her claws against the reinforced barrier, the sound reverberating through the observation room like a ghostly shriek. "She's been at it for over an hour," he muttered, his voice low and uneasy as he jotted hurried notes onto his clipboard. "She hasn't stopped once. She's —"

A thunderous *thud* cut him off. The girl hurled herself against the glass with a force that rattled the nearby equipment, her teeth gnashing audibly as she lunged for the lock mechanism. Her jaws clamped down hard, a sharp *clink* ringing out as she tested the metal with relentless precision.

The assistant paled, his grip tightening on the clipboard. Her low, guttural growls had deepened into something more—something raw and primal that sent a cold shiver down his spine.

Rick stormed into the observation room, his boots striking the floor with purpose. His expression was grim, his patience clearly worn thin.

"What the hell is she doing now?" he asked, his voice low but sharp, his eyes narrowing at the display on the console.

The assistant glanced up, visibly nervous. "Trying to chew through the lock," he said, gesturing at the monitor. "She hasn't stopped since she started. We thought she'd wear herself out, but—"

"She won't," Rick interrupted, his tone flat. He straightened, his jaw tightening as he watched the girl's frantic movements through the glass. Her desperation was palpable, her snarls echoing in the small room like the growl of a cornered animal.

Rick exhaled through his nose, his frustration tempered by experience. "You can't be soft with them when they get like this," he muttered, rolling his sleeves up. "Not when they're this far gone."

He strode toward the door, his movements quick and deliberate. The assistant took a cautious step back, his fingers tightening around the clipboard. "You're going in there?"

Rick didn't bother responding. He hit the button to unlock the door, the sharp metallic *click* silencing the room momentarily. Inside, the girl froze mid-swipe, her body coiled and tense. Her head snapped toward him, her wide eyes glowing faintly under the sterile light.

Her growl deepened, low and guttural, as Rick stepped into the room. She didn't lunge—yet—but every muscle in her body screamed readiness, waiting for the moment to strike.

Rick's gaze locked on hers, unwavering. He closed the door behind him with a loud *clang*, the sound echoing in the small space. "Alright," he said evenly, his voice cutting through the tension. "You want to fight? Fine. But you'll do it on my terms."

She snarled, pacing in tight, jerky circles like a predator sizing up its prey. Rick stayed still, his arms loose at his sides, his posture deliberately relaxed. He knew better than to react too quickly—ferals thrived on panic, and he wasn't about to give her the satisfaction.

The girl lunged suddenly, her claws outstretched, aiming straight for his face. Rick sidestepped with practiced ease, his boots scraping against the floor as he pivoted. She hit the wall behind him, rebounding with a snarl, her movements wild but calculated.

"Not bad," Rick muttered under his breath, watching her closely. "But you're not the first."

He took a step forward, forcing her to shift her weight and back up slightly. The feral's growls grew louder, her frustration bubbling over as she swiped at him again, missing by inches. Rick moved deliberately, keeping his steps slow and controlled, making her work for every inch of ground.

"You're not in charge here," he said firmly, his tone calm but commanding. He raised his hand, palm out, and took another step forward. "You want to act like that? Fine. But you'll learn."

The girl hesitated, her body trembling with barely contained energy. She snarled again, baring her teeth, but didn't lunge this time. Her eyes darted between Rick and the door, calculating her options.

Rick kept his gaze steady, his expression unyielding. "Good," he said softly. "You're starting to think. That's better than clawing at glass."

She growled again, softer this time, though her claws remained out. Rick took another step closer, closing the distance between them. When she didn't lunge, he reached into his pocket and pulled out a small piece of dried meat, holding it up just enough for her to see.

Her eyes locked onto it immediately, her nostrils flaring as the scent hit her. Rick crouched slightly, keeping his movements slow and deliberate as he placed the meat on the floor between them.

"There," he said, standing back up. "It's yours. But you'll take it the right way."

The girl hesitated, her growl fading into a low rumble as she eyed the meat. Her gaze flicked back to Rick, watching him warily as she edged closer. Her movements were cautious, her body low to the ground as she reached for the food.

When her claws scraped against the floor, Rick raised a hand sharply, stopping her. She froze, her eyes narrowing.

"Gentle," he said firmly, demonstrating the motion with his hand. He picked up the piece of meat and placed it down again, this time moving slower, more precise. "Like this. Gentle."

She growled softly, but her movements slowed. Her claws retracted slightly as she reached for the food again, this time grasping it with less force.

Rick nodded faintly, stepping back as she devoured the meat. It wasn't perfect—far from it—but it was enough.

"You'll learn," he said quietly, his voice low enough that only he could hear. "One way or another, you'll learn."

Rick stepped out of the glass room, letting the door seal shut behind him with a sharp hiss. He rolled his sleeves back down, the practice so casual it looked almost routine. The assistant stood nearby, clutching his clipboard like it was a lifeline. His posture was stiff, his gaze darting nervously between Rick and the feral girl, who was still pacing inside the room, her claws occasionally scraping against the glass.

Rick leaned against the counter, crossing his arms over his chest as he regarded the younger man. "You can't be nice all the time," he said, breaking the tense silence. He nodded toward the feral, her glowing eyes fixed on the door he'd just exited. "If they think you're weak, they'll take advantage of that. Every time."

The assistant shifted uncomfortably, his grip on the clipboard tightening. "I... yeah, I get that," he said, though his voice lacked confidence. "It's just... I don't know. She's young, right? Feels wrong being that harsh with her."

Rick raised an eyebrow, his smirk faint and dry. "That wasn't harsh," he said simply, his tone carrying just a hint of amusement. "That was measured. Harsh would've been me pinning her to the ground the second she started clawing at the glass."

The assistant blinked, startled by the bluntness of Rick's words. "You're joking... right?"

Rick's smirk faded, his expression hardening. "Do I look like I'm joking?" He let the words hang in the air for a moment before continuing. "You're new, so I'll cut you some slack, but let me be clear: this isn't about being cruel. It's about control. You don't show control, and they'll walk all over you—or worse."

The assistant hesitated, his eyes darting to the girl in the observation room. She was still pacing, her movements sharp and agitated, her claws occasionally swiping at the glass with audible screeches. "I just... I guess I didn't expect it to be this intense," he admitted, his voice quieter now. "This is only my first week."

"That much is obvious," Rick said, his tone flat but not unkind. He pushed off the counter with deliberate ease, his movements unhurried, like a predator that didn't need to prove itself. Straightening to his full height, he gestured toward the girl in the glass enclosure. Her pacing halted as his gaze settled on her, her glowing eyes narrowing as though daring him to move closer.

"See that?" he said, his voice low but steady. "Listen, ferals don't think like we do." He tilted his head slightly as the girl let out a guttural growl, claws scraping faintly against the reinforced glass. Rick didn't flinch, didn't even blink, his calm expression almost daring her to keep trying. "They don't care about rules, politeness, or decency."

The assistant fidgeted near the clipboard, his grip tightening every time the girl shifted abruptly. She swiped at the glass again, a sharp screech reverberating through the room, but Rick remained still. He glanced back toward the assistant briefly, his mouth curling into something between amusement and warning.

"They care about survival," Rick continued, his voice cutting through the tension like a knife. "Everything they do—every growl, every swipe, every damn glare—is a test." He gestured lightly, his movements controlled, as if showing the assistant a lesson etched into muscle memory. "They're testing *you*. Testing the room. Testing the limits of what they can get away with."

Another thud rattled the glass as the girl lunged suddenly, her sharp teeth bared in frustration. The assistant flinched, a muffled curse escaping his lips, but Rick barely glanced at her. Instead, he stood upright, hands at his sides, calm as ever.

"You let them think they're in charge," Rick said, his tone dropping just slightly, an edge creeping into his words. "Even for a second..." He let the silence stretch, his meaning hanging heavy in the air. "And you've already lost."

The assistant swallowed hard, glancing at the feral again. Her pacing had slowed slightly, but her eyes were still locked on the door, her growls a low, constant hum. "So... what, you just... stand your ground? Every time?"

"Every time," Rick confirmed. "It's not about being aggressive; it's about being in control. They need to know where the boundaries are, and they need to know you're the one setting them."

"But isn't that risky?" the assistant asked, his brows knitting together. "What if they don't back down?"

Rick shrugged, his expression unreadable. "Then you hold the line until they do. Ferals are instinct-driven, sure, but they're not stupid. They don't waste energy on fights they know they can't win. Eventually, they figure out who's in charge."

The assistant hesitated again, his grip on the clipboard loosening slightly. "And if they don't?"

"They will," Rick said firmly. "If they don't, it's because you didn't hold firm. This isn't a job for people who second-guess themselves."

The assistant nodded slowly, though his uncertainty was still evident in the furrow of his brow. "I guess... I guess I've just got a lot to learn."

Rick snorted softly, a hint of a smirk returning to his lips. "Yeah, you do. But you'll get there—assuming you don't piss yourself the next time one of them snarls at you."

The assistant flushed, looking away as he muttered something under his breath. Rick chuckled, shaking his head. "Relax, kid. It's a lot, I know. But if you're going to stick around, you've got to toughen up. Ferals don't respect fear, and they sure as hell don't respect hesitation. They respect strength, consistency, and control. Show them that, and you'll do fine."

The assistant glanced back at the girl, who had finally stopped pacing. She sat near the far wall, her breathing heavy but slowing, her growls fading into silence. "She's... calming down," he said, almost surprised.

Rick nodded, his gaze steady. "Told you. She's testing the boundaries. She pushed, she didn't get what she wanted, and now she's reevaluating. That's how they work."

The assistant frowned slightly, tilting his head. "So... what happens now? Do we just leave her in there?"

"For now," Rick said simply. "She'll learn there's no point in fighting what she can't win against. When she's ready, we'll take the next step. It's all about conditioning—teaching them to respond the way we want them to."

The assistant scribbled a note on his clipboard, his expression thoughtful. "And... you've done this before? Like, a lot?"

Rick chuckled dryly, turning to lean against the counter again. "More times than I can count. Some take longer than others, but the principle is always the same. You stay calm, you stay firm, and you don't let them dictate the terms."

The assistant nodded slowly, his gaze still on the feral. "I guess it makes sense... I just didn't think it'd be this... intense."

Rick smirked faintly. "You're not wrong. It's intense. But it's also necessary. These aren't house pets we're dealing with—they're ferals. You want to help them? You've got to prove you're worth respecting first."

The assistant didn't respond immediately, his pen tapping against the edge of his clipboard. Finally, he nodded again, his posture relaxing slightly. "Alright," he said quietly. "I'll do better next time."

Rick clapped him on the shoulder, his smirk softening into something almost encouraging. "Good. You'll get there, kid. Just don't flinch every time they growl, and you'll be fine."

With that, Rick straightened and turned toward the hallway, his boots echoing faintly as he walked away. The assistant stayed behind, glancing once more at the feral girl through the glass. She was quiet now, her eyes half-closed as she rested against the wall, her earlier aggression replaced by a wary stillness.

The assistant exhaled slowly, muttering under his breath as he jotted down another note. "Guess I've got a long way to go."

CHAPTER 3

Later that day, the assistant stood outside the glass room, tray in hand, his palms slick with sweat despite the cool air of the observation wing. On the tray was the same basic offering—a blood bag and a piece of raw meat—meant to keep the feral satiated enough to avoid further incidents. He swallowed hard, his grip tightening on the edges of the tray as he glanced through the glass at the girl.

She was sitting in the far corner, her body hunched and still, but her eyes told a different story. They glowed faintly in the dim light, locked on him with an intensity that sent a chill down his spine. Her movements were subtle, but the tension in her coiled frame was unmistakable. She was waiting.

"She knows I'm scared," he muttered under his breath, though no one was there to hear him. He took a deep breath, willing himself to calm down. "You can do this. It's just… just feeding her. That's all."

The assistant looked down at the tray, then back at the girl. She hadn't moved an inch, but her piercing gaze hadn't wavered either. He fumbled with the door controls, his hand shaking slightly as he swiped his badge. The lock disengaged with a soft *click*, and he stepped inside, his shoes scuffing against the tile floor.

The girl's head tilted ever so slightly, her sharp eyes tracking his every move. She didn't growl or hiss, but the weight of her presence was suffocating. The assistant swallowed again, trying to ignore the way his heart pounded in his chest.

"Alright," he said quietly, his voice shaking. "Here you go. Just... take it easy, okay?"

He set the tray on the floor and took a small step back, his movements hesitant and unsure. The girl didn't lunge immediately, but the way her muscles tensed was a clear warning. She was waiting for something—for him to make a mistake.

He tried to mimic what he'd seen Rick do earlier, holding his hands up slightly, palms out, in what he hoped was a non-threatening gesture. "See? It's all yours," he said, forcing a nervous smile.

The girl's head lowered slightly, her posture shifting as her claws tapped against the floor. She took one slow step forward, then another, her eyes never leaving him. Her growl started low, barely audible, but it sent a shiver down his spine.

The assistant's breathing quickened. He took another step back, his heel catching slightly on the tile. The tray rattled faintly on the floor, and that was all it took.

The girl lunged.

Her claws scraped against the tray as she grabbed the meat, but she didn't stop there. Her snarl deepened as she snapped her head toward the assistant, baring her teeth in a warning that was anything but subtle. She wasn't just taking the food—she was taking control.

The assistant stumbled backward, his clipboard clattering to the floor as he raised his hands defensively. "Whoa, hey! Calm down!" he stammered, his voice rising with panic.

The girl advanced, her growl escalating into a full-blown snarl. Her claws scraped against the floor as she closed the distance, her movements sharp and deliberate. She wasn't going for the tray anymore—she was going for him.

Before he could react, the door swung open, and Rick strode in with the force of a storm. His boots struck the floor with purpose, the sound sharp and commanding.

"Enough!" Rick's voice cut through the tension like a knife, his tone firm and unyielding.

The girl froze mid-step, her head snapping toward Rick. Her growls didn't stop, but her movements halted, her glowing eyes narrowing as she assessed him.

Rick didn't slow down. He stepped between the assistant and the girl, his posture tall and steady, his gaze locked on hers. "You're not in charge here," he said, his voice low and deliberate. "I am. And you'll remember that."

The girl snarled again, louder this time—a sound that vibrated through the room like a warning shot. Rick didn't flinch. He held her gaze, steady and unblinking, every muscle in his body radiating a quiet, unshakable control. Slowly, he raised a hand, palm out, the same deliberate gesture he'd used earlier.

"Back off," he said, his voice low, firm, leaving no room for argument.

For a breathless moment, the tension hung thick in the air. The girl's claws flexed, scraping faintly against the reinforced floor as her growls deepened into a low, guttural rumble. Her sharp eyes burned into him, defiant and primal, as though daring him to make the next move.

Rick didn't waver. He held his position, his hand steady.

The girl's snarl faltered. With a reluctant hiss, she stepped back—one clawing step, then another. The growl ebbed, her shoulders dropping as she slunk toward her corner. Even then, she didn't break eye contact, her predatory stare lingering on Rick with wary calculation.

Rick exhaled slowly, letting his hand drop. The room seemed to release a breath with him, the heavy tension easing just enough to let sound creep back into the silence. He turned his head slightly, his gaze falling on the assistant, who was still crumpled on the floor. Pale-faced and trembling, the younger man's chest rose and fell in shallow, rapid bursts, his wide eyes darting between Rick and the girl.

"You alright?" Rick asked, his voice more measured now, the earlier edge softening just a fraction.

The assistant nodded shakily, his trembling hands pressing against the floor as he scrambled clumsily to his feet. "Yeah, I... I think so," he stammered, swallowing hard. "She just... she came at me. I didn't know what to do."

Rick's eyes flicked back to the girl. She'd resumed pacing in her corner, though her movements were tight and deliberate, like a spring coiled just short of snapping.

"She came at you because you gave her an opening," Rick said bluntly, his tone matter-of-fact but not unkind. "You hesitated. You flinched. And she took advantage of it."

The assistant's face fell, his shoulders slumping as he dropped his gaze to the floor. "I was trying to stay calm," he muttered, frustration tugging at the edges of his voice. "I thought I was doing what you said."

Rick shook his head slowly, his gaze sharp but steady. "You don't *act* calm. You have to *be* calm. They can smell it—fear, doubt, hesitation. Doesn't matter how still you stand or what you tell yourself. You go in there second-guessing? They'll see it, feel it. And they'll tear you apart."

He paused, his words hanging heavy in the air, deliberate and unrelenting. "Maybe not physically. But mentally? Every damn time."

The assistant swallowed thickly, his throat bobbing as he absorbed Rick's words. "I'll... I'll do better next time," he said, though the lack of conviction in his voice betrayed him.

Rick studied him for a long moment, his expression unreadable. Then, with a quiet grunt—half acknowledgment, half skepticism—he clapped a firm hand on the younger man's shoulder. The assistant stiffened, but Rick's grip was steady, grounding.

"You will," Rick said, his voice steady and certain. "But you've got to stop overthinking it. Intentions don't mean a damn thing to them. It's what you show that matters."

His hand lingered briefly on the assistant's shoulder, the gesture firm but reassuring. "You hesitate? They'll see weakness. You panic? They'll see an opening. You want her respect? You've got to *earn* it—every damn time."

The assistant nodded shakily, the weight of Rick's words pressing down on him as much as the hand on his shoulder.

Rick turned his attention back to the girl. She'd stopped pacing, crouched now in her corner, her glowing eyes still watching them, sharp and unblinking.

"She's still testing you," Rick murmured, half to himself, half to the assistant. "They always are."

"She's still testing you," Rick murmured, his voice low, almost as though speaking to himself. "They always are."

The assistant nodded, swallowing hard as his grip on the clipboard tightened, his knuckles pale against the strain. "Got it," he said quietly, his tone more measured this time. "No hesitation."

"Good." Rick turned back to the girl, his eyes narrowing as he watched her pace. "She's smart. Too smart, maybe. She's going to keep testing you until you prove she can't win. And even then, she'll try again eventually. That's just how they are."

The assistant glanced at the feral, then back at Rick. "And you're sure it's worth it? Trying to work with them?"

Rick didn't answer immediately. His gaze lingered on the girl, his expression unreadable. Finally, he said, "It's worth it if you make it worth it. If you don't? Then you're just wasting everyone's time."

The assistant didn't respond, but his expression hardened slightly, the doubt in his eyes replaced with determination. Rick nodded faintly, satisfied.

"Alright," Rick said, stepping toward the door. "Clean up your mess, and we'll try this again tomorrow. Just don't screw it up next time."

The assistant gave a small, nervous laugh, bending to pick up the fallen tray. As Rick left the room, his footsteps echoing down the hall, the assistant glanced back at the feral girl. She was still watching, her glowing eyes unblinking.

This wasn't going to get any easier.

CHAPTER 4

The following day, the sound of heavy boots and muffled voices filled the observation wing as a second feral was moved into the neighboring glass room. Rick stood with his arms crossed, leaning casually against the counter as he watched the transfer through the reinforced observation window. A team of handlers escorted the girl inside, her movements wild and resistant, her snarls echoing down the hallway.

The new feral was smaller than the first, her frame lean but wiry, with scars crisscrossing her arms and legs. Her eyes glowed with the same animalistic intensity, darting around the room as she took in her surroundings. She clawed at the air toward one of the handlers before they quickly stepped back and exited, leaving her alone in the enclosed space. The door sealed with a loud hiss, and the room fell silent except for the faint sound of her growling.

Rick's eyes shifted to the first feral, who had pressed herself against the glass of her own room, her lips curled back in a vicious snarl. Her claws scraped audibly against the barrier, her posture rigid and aggressive. The second feral immediately responded, whipping her head around to face the sound. For a moment, the two locked eyes, and the hostility was palpable.

"They're not friends," Rick muttered, more to himself than anyone else, a faint smirk tugging at his lips. He shook his head as though the thought amused him. "Didn't think they would be."

The assistant, noticeably more cautious after the previous day's events, hovered a step behind Rick, his movements hesitant. "What gave it away?" he asked dryly, his voice laced with nervous sarcasm as his eyes darted between the two ferals. "The snarling? Or the fact that they look like they'd rip each other apart the second we took the glass away?"

Rick chuckled softly, the sound low and unhurried as his gaze stayed fixed on the girls. "That, and the fact that ferals don't do 'friends.'" He glanced briefly over his shoulder at the assistant, the faintest edge of amusement lingering in his expression. "At least, not in the way you're thinking. Their idea of socializing is seeing who can claw the other's throat out first."

He gestured toward the glass enclosures where the two ferals paced along the length of their respective rooms, steps measured and deliberate, their glowing eyes locked on each other. They mirrored each movement like two predators testing boundaries, their bodies taut with barely-contained energy.

"What you're seeing right now?" Rick continued, his tone calm and knowing. "That's posturing. They're sizing each other up, figuring out who's stronger."

The assistant frowned, shifting the clipboard nervously in his grip. His gaze flicked from Rick to the ferals, lingering on the rhythmic pacing and low growls reverberating through the glass. "Is that... normal? For them to be this hostile right away?"

"Completely normal," Rick replied without hesitation, his voice steady and matter-of-fact, as though discussing the weather. "They're territorial by nature. You put two ferals this close together, and they'll either fight for dominance or avoid each other altogether."

He paused, studying the ferals with an almost analytical calm as one of the girls bared her teeth, a sharp, warning hiss filling the room. The other froze briefly, muscles coiling beneath her pale skin before resuming her pacing.

"Judging by these two," Rick added, his smirk faint but unmistakable, "I'd say we're looking at the first option."

As if on cue, the first feral slammed her palm against the glass, the sharp screech of her claws scraping against the surface slicing through the room. The sound was enough to make the assistant wince, his shoulders tensing as the second feral answered with a low, guttural snarl. She lunged at the barrier, her fangs bared and her movements so sudden and violent that the assistant instinctively took a step back.

"Jesus," he muttered under his breath, his voice tight. "They're going to kill each other."

Rick didn't react to the commotion. He stood still, his face unreadable as his eyes tracked the ferals' movements. "Not unless we're stupid enough to let them," he replied, his tone even, almost bored. He rapped his knuckles twice against the observation window—*thunk, thunk*—the sound flat but reassuring. "The glass is reinforced. It can handle it."

The assistant's gaze darted nervously between the ferals, their clawed hands leaving faint streaks across the barrier as they prowled, each movement deliberate and predatory.

"This isn't about killing," Rick continued, his voice calm but firm, as though explaining something obvious. "It's about control. They're testing boundaries, trying to figure out where they stand in the hierarchy." He gestured toward the two ferals, who now paced in mirrored lines, their sharp eyes locked on each other like two forces waiting for the first crack.

"Right now," Rick added, his gaze narrowing slightly, "they're just figuring out who's alpha."

The assistant raised an eyebrow. "And what happens when they figure that out?"

Rick shrugged. "Depends on how long it takes. If one of them backs down, the other will take the lead. If neither backs down..." He paused, his gaze narrowing slightly. "Then we've got a bigger problem."

Inside the rooms, the ferals continued their standoff. The first girl paced along the glass, her claws scraping in short bursts as she growled low in her throat. The second feral mirrored her movements, occasionally lunging forward to test the barrier. The intensity in their eyes was unmistakable—neither of them was backing down anytime soon.

The assistant shifted uncomfortably, his grip tightening on the clipboard. "Should we... I don't know, do something? Try to calm them down?"

Rick gave him a sidelong glance, his smirk faint but sharp. "You think you can 'calm' them down?" He chuckled softly, shaking his head. "These aren't house cats, kid. You don't 'calm' a feral. You observe you learn, and you let them work it out—within reason."

"And if 'within reason' doesn't happen?" the assistant asked, his tone hesitant.

Rick's smirk faded slightly, his expression turning serious. "Then we intervene. But only if we have to."

The assistant nodded, though the unease on his face didn't disappear. He glanced at the girls again, his brow furrowing as the second feral lunged forward once more, slamming her hands against the glass with a loud *thud*. The first feral responded immediately, clawing at the barrier with renewed vigor, her screech rising in pitch.

"They really hate each other, don't they?" the assistant said quietly.

Rick didn't answer right away. He watched the two ferals, his eyes narrowing as he studied their movements. There was something almost methodical about the way they circled each other, their hostility underpinned by a strange sort of calculation. It wasn't just blind rage—it was something deeper.

"They don't hate each other," Rick said finally, his tone thoughtful. "Not the way we think about hate. For them, this is instinct. Survival. They're not mad at each other—they're just following the rules of their world."

The assistant frowned, his gaze lingering on the ferals. "Still seems like a bad idea to keep them this close."

Rick shrugged again, his smirk returning faintly. "Maybe. But it's not my call to make. They're here now, so we deal with it." He pushed off the counter, adjusting the cuffs of his sleeves as he turned toward the door. "Keep an eye on them. If it looks like they're getting too riled up, call me."

"Where are you going?" the assistant asked, his tone almost panicked.

"To get some coffee," Rick replied, his smirk widening. "You'll be fine. Just don't flinch every time they growl, and they'll probably ignore you."

"Probably?" the assistant muttered, his expression skeptical.

Rick chuckled as he walked away, leaving the assistant alone with the snarls and screeches of the two ferals. Through the glass, the girls continued their posturing, their glowing eyes never leaving each other as the tension in the room simmered just below the boiling point.

When Rick returned, steaming cup of coffee in hand, he immediately noticed the change in the atmosphere. The snarls and screeches that had filled the observation wing earlier were gone, replaced by an almost eerie silence. He glanced toward the glass rooms and raised an eyebrow.

The two ferals were no longer pacing or clawing at the barriers. Instead, they were each in their respective corners, their bodies curled in tense but quiet postures. The first girl sat with her back against the wall, her glowing eyes half-closed as she watched the room lazily. The second feral mirrored her on the opposite side, crouched low with her head resting on her arms, though her sharp gaze occasionally flicked toward her rival.

The assistant stood near the console, his face a mix of confusion and relief. He turned as soon as Rick entered, his expression incredulous. "They just... stopped," he said, gesturing toward the glass. "One minute they're trying to tear through the barrier to get at each other, and now... this?"

Rick sipped his coffee, his gaze drifting to the girls. He studied their postures for a long moment before shrugging. "Makes sense," he said casually, leaning against the counter.

"Makes sense?" the assistant repeated, his voice rising slightly. "They looked like they were about to kill each other an hour ago. Now they're just... sitting there? How does that make sense?"

Rick smirked faintly, swirling the coffee in his cup. "Ferals don't waste energy. They test each other, figure out who's dominant, and when they decide it's not worth the fight, they stop. It's all instinct."

The assistant frowned, glancing back at the girls. "But they didn't fight. They didn't decide anything."

Rick raised an eyebrow. "Didn't they?" He gestured toward the two rooms with his coffee cup. "Look at them. They're in opposite corners, keeping their distance. That's not an accident."

The assistant stared at the girls, his brow furrowing as he processed Rick's words. "So... what, they just called it a draw?"

"Not exactly," Rick said, setting his coffee on the counter. "They're not equals. One of them backed down first, even if it wasn't obvious. The other one picked up on it and didn't press the issue. That's how it works. No fight, no wasted energy. Just understanding."

The assistant tilted his head, glancing between the two ferals again. "How can you even tell? They're just sitting there."

Rick chuckled softly, shaking his head. "You're thinking like a human. Stop that." He pointed toward the first feral. "See how she's leaning back, her posture relaxed? She's confident. She knows she doesn't need to keep posturing anymore. She's claimed the space."

He turned his finger toward the second girl. "And her? She's tense. Crouched low. Keeping her head down. That's submission. She knows she can't win, so she's staying out of the way."

The assistant blinked, his grip tightening on his clipboard. "That's... subtle," he admitted, his tone hesitant. "I didn't think ferals could be that... I don't know, strategic."

"It's not strategy," Rick corrected. "It's survival. They're hardwired to figure out who's in charge and who isn't. Once they know, the dynamic's set—at least until something changes."

The assistant scratched his head, clearly still puzzled. "So... what do we do now?"

"Nothing," Rick said simply, picking up his coffee again. "Let them be. The worst thing we could do is mess with them now. They've found their balance, and as long as we don't disrupt it, they'll keep to their own corners."

The assistant sighed, looking down at his notes. "This job gets weirder by the hour."

Rick smirked, taking another sip of his coffee. "Welcome to Spearhead."

The assistant chuckled nervously, shaking his head. "I still don't get how you're so calm about all this."

Rick glanced at the ferals again, his expression unreadable. "Because I've seen worse. A lot worse. This?" He gestured toward the glass. "This is easy. Trust me, you'll learn to read them. Eventually, you'll start seeing the patterns. They're not as unpredictable as you think."

The assistant nodded slowly, though his uncertainty lingered. "I guess I've got a lot to learn."

"You do," Rick said bluntly. "But you're here, so you'll figure it out. Just remember—don't overthink it. Ferals don't live in their heads like we do. They live in the moment. You start doubting yourself, and they'll see it before you even realize it's there."

The assistant nodded again, glancing at the girls one last time. "Alright," he said softly. "I'll keep that in mind."

Rick grunted in acknowledgment, finishing the last of his coffee. He placed the empty cup on the counter and rolled his shoulders, his gaze never leaving the ferals. "Good. Because this is just the beginning. If you think two ferals are hard to deal with, wait until you see what happens when we have to bring in a third."

The assistant froze, his eyes widening. "A third?"

Rick smirked, his tone laced with dark humor. "Relax, kid. You've got time. For now, just keep an eye on them. If anything changes, let me know." He turned toward the door, his boots echoing faintly as he walked away.

Behind him, the assistant exhaled slowly, muttering under his breath as he jotted down another note. Through the glass, the ferals remained in their respective corners, their unspoken truce holding steady—for now.

CHAPTER 5

The quiet hum of the observation wing was broken only by the occasional scratch of a pen on paper and the soft rustle of reports being flipped. Rick sat at the counter, methodically sorting through the stacks of documents, though his attention never fully drifted from the glass enclosures. Inside, the two feral girls had retreated to their respective corners, their earlier aggression now smoldering into a wary, uneasy silence.

Across the room, the assistant sat perched on the edge of his chair, his clipboard balanced on his knees. He tapped the end of his pen against it, hesitating just long enough for Rick to notice.

"Hey, Rick?"

Rick didn't look up, his focus still trained on the reports spread before him. "What?"

The assistant shifted, clearing his throat as he fumbled for his words. "Why don't we... I mean, why doesn't Spearhead work with younger ferals? Like, kids?"

That got Rick's attention. His pen paused mid-stroke, the tip hovering above the page before he slowly glanced up. One eyebrow arched as he regarded the assistant with faint incredulity. "Kids?"

"Yeah," the assistant said, nodding toward the glass rooms. "Like, if you got them younger, wouldn't it be easier to rehabilitate them? You know, before they've... gone completely feral?"

Rick leaned back in his chair, the faint creak of the worn wood filling the pause. He crossed his arms over his chest, his gaze sharp and unwavering. "Easier? Sure. In theory. But it's not that simple."

The assistant tilted his head, clearly unsatisfied with the answer. "Why not? I mean, wouldn't they be less dangerous? More... manageable?"

Rick let out a low, dry snort, shaking his head. "You're thinking about this all wrong," he said, his tone carrying the weight of someone who'd seen too much. "Younger doesn't mean safer. If anything, it's harder. A hell of a lot harder."

The assistant frowned, leaning forward slightly. "How so?"

Rick set his pen down and tapped a finger against the counter as he began to explain. "First off, you have to find a feral kid. And that's not easy. They're small, fast, and smart as hell when it comes to hiding. You think adult ferals are good at staying out of sight? Kids are even better. They know how to vanish the second they feel threatened. You could walk right past one and never even know they were there."

The assistant blinked, surprised. "Seriously? They're that good?"

Rick nodded. "Survival instinct. It's built into them from the moment they're born. They don't trust anyone or anything, and they've got the skills to back it up." He gestured toward the two girls in the glass rooms. "Those two? They were probably the same way when they were younger. They only got caught because someone made a mistake, or they were too hungry to keep running. Otherwise, they'd still be out there."

The assistant scribbled a note on his clipboard, his brow furrowing. "Alright, so... finding them is hard. But it's not impossible, right? What about when you do find one?"

Rick's expression darkened slightly. "That's the second problem. The mother."

The assistant froze, his pen hovering over the page. "The mother?"

Rick nodded, his tone grim. "If there's a feral kid, there's almost always a mother nearby. And let me tell you something—you do not want to mess with a feral mother. They'll kill anyone who so much as looks at their kid the wrong way. And they won't hesitate, either. You think adult ferals are dangerous? A mother protecting her kid is ten times worse. She'll fight to the death, no questions asked."

The assistant swallowed hard, his hand tightening around the pen. "That bad, huh?"

"Worse," Rick said flatly. "And let's say, somehow, you manage to get past her. Maybe you're lucky, or maybe you've got a damn good team backing you up. That's not the end of it."

The assistant tilted his head, confused. "It's not?"

"Nope." Rick leaned forward slightly, his expression serious. "Because now you've got the kid. And if you think the mother's reaction is bad, wait until you see what happens to the kid after you take her away."

The assistant frowned, his confusion deepening. "What do you mean?"

Rick exhaled through his nose, the sound heavy with something unspoken. "We tried. Once."

The assistant glanced at him, curiosity flickering across his face, but Rick didn't elaborate—not yet. His gaze stayed fixed on the ferals, their muscles coiling and tensing as they paced. Their movements were almost synchronized, an unsettling rhythm broken only by the scrape of claws against the reinforced glass.

That sound—slow, deliberate—pulled Rick back, unbidden, to another time.

The observation room had felt smaller then, its walls pressing in with a stifling weight. The hum of machinery was louder, the fluorescent lights too bright, cutting harsh lines into the sterile space.

On the other side of the glass, a young feral crouched in the corner. She was trembling under a tattered blanket, her glowing eyes darting erratically as if searching for something that wasn't there. Her breaths came in shallow, panicked bursts, and the keening sound that escaped her throat was a fragile, broken thing—neither a growl nor a cry, but something in between.

Rick stood where he was now, his arms crossed tightly over his chest, his jaw clenched. Beside him, a Spearhead doctor scrolled through a datapad, her expression drawn with frustration.

"She's not stabilizing," the doctor muttered, shaking her head. "Stress levels are spiking. Vitals are dropping. If this keeps up—"

"She's shutting down," Rick interrupted, his tone grim. He didn't need the datapad to see what was happening. The signs were all there—too familiar, too final. "She's not going to make it."

The doctor tightened her grip on the datapad, her lips pressing into a thin line. "We've done everything we can. She just... won't respond."

The young feral shifted slightly, clutching the blanket tighter around her small frame. Her claws scraped weakly against the floor, leaving faint marks over the already-scored surface. Rick's eyes narrowed as he studied her, the faint tremors wracking her body like a tremble in the earth before it gave way completely.

"She hasn't eaten in two days," the doctor said, her voice softer now. "We've tried raw meat, blood, even basic sustenance. Nothing works."

"Because it's not from her mother," Rick said, his voice as flat and certain as the reinforced glass between them. His eyes stayed on the girl. "She doesn't want food. She wants her."

The doctor glanced at him, sympathy flickering across her sharp features. "There's nothing we can do about that," she said quietly.

Rick didn't answer. He just watched as the feral's trembling slowed, her movements growing eerily still. Her glowing eyes no longer darted; they stared blankly into the distance, unseeing.

The memory shifted, sharp and unforgiving, to the last time they'd seen the mother.

The capture had been brutal—messy. Rick could still hear the feral mother's growls, the guttural, almost human wails that had torn through the air. She had fought with a ferocity that left even the most seasoned agents shaken, her claws slicing through the air like weapons forged in rage.

It had taken four agents to bring her down. Even then, the injuries she'd sustained sealed her fate long before they could reach the lab.

Rick remembered standing over her crumpled form, the world quiet except for her ragged, fading breaths. Her glowing eyes had dimmed, the fire in them replaced by something hollow. Her claws were clutching something—a scrap of cloth, torn and frayed.

Later, they realized it was from the youngling's bedding.

Back in the present, Rick blinked, the weight of the memory settling over him like a stone.

"She didn't make it," he said quietly, his voice roughened by the edges of the past. "We gave her everything we could. Food, shelter, warmth. None of it mattered. Without her mother..." His voice trailed off, and he gestured vaguely toward the glass, where one of the adult ferals let out a low, guttural growl. "They don't survive."

The assistant's grip on his clipboard tightened, his knuckles white against the hard edges. "Why? I mean... why can't they just adapt?"

Rick's jaw tightened, his gaze hardening. "Because it's not about comfort. It's not even about survival. That bond between a feral mother and her youngling? It's instinct. It's survival. You take that away, and it's like ripping the ground out from under them. They don't know how to stand without it."

The assistant stared at him, his expression pale and unreadable. He turned back to the ferals, watching as one of them paced near the edge of the enclosure, her claws clicking softly against the floor.

"And that's why we don't try anymore," the assistant murmured, the words heavy in the quiet room.

Rick nodded, his lips pressed into a thin line. "Yeah," he said, his voice steady but edged with something raw, like the memory itself had left a scar. "That's why."

The observation room hummed softly, a blend of machinery and the faint buzz of overhead lights that flickered once before steadying again. Rick leaned against the counter, his arms loose at his sides but his shoulders tight. Beyond the glass, the two feral girls remained in their corners, the earlier snarls replaced by a watchful silence. One shifted, her claws scraping faintly against the reinforced floor as she adjusted her weight, her glowing eyes narrowing. Across the room, her counterpart mirrored the movement, every twitch calculated, every glance a challenge.

Behind Rick, the assistant fidgeted with his pen, the faint tap-tap-tap breaking the quiet rhythm of the machines. The sound blended with the soft hiss of air conditioning, the occasional creak of a shifting chair, and the muffled voices of distant conversations in other parts of the facility.

"So…" the assistant began, his voice hesitant as he glanced at Rick. "This is why you don't work with the kids anymore? Too risky?"

Rick didn't respond immediately. The faint whir of a camera repositioning somewhere overhead filled the silence. His shoulders rose and fell with a deliberate exhale, his gaze locked on the ferals. "Risky doesn't cover it," he said finally, his voice low and even. "You've got to find them first. That's the easy part. Then you survive the mother—if you're lucky. And somehow, you separate them without breaking either one."

The assistant shifted, his weight creaking the floor beneath him as he glanced uneasily at the glass. Inside, one of the ferals raised her head, her fangs flashing briefly before she lowered herself back into a crouch. Her claws flexed against the floor, the faint scratches catching the overhead light.

"And even then," Rick continued, his voice quieter now, "it's a crapshoot if the kid makes it."

The assistant's pen stilled mid-tap, the faint rhythm vanishing into the background hum. "It's kind of sad," he murmured, almost to himself, his voice barely cutting through the quiet buzz of the room. Somewhere down the hall, the faint clang of a closing door echoed, followed by the steady click of approaching footsteps that faded just as quickly.

Rick finally turned, his arms crossing loosely over his chest as he studied the younger man. "Sad?" he echoed, his tone soft but flat, as if weighing the word. "Yeah. It is." He tilted his head slightly toward the glass. "But that's reality. They don't live by our rules. They've got their own. And trying to change that?" He shook his head slowly, the motion deliberate. "It usually ends worse than it started."

The assistant's brow furrowed as he nodded faintly. His pen hovered over the clipboard, the sound of its faint scratch joining the background noise. Rick's gaze sharpened, catching the motion.

"You're still trying to see them like us," Rick said, his tone softening but still firm. "They're not. And the sooner you figure that out, the better off you'll be."

The assistant hesitated, his lips parting slightly as though to argue, but no words came. His eyes drifted back to the glass. One of the ferals had risen, pacing along the edge of her enclosure. Each step was deliberate, her glowing eyes darting between her counterpart and the observation window. Across the room, the other feral mirrored her movements, coiled like a spring, every muscle tensed and ready.

The faint hum of the machines seemed louder now, filling the silence as the assistant's pen stilled once more. "Do you think they ever... miss their mothers?" he asked finally, his voice hesitant and low, as though afraid the question might be too much.

Rick's gaze followed the pacing feral. She stopped abruptly, her head snapping up as her eyes locked onto her counterpart. For a moment, neither moved, the tension between them a palpable force, thick enough to smother the air in the room.

"Maybe," Rick said at last, his voice distant. His jaw tightened as he pushed off the counter and stepped closer to the glass. He stood there, his hands loose at his sides, his posture steady as his eyes tracked the ferals' movements. "But if they do, they don't show it. Ferals don't dwell on the past. They live in the moment. That's all they know."

Behind him, the assistant shifted uneasily, the chair creaking as he leaned forward slightly. Inside the glass enclosure, one feral lowered her head, baring her teeth silently as the other finally broke eye contact and resumed her pacing. The scrape of claws against reinforced flooring filled the room, an eerie rhythm that seemed to echo Rick's words.

Rick glanced back at the assistant, his expression unreadable but his tone lighter, almost teasing. "You'll figure it out," he said, his words cutting through the quiet like a challenge.

The assistant nodded again, though his expression remained thoughtful. Rick picked up his pen and returned to his paperwork, his focus shifting back to the reports in front of him. But the assistant's gaze lingered on the glass rooms, the silent tension between the two ferals a stark reminder of the world they came from.

The quiet rhythm of paperwork and occasional observation was broken by the soft *click* of boots on the tiled floor. Rick didn't look up immediately, but the assistant did, his brow furrowing as a woman stepped into the room. She was tall, her figure lean and sharp, dressed in Spearhead's standard black uniform. Her pale skin gave away her nature instantly, though the faint red glint in her eyes was the real giveaway. A vampire.

Rick finally glanced up, a small smirk tugging at the corner of his mouth. "Well, well. Look who decided to show up. Didn't think you'd be back for another week, Emma."

The woman crossed her arms and leaned against the counter, a knowing smile playing on her lips. "And let you handle this circus alone? Please, Rick. I'd come back early just to make sure you're not screwing it all up."

Rick chuckled, leaning back in his chair. "Always nice to see you, too."

Emma turned her attention to the assistant, who was still staring at her with a mix of curiosity and unease. "You must be the new guy," she said, her voice smooth and unhurried. "What's your name?"

The assistant blinked, snapping out of his daze. "Uh, Kyle," he said quickly. "Kyle Sanders."

Emma nodded, her smile widening slightly. "Nice to meet you, Kyle. Don't worry, you'll get used to the chaos. Eventually."

Kyle managed a nervous chuckle, his grip on his clipboard tightening. "Yeah, uh... sure."

Rick snorted. "Don't scare the kid too much, Em. He's barely survived his first week."

Emma raised an eyebrow, glancing at the glass rooms. "Barely survived? Let me guess—you threw him in with a feral and watched from the sidelines?"

Rick smirked. "Not quite. He volunteered."

Kyle turned bright red. "I didn't know what I was doing."

Emma laughed softly, shaking her head. "Don't worry, Kyle. Nobody knows what they're doing their first week. The trick is to fake it until you figure it out. Just stick close to Rick—he's stubborn enough to keep you alive."

Rick rolled his eyes, but there was a faint glint of amusement in his expression. "Thanks for the vote of confidence."

Emma shrugged, her gaze drifting to the two ferals in the glass rooms. "So, what's the story with these two? They look like they're ready to tear each other apart."

"They were," Rick said, sipping his coffee. "Then they figured out it wasn't worth the energy. Now they're keeping to their own corners."

Emma's lips curved into a faint smirk. "Smart girls. I like them already."

Kyle frowned, glancing between Rick and Emma. "Wait... you *like* them? They were trying to kill each other."

Emma shrugged again, her tone casual. "That's just how they are. Ferals don't do friendship, Kyle. They do survival. And these two are doing exactly what they're supposed to—finding balance."

Kyle looked at Rick for confirmation, and Rick nodded. "She's not wrong. You'll get used to it."

Emma tilted her head, studying the girls through the glass. "The smaller one's new, right?"

"Came in yesterday," Rick confirmed. "Not thrilled about her accommodations, but she's settling in."

Emma's gaze lingered on the second feral, her eyes narrowing slightly. "She's young. Barely out of her teens, if that."

"Yeah," Rick said, his tone shifting slightly. "She's a fighter, though. Got into it with the handlers when they brought her in. Nearly took a chunk out of one of them."

Emma's smirk returned. "Sounds like a handful. Reminds me of that one we handled in Sector 8 last year."

Rick groaned, rubbing his temples. "Don't remind me. I still have the scar from that one."

Kyle's eyes widened. "You got hurt? I thought you were, like, invincible or something."

Rick snorted. "Invincible? Hardly. Ferals don't play fair, kid. You make one wrong move, and they'll make you pay for it."

Emma chuckled, shaking her head. "He's being modest. That feral in Sector 8 was a nightmare. Fast, smart, and mean as hell. Rick kept her contained long enough for backup to arrive. Saved a lot of lives that day."

Rick waved her off. "Yeah, yeah. Let's not make a big deal out of it."

Kyle stared at Rick, his expression a mix of awe and nervousness. "You've been doing this for a long time, haven't you?"

"Too long," Rick said, leaning back in his chair. "Emma and I go way back. We've been through more feral incidents than I care to count."

Emma nodded, her expression softening slightly. "That's true. And somehow, he's still the same stubborn, coffee-addicted mess he was when we started."

Rick smirked. "And you're still the bossy vampire who thinks she knows everything."

"Because I do," Emma shot back, her tone teasing.

Kyle watched the exchange, his tension easing slightly as he realized how natural their banter was. "You two seem… close."

Rick and Emma exchanged a glance, and Rick shrugged. "You could say that. When you've worked with someone as long as we have, you either become friends or you kill each other. We chose the first option."

Emma chuckled. "Mostly because I'm too patient to put up with his nonsense otherwise."

"Patient, my ass," Rick muttered, though there was no malice in his tone.

Kyle smiled faintly, the atmosphere in the room feeling lighter despite the ever-present tension of the ferals behind the glass. Emma crossed her arms again, her gaze returning to the two girls.

"Well, I'm here now," she said. "What's the plan?"

Rick picked up his coffee, his smirk widening. "Same as always. We watch, we learn, and we figure out what the hell to do with them."

Emma grinned. "Sounds like a typical day in paradise."

Emma leaned casually against the counter, her gaze flicking

between the glass rooms and Rick. "So, Rick," she began, her tone light but laced with curiosity, "how's it feel babysitting these two? A step down from wrangling ferals in the wild, don't you think?"

Rick rolled his eyes, taking a slow sip of his coffee. "Babysitting, huh? I don't remember you being this chatty last time we worked together. What's with the commentary?"

Emma smirked. "What can I say? I missed you."

Kyle raised an eyebrow, glancing between the two. "Wait... have you guys worked together on, like, big feral hunts? Out in the field?"

Emma chuckled softly. "Oh, we've done plenty of fieldwork. Sector 8, Sector 12... that mess in the Blackridge mountains—"

"Don't remind me," Rick interrupted, rubbing his temple as if the memory alone gave him a headache. "I'm still washing Blackridge mud out of my boots."

Emma's laugh was genuine, a soft and musical sound. "That was years ago, Rick. You really need to let it go."

CHAPTER 6

Kyle's curiosity got the better of him. "Okay, hold on. You've been doing this for how long exactly? I mean, you're—what, mid-thirties? You've been with Spearhead for what, ten years?"

Rick glanced at Emma, his smirk faint but knowing. "Mid-thirties, huh? Nice of you to think so."

Emma grinned, her sharp canines showing faintly. "Rick's been at this a lot longer than you'd think, Kyle. You're looking at one of Spearhead's finest anomalies—a guy who's technically older than he looks."

Kyle tilted his head, clearly confused. "Older than he looks? What, are you saying—" His voice trailed off as realization dawned. "Wait... are you a vampire?"

Rick snorted, shaking his head. "Not quite. Half-vampire."

Kyle blinked, his jaw dropping slightly. "Half-vampire? That's a thing?"

Emma crossed her arms, her smile turning more amused. "It's rare, but it happens. Rick's mom was one of us—a full vampire. His dad? Human."

Rick shrugged, his tone nonchalant. "Yeah, it's a fun little mix. I get the perks without some of the drawbacks. Can walk in the sun, eat garlic, all that good stuff. But I've got the speed, strength, and heightened senses to keep me alive out here."

Kyle's expression shifted from surprise to curiosity. "So... what's it like? I mean, being half of both?"

Rick leaned back in his chair, his gaze distant for a moment. "It's… complicated. You don't really fit in with either side. Vampires see you as too human. Humans see you as too… other. Growing up wasn't exactly a picnic."

Emma nodded, her expression softening slightly. "His mom did her best, though. She was one hell of a woman."

Rick's smirk returned, though it was faint. "Yeah, she was. My dad, too. They weren't exactly thrilled about the risks of raising someone like me, but they made it work."

Kyle tilted his head, intrigued. "What happened to them?"

Rick's smirk faded, his eyes darkening slightly. "They're gone. Long time ago."

Emma stepped in, her tone lightening. "But their stubbornness lives on in Rick. Trust me, he's every bit as impossible as they were."

Rick chuckled softly, the tension easing. "I'll take that as a compliment."

Kyle looked between them, still processing everything. "So… does being half-vampire make you better at this job? Like, dealing with ferals?"

Rick shrugged. "It helps. The speed and strength are useful. The senses, too. But honestly? The biggest advantage is just understanding them. I know what it's like to live by instinct, to feel like you don't belong. Ferals? They're not monsters. They're just… stuck. They're doing what they have to do to survive."

Emma nodded, her gaze thoughtful. "It's why you're so good at this. You don't just see them as threats—you see them as people. Most agents can't do that."

Rick smirked faintly, his tone dry. "Don't get all sentimental on me, Em."

She laughed softly, shaking her head. "Wouldn't dream of it."

Kyle leaned forward slightly, his curiosity still burning. "So, wait—how did you two meet? I mean, you've obviously been working together for years."

Emma grinned, glancing at Rick. "You want to tell him, or should I?"

Rick groaned, rubbing the bridge of his nose. "It's not that interesting."

Emma raised an eyebrow. "You tackled me the first time we met, Rick. How is that not interesting?"

Kyle's jaw dropped. "Wait—you tackled her? Why?"

Rick exhaled, leaning back in his chair. "It was a misunderstanding. I thought she was sneaking into a restricted area—no clearance, no badge that I could see. So, I did what I was trained to do." He smirked slightly. "She, on the other hand, thought I was an idiot. Turns out, we were both right."

Emma burst into laughter, shaking her head. "You didn't just react—you tackled me! One second, I'm minding my own business, and the next, I'm flat on the ground with some guy shouting about protocol."

Kyle couldn't help but laugh, though he quickly tried to stifle it. "That's... kind of hilarious."

Rick shrugged, smirking. "She's never let me live it down."

"Because it was ridiculous," Emma said, her tone teasing. "But, to be fair, you did make up for it later. That feral pack in Sector 4? You saved my ass."

Rick's expression softened slightly. "Yeah, well, you've returned the favor plenty of times since then."

Emma smiled faintly, her tone more genuine now. "That's what partners do."

Kyle watched the exchange, his respect for both of them growing. "You guys really are close, huh?"

Rick and Emma exchanged a glance, and Rick nodded. "Yeah. We've been through a lot together. You don't come out of that without a bond."

Emma grinned. "Besides, somebody's got to keep him in line."

Rick rolled his eyes, but the corner of his mouth twitched in a faint smile. "Sure, Em. Whatever you say."

The three of them were walking down the corridor, their conversation drifting to lighter topics as they headed toward the cafeteria. The sterile, fluorescent-lit halls of the facility buzzed faintly, punctuated by the occasional muffled voice or distant clang of equipment.

Emma was in the middle of recounting a particularly chaotic mission in Sector 5 when a commotion erupted further down the hall. A feral, being escorted by a team of guards in full containment gear, was thrashing violently against its restraints. The growls and snarls grew louder as it fought against the handlers, its movements erratic but powerful.

"Looks like someone's having a bad day," Emma muttered, her eyes narrowing as she watched the scene unfold.

Rick stopped mid-stride, his body tensing as he assessed the situation. The feral was a young male, wiry but muscular, with glowing eyes that darted around wildly. It let out a guttural snarl, twisting suddenly and catching one of the guards off-balance. The handler stumbled, and the feral seized the opportunity, tearing free from its restraints with a sharp, guttural roar.

"Shit," Kyle muttered, gripping his clipboard like it would somehow protect him.

The feral didn't hesitate. It charged down the hall, its claws scraping against the tiled floor as it bolted straight toward them. Its snarls echoed off the walls, primal and unrelenting, its glowing eyes locked on the closest target—Rick.

Emma instinctively stepped back, her hand darting toward the tranquilizer gun holstered at her side. Kyle froze, his eyes wide as he fumbled to move behind Rick. But Rick didn't move to draw a weapon. He didn't even flinch.

As the feral closed the distance, Rick sidestepped fluidly, his movements precise and practiced. In one swift motion, he grabbed the feral's arm, using its own momentum to twist it around. The feral snarled and clawed at the air, but before it could react further, Rick's other arm looped around its neck. He locked it into a chokehold with practiced ease, his grip firm but controlled.

The feral thrashed wildly, its claws scraping against Rick's jacket, but he held his ground. "Settle down," Rick growled, his tone low and commanding. "You're not going anywhere."

Emma lowered her hand, her lips quirking into an impressed smirk. "Show-off."

Kyle stared, his mouth agape. "How the hell did you do that so fast?"

"Practice," Rick muttered, his focus entirely on the feral. The creature's struggles began to weaken as the lack of air took its toll, though its snarls didn't completely fade. Rick adjusted his grip slightly, making sure he wasn't cutting off too much airflow. "You done yet? Or are we going to keep dancing?"

The feral let out one last guttural growl before going limp, its body sagging in Rick's grip. Rick eased up slightly, ensuring it was subdued but not unconscious. He glanced over his shoulder at the guards, who were scrambling to recover.

"You want to help here?" Rick called out, his tone sharp.

The lead guard nodded quickly, jogging over with a set of reinforced cuffs. "Sorry, sir. He caught us off-guard. Won't happen again."

Rick raised an eyebrow but didn't comment. He held the feral steady as the guards secured its wrists and ankles with reinforced restraints. Once the feral was fully contained, Rick released it, stepping back and adjusting his jacket.

Emma crossed her arms, her smirk widening. "Smooth as ever. You make it look easy."

"It's not," Rick muttered, brushing off his sleeves with a practiced flick. "But you can't hesitate. They see it, they use it."

Kyle was still frozen in place, his wide eyes locked on Rick, the clipboard clutched tightly to his chest like a shield. "You just… took it down. Like it was nothing."

Rick turned to him, his faint smirk carrying a mix of amusement and challenge. "That's the difference between watching and doing, kid." He held Kyle's gaze for a beat, the weight of his words settling in. "You'll get there."

The guards hauled the subdued feral back down the hall, their steps quick and deliberate. The creature let out a weak snarl but didn't resist further, its energy spent.

"Seriously, though," Emma said as the group resumed their walk toward the cafeteria. "You didn't even blink. I've seen seasoned agents hesitate in situations like that."

Rick shrugged, his tone casual. "Hesitation gets you killed. You see them coming, you act. Simple as that."

Kyle frowned, his brow furrowing. "But… how do you not panic? I mean, it was coming right at you."

Rick glanced at him, his smirk fading slightly. "You think that was the first feral that's come at me? After a while, you learn to stop panicking. You just see the threat and handle it."

Emma tilted her head, her gaze thoughtful. "It's not just experience, though, is it? It's instinct."

Rick's smirk returned, faint but knowing. "Maybe. Guess I've got a bit of an edge there."

Kyle hesitated, then nodded slowly. "That's the half-vampire thing, right?"

Rick raised an eyebrow. "Caught on quick, didn't you?"

Kyle gave a nervous chuckle. "I mean, it makes sense. The speed, the reflexes... it's not exactly normal."

Emma laughed softly. "Rick hasn't been normal a day in his life. But that's what makes him so damn good at this."

Rick rolled his eyes, though the corner of his mouth twitched in a faint smile. "Thanks for the glowing endorsement."

"Anytime," Emma said with a grin.

The group reached the cafeteria, the earlier tension dissipating as they stepped inside. Rick grabbed a tray and glanced at Kyle, who still seemed a bit shaken.

"Relax, kid," Rick said, his tone lighter now. "If you're sticking around, you'll see a lot more of that. Might as well get used to it."

Kyle gave a weak smile, though his hands still trembled slightly. "Yeah... I'll work on that."

Emma clapped Kyle on the shoulder, her smile encouraging. "Don't worry. You've got two of the best showing you the ropes. You'll be fine."

Rick smirked, grabbing a coffee from the counter. "Assuming he doesn't trip over his own feet again."

Kyle groaned, his face reddening. "I'm never going to live that down, am I?"

"Nope," Rick and Emma said in unison, their laughter echoing through the cafeteria.

The following day, the observation wing was anything but quiet. The sounds of snarling, screeching, and claws raking against reinforced glass echoed through the halls, accompanied by the frantic scribbling of Kyle's pen against his clipboard. He paced nervously near the console, glancing between the two feral girls in their respective rooms.

They were back at it again, each one pacing aggressively along the glass that separated them, claws scraping and striking the barrier in bursts of feral frustration. Their eyes glowed brightly, and their guttural growls seemed to bounce off the walls, amplifying the tension in the room.

Kyle ran a hand through his hair, exhaling sharply as he muttered to himself. "Okay, uh... what do I do? What do I do?"

One of the girls lunged at the glass, her claws screeching against it, while the other bared her teeth in a vicious snarl, pressing her hands against the barrier in response. The sound made Kyle flinch, and he nearly dropped his clipboard.

"Damn it," he muttered, glancing toward the hallway as if salvation might walk through the door at any second.

As if on cue, the door opened, and Emma stepped in, followed by Rick, who was holding a steaming cup of coffee. Emma stopped mid-stride, her eyes narrowing as she took in the scene. "Well, this is cozy," she said dryly, crossing her arms. "What the hell's going on here?"

Kyle turned toward them, his face a mix of relief and frustration. "They started this about twenty minutes ago! I've tried everything—well, everything I could think of—but they're just getting worse."

Rick stepped beside Emma, taking a long sip of his coffee before raising an eyebrow. "Let me guess. You tried talking to them?"

Kyle nodded, though he looked sheepish. "Yeah... I figured maybe if I—"

"Stop," Rick interrupted, holding up a hand. "Talking doesn't work. Not with ferals. All you're doing is giving them background noise to ignore."

Emma smirked, leaning against the counter. "He's learning, Rick. Slowly, but he's learning."

Kyle flushed, looking down at his clipboard. "Well, what do I do, then? They're going to break the damn glass at this rate."

Rick tilted his head, studying the girls for a moment. One of them let out a high-pitched screech, slamming her hands against the glass again, while the other lunged in response, her snarls loud and guttural.

"They're feeding off each other's energy," Rick said calmly. "It's not about the glass—it's about dominance. They're still trying to figure out who's in charge. This is just the next round of their little power struggle."

Emma nodded, her gaze thoughtful. "And if we don't step in, it'll just keep escalating."

Kyle frowned, glancing between the two. "Okay... so how do we stop it?"

Rick set his coffee down on the counter, rolling up his sleeves. "Simple. We remind them who's actually in charge."

Emma smirked, straightening. "This should be fun."

Rick shot her a dry look. "You're helping."

"Obviously," Emma said, her tone amused.

Kyle blinked, confused. "Wait—you're both going in there? At the same time?"

"Relax, kid," Rick said, grabbing a pair of heavy gloves from the nearby rack. "We've done this before."

Emma adjusted her own gloves, her movements calm and practiced. "You might want to take notes, Kyle. This is how you handle ferals."

Kyle hesitated, his grip tightening on his clipboard. "Uh... right. Notes. Got it."

Rick hit the button to unlock the first feral's door, the sharp *click* of the mechanism drawing both girls' attention instantly. They froze, their glowing eyes snapping toward him as he stepped inside. Emma followed close behind, her posture relaxed but alert.

The first girl snarled, her claws flexing as she crouched low, her eyes darting between Rick and Emma. The second feral pressed her hands against the glass, her growls growing louder as she watched them enter.

Rick stopped a few feet from the first girl, his stance steady. "Alright," he said firmly, his voice low and commanding. "Enough."

The girl responded with a sharp screech, lunging forward with surprising speed. Rick sidestepped smoothly, grabbing her wrist and twisting it just enough to halt her momentum. She thrashed, snapping her teeth, but Rick's grip didn't waver.

"Calm," he said, his tone unyielding. "You're not in charge here."

Emma moved to the side, positioning herself between the girl and the door. She didn't speak, but her presence was enough to block any attempt at escape. The second feral let out a guttural growl from behind the glass, slamming her fists against it in frustration.

"She's feeding off her," Emma said, nodding toward the second girl. "They're egging each other on."

Rick nodded, his grip still firm on the first feral. "Then let's remind her who's boss, too."

He guided the struggling girl toward the far corner, his movements calm but deliberate. Once she was positioned, he released her, taking a step back but keeping his posture dominant. She growled low, her claws twitching, but she didn't lunge again.

Emma moved to the console, hitting the button to unlock the second feral's door. The girl stormed out immediately, her snarls echoing in the small space. Emma blocked her path with a raised hand, her eyes narrowing.

"Not so fast," she said evenly. "You're not in charge here, either."

The second feral hesitated, her glowing eyes flicking between Emma and Rick. Rick stepped forward, his gaze steady. "Back off," he said, his tone sharp. The feral snarled but didn't advance.

Slowly, the second girl retreated a few steps, her growls softening. Emma and Rick exchanged a glance, both nodding subtly. They stood their ground for a few more moments, ensuring the girls had settled before retreating to the hallway.

Kyle was waiting for them, his expression a mix of awe and disbelief. "You just... walked in there. And they listened to you."

"Of course they did," Emma said, pulling off her gloves. "That's how you handle ferals. Firm, clear, and no room for hesitation."

Rick smirked, grabbing his coffee. "And a little practice doesn't hurt."

Kyle shook his head, still processing what he'd seen. "You guys make it look easy."

"It's not," Rick said bluntly. "But you'll get there. Eventually."

Emma grinned, clapping Kyle on the shoulder. "If he survives long enough."

Kyle groaned, rubbing his temples. "Great. No pressure."

Rick chuckled softly, sipping his coffee as he glanced back at the observation rooms. The two girls had retreated to their respective corners again, their posturing temporarily subdued. For now.

The observation wing had settled into a rare moment of quiet. The two feral girls were back in their respective corners, the tension between them reduced to occasional growls and sharp glances. Rick was leaning against the counter, flipping through a report with his usual casual air, while Emma sat nearby, jotting notes on her tablet. Kyle, seated across from them, was tapping his pen against the edge of his clipboard, his expression thoughtful.

After a few moments, Kyle broke the silence. "So… I've been thinking," he began hesitantly, glancing between Rick and Emma. "Are ferals smart enough to, like… open doors? Or… I don't know, drive a car?"

Rick raised an eyebrow, smirking faintly. "Drive a car? You've been watching too many movies, kid."

Kyle flushed slightly but pressed on. "No, I mean, they're clearly not stupid, right? So how far does it go? Could they figure out something like that?"

Rick opened his mouth to respond, but Emma held up a hand, her expression amused. "Hold on, Rick. This one's actually my wheelhouse."

Rick leaned back, smirking. "All yours, professor."

Emma set her tablet down, crossing one leg over the other as she turned her full attention to Kyle. "Alright, Kyle, let's start with the basics. Ferals aren't stupid—far from it. Their intelligence isn't the same as ours, but that doesn't mean they're mindless animals. They operate on instinct, sure, but there's a level of problem-solving ability that can't be ignored."

Kyle tilted his head, intrigued. "Problem-solving? Like... what kind?"

Emma nodded, her tone shifting into the calm, measured cadence of an expert in her field. "Take doors, for example. A feral might not know how a lock works in the way you or I would, but that doesn't mean they won't figure it out. They'll observe, test, and experiment until they find a way through—whether that's by manipulating the handle, smashing it, or even finding an alternate route."

Kyle blinked, clearly surprised. "So... they're adaptable?"

"Extremely," Emma said. "Their adaptability is one of their greatest strengths. It's why they're so hard to track and capture. They don't rely on a single method of survival—they adjust to their environment and circumstances in real time. If one approach doesn't work, they'll try another."

Rick sipped his coffee, nodding in agreement. "She's right. Seen it happen plenty of times. You think you've got them contained, and then suddenly they're three steps ahead, using stuff you didn't even think they'd notice."

Kyle frowned, processing the information. "Okay, but... driving? That's a bit more complicated than opening a door."

Emma smiled faintly. "You're right—it is. And the answer there is a bit more nuanced. Ferals don't have the same kind of higher reasoning or long-term planning skills that we do. They're not going to learn to drive a car in the traditional sense. But if you put one in a vehicle and something happens—say, the car moves when they press a pedal—they might figure out how to replicate the action through trial and error."

Kyle's eyes widened. "So they *could* drive?"

"Not the way you're thinking," Emma clarified. "They wouldn't understand traffic laws, navigation, or even the concept of a destination. But they might figure out the mechanics—like turning a wheel or pressing pedals—if it served their immediate needs."

Rick chuckled, shaking his head. "I don't know, Em. Last thing we need is ferals behind the wheel. They're bad enough on foot."

Emma laughed softly, her tone lightening. "Agreed. But the point stands—they're more intelligent than most people give them credit for. It's just that their intelligence is focused on survival. They don't waste time on abstract thinking or complex reasoning. Everything they do serves a purpose."

Kyle scribbled notes furiously, his expression a mix of fascination and concern. "So... they're not just dangerous because of their strength and instincts. They're dangerous because they can *learn*."

"Exactly," Emma said, her tone serious now. "And that's what makes them so challenging to manage. Every encounter is different because every feral is different. They learn from their experiences, adapt to their environment, and develop unique behaviors based on what works for them."

Rick leaned against the counter, his expression thoughtful. "That's why containment's so important. You let one of them loose, and it's not just about tracking them down—it's about dealing with whatever tricks they've picked up along the way."

Kyle looked up from his notes, his brow furrowed. "Has there ever been a feral that... I don't know, seemed smarter than the others? Like, unusually intelligent?"

Emma and Rick exchanged a glance, and Rick's smirk faded slightly. "Yeah," he said quietly. "Once or twice. And those are the ones you don't forget."

Emma nodded, her expression serious. "Most ferals operate on instinct, but every now and then, you'll come across one that pushes the limits. They're rare, but they exist. And when they do…" She paused, her gaze distant. "Let's just say it's not something you want to deal with unprepared."

Kyle hesitated, then nodded slowly. "So… how do you stop something like that?"

Rick smirked faintly, though it didn't quite reach his eyes. "You don't. You contain it, study it, and pray it doesn't figure out how to turn the tables."

Kyle swallowed hard, glancing toward the glass rooms. The two feral girls were quiet now, their earlier aggression replaced by a tense stillness. "Guess I've got a lot more to learn," he muttered.

Emma smiled faintly, her tone softening. "That's why you're here. You'll figure it out."

Rick picked up his coffee, his smirk returning. "Assuming these two don't scare you off first."

CHAPTER 7

The hum of the Spearhead vehicle filled the cabin, a steady drone beneath the rhythmic patter of rain against the windows. Rick's hands gripped the wheel with practiced ease as he guided the truck down the narrow, tree-lined road. The headlights sliced cleanly through the darkness, their beams catching on wet pavement and glinting off slick leaves.

From the backseat, Kyle shifted, the clipboard balanced on his lap tapping softly against his knee with every nervous bounce of his leg. The silence had stretched too long, heavy and unyielding, before he finally broke it.

"So, uh… how often do you guys get called out for this kind of thing?" His voice was casual, but the edge of unease wasn't hard to miss.

Rick didn't glance away from the road, his expression unreadable. "More than you'd think," he said, his tone flat but unhurried, like this was nothing worth talking about.

In the passenger seat, Emma smirked faintly, her lips tugging upward as if she'd been waiting for Kyle to crack. She didn't bother turning around. "What's the matter, Kyle? Starting to feel the pressure?"

Kyle hesitated, his fingers gripping the clipboard just a little tighter, the paper edges crumpling faintly beneath his thumb. "Not pressure, exactly," he muttered, though the words came a little too quickly. "Just, you know… trying to be ready for whatever happens."

Rick let out a low chuckle, though it carried no warmth. "Ready? You can train all you want, but this job doesn't care about plans. Once you're in there, it's all instincts and fast thinking."

"Great," Kyle muttered under his breath, earning a quiet laugh from Emma.

The vehicle slowed as the address came into view: a two-story house partially obscured by a line of bare trees. The area was eerily quiet, save for the occasional rustle of leaves in the wind. A Spearhead vehicle was already parked crookedly in the driveway, its lights dimmed. Several agents stood clustered near the front porch, their rain-soaked gear glistening in the faint glow of their flashlights.

Rick eased the vehicle into park and cut the engine. "Stay close," he instructed as they stepped out, the chill of the rain biting through their jackets. Emma pulled up her hood, her sharp gaze sweeping across the scene.

"Already a mess," she muttered, gesturing toward the shattered front window. Shards of glass glittered on the wooden porch like a warning.

One of the agents approached, his rifle slung across his chest. "Glad you're here," he said, his voice tight with restrained urgency. "It's bad inside."

Rick's expression remained calm but unreadable. "What are we dealing with?"

"Two, maybe three ferals," the agent said grimly. "Neighbors reported screams and breaking glass. We arrived to find the place torn apart. Haven't spotted them yet, but there's no mistaking the signs—they're here."

Rick's gaze flicked to the house, narrowing as he noted the deep claw marks etched into the doorframe. "And the family?"

The agent shook his head. "No sign. The car's still here, but the house is empty. Either they bolted, or..." He let the sentence hang, his meaning clear.

Kyle shifted uncomfortably, clutching his clipboard like a lifeline. "What's the protocol for this?" he asked, his voice quieter now.

Rick glanced over his shoulder, his faint smirk not quite reaching his eyes. "We go in, find the ferals, and take them out. Alive, if possible."

"And if they don't come quietly?" Kyle asked, his unease clear.

Emma turned to answer, her voice even. "Then we make them. But we only use the force we need—nothing more."

Rick nodded, pulling the tranquilizer gun from his holster and checking the chamber. "Non-lethal first," he confirmed. "Always."

The lead agent gestured toward the house. "Perimeter's secure, but we haven't gone in. We figured it'd be better to wait for you."

"Smart," Rick said with a nod. "You've got your team ready?"

The agent straightened slightly. "Ready and waiting."

Rick turned to Emma and Kyle, his voice steady. "Alright. Let's move."

The team moved into position, rain dripping from their gear as they lined up near the front door. Rick signaled with two fingers, motioning for silence. The agents nodded in unison, their faces set with focused determination.

"Alpha team, ready," Rick whispered into his comm. "Bravo, hold position outside. Cover the perimeter."

"Copy," came the quiet response from Bravo's lead.

Rick adjusted his earpiece and turned to the group. "Emma, you're with me. Kyle, stay in the middle. Follow our lead, keep your head down, and don't try to play hero."

Kyle gave a shaky nod, gripping his flashlight and tranquilizer gun tightly. "Got it."

Emma smirked faintly, her eyes gleaming under the shadow of her hood. "Let's make this quick. No unnecessary risks."

Rick stepped toward the shattered door, his boots crunching softly on the glass shards. He crouched slightly, glancing through the jagged opening. The entryway was dim, the faint glow of their flashlights catching on scattered debris and deep claw marks along the walls. The house smelled stale and metallic, a sharp tang of blood and damp wood.

"Stack up," Rick muttered, motioning for the team to line up behind him. He reached for the door, pushing it open with a controlled movement. It creaked loudly, the sound making Kyle flinch.

"Go," Rick ordered, slipping inside.

The team entered in single file, their flashlights cutting through the darkness. The living room was a mess—overturned furniture, broken picture frames, and muddy footprints crisscrossing the floor. Rick held up a fist, signaling the team to stop.

"Clear the first floor," he whispered. "Emma, take the right. Kyle, with me."

The agents fanned out, their movements precise and silent. Rick led Kyle through the living room, his eyes scanning every shadow. Emma moved toward the adjacent dining area, her flashlight sweeping across the room as she kept her tranquilizer gun raised.

"Movement in the kitchen," one of the vampire agents whispered through the comms. "Far corner."

"Copy," Rick replied. "Hold position."

He and Kyle crept forward, their steps measured. The kitchen came into view, the wreckage there even more pronounced. Cabinet doors hung open, their contents spilled across the floor. Claw marks gouged deep into the counters spoke of raw aggression.

Rick held up a hand, motioning for Kyle to stay back. He crouched low, his flashlight angled upward to catch every surface. A faint, guttural growl echoed from somewhere in the shadows, low and menacing.

"They're here," Rick whispered into his comms. "At least one. Possibly more."

Emma's voice came through, steady and calm. "Hallway clear. Looping back to your position."

The growling grew louder, a sharp, chittering noise joining it. Kyle's grip tightened on his tranquilizer gun, his breath coming in shallow bursts.

Suddenly, a blur of motion shot out from the darkness—a feral darting across the ceiling, its claws scraping against the plaster. Kyle yelped, stumbling back as Rick moved instantly, raising his tranquilizer gun and firing. The dart struck the feral in the shoulder, but it only faltered for a moment before leaping onto the wall, snarling viciously.

"Corner it!" Rick barked, his voice sharp.

Emma appeared in the doorway, her weapon raised. She fired, the second dart embedding itself in the feral's side. The creature screeched, its movements growing erratic as the tranquilizers took effect. It fell from the wall, landing heavily on the counter before slumping to the floor.

"Target down," Emma reported, lowering her weapon. "Still breathing."

Rick moved forward cautiously, his flashlight trained on the feral's still-twitching form. He grabbed a pair of reinforced restraints from his belt, securing the creature's wrists and ankles.

"First one's secured," Rick said. "Keep moving. There's at least one more."

With the first feral restrained, the tension in the air remained palpable. Rick stood, his gaze sharp as he turned to the rest of the team. "Bravo, maintain perimeter. We're moving upstairs."

"Copy," came the reply over the comms.

Rick glanced at Kyle, who was still catching his breath. "You good?"

Kyle nodded quickly, though his grip on the flashlight remained tight. "Yeah. Yeah, I'm fine."

Emma smirked faintly, stepping past him. "Don't worry, Kyle. First encounter's always the worst."

Rick motioned for them to follow, leading the way toward the staircase. The wooden steps groaned under their weight, the sound unsettling in the otherwise silent house. Flashlights swept across the narrow hallway at the top, revealing closed doors and debris scattered across the floor.

"Stay sharp," Rick murmured. "Ferals love tight spaces like this."

The team split into pairs, Emma taking the right side while Rick and Kyle moved left. Each door was opened cautiously, flashlights illuminating the rooms one by one. The first was a bedroom, its bed shredded and walls marred with deep claw marks. Rick moved inside, scanning the shadows for any signs of movement.

"Clear," he whispered.

Kyle stayed close behind, his flashlight trembling slightly. "You think the others are still upstairs?"

Rick nodded, his gaze still sweeping the room. "Probably. They're territorial. If one's up here, the others won't be far."

Emma's voice came through the comms. "Left hallway clear. Moving to the master bedroom."

Rick motioned for Kyle to follow as they stepped back into the hallway. The master bedroom door was slightly ajar, a faint creaking sound coming from within. Rick held up a hand, signaling for silence as he approached.

He pushed the door open slowly, his flashlight cutting through the darkness. The room was larger than the others, its furniture overturned and a large window shattered, letting in the faint sound of rain. In the far corner, a shadow shifted.

"There," Rick said quietly, pointing.

The feral crouched low, its glowing eyes locked onto the intruders. It growled low, its claws flexing against the floor as it prepared to lunge. Rick raised his tranquilizer gun, his aim steady.

"Easy," he said softly. "No sudden moves."

The feral let out a piercing screech, darting toward the window. It moved with astonishing speed, scrambling up the wall and clinging to the ceiling like a spider. Kyle's flashlight jerked upward, catching the creature's wild, snarling face as it crawled toward the doorway.

"On the ceiling!" Kyle shouted, stumbling back.

Emma appeared in the hallway, her gun already raised. "I see it."

The feral lunged, its claws outstretched as it launched itself toward Rick. He sidestepped smoothly, firing his tranquilizer gun as the creature sailed past him. The dart struck its leg, but it didn't stop the feral from hitting the floor and scrambling toward Kyle.

"Kyle, move!" Rick barked.

Kyle froze for a split second, his eyes wide as the feral closed in. Emma fired again, the dart striking the creature in the side just as it reached Kyle. It screeched, its movements slowing as the tranquilizers took effect. Rick stepped in, grabbing the feral by the scruff and pinning it to the floor.

"Second target down," Rick said, his voice even as he restrained the feral. "Emma, any more movement?"

Emma scanned the room and hallway with her flashlight, her sharp eyes missing nothing. "Negative. I think that's all of them."

Rick nodded, securing the restraints on the feral before stepping back. "Kyle, you alright?"

Kyle exhaled shakily, nodding. "Yeah... yeah, I'm good."

Emma grinned, holstering her weapon. "Well, you didn't get eaten. I'd call that a win."

Rick smirked faintly, pulling out his comm. "Bravo, ground floor status?"

"Perimeter secure," came the reply. "No additional movement."

Rick glanced at Emma. "Looks like we're clear."

"Good," Emma said, her tone light. "Now let's get these two out of here before they wake up."

Rick straightened, adjusting his gloves as he stood over the second restrained feral. Its breathing was shallow, the tranquilizers keeping it subdued but not entirely unconscious. He nudged the creature's side with his boot, ensuring it wasn't faking its current state. Satisfied, he turned to Emma.

"Get the extraction gear," he said. "Let's secure them for transport."

Emma nodded, moving to the hallway and signaling to the vampire agent who had joined Bravo team. The agent carried a small case, setting it down on the floor as Emma opened it to reveal reinforced collars and transport harnesses.

"These two are lightweights," Emma said, inspecting the gear. "Teenagers, maybe younger. Shouldn't be too much trouble, but we'll double up on restraints just to be safe."

Kyle hovered near the doorway, his flashlight shaking slightly in his grip. "So... we're just going to carry them out like this? Won't they freak out once they wake up?"

Rick gave him a flat look. "That's why we don't let them wake up until we're back at the sanctuary. The tranquilizers buy us enough time."

Kyle shifted uncomfortably. "And if they don't?"

"Then you'll get some on-the-job experience," Emma quipped, a sly grin on her face.

Rick crouched beside the first feral, snapping a collar around its neck and securing the harness. The device clicked into place with a faint hum, the reinforced material designed to withstand even the strongest feral's thrashing.

"These collars are synced to the transport cage," Rick explained, tightening the straps. "Once we load them in, they won't be able to move much, even if they wake up."

Emma was already securing the second feral, her movements practiced and efficient. The creature let out a faint growl as she tightened the harness, but it didn't stir. "Kyle, grab the other end," she said, nodding toward the straps. "We'll carry this one down together."

Kyle hesitated but stepped forward, taking the straps with trembling hands. The weight of the feral surprised him, and he staggered slightly before Emma steadied him with a sharp look.

"Relax," she said. "It's not going to bite you. Not yet, anyway."

Rick smirked faintly as he lifted the first feral onto his shoulder with ease. "Let's move. The sooner we're out of here, the better."

The team descended the staircase carefully, their flashlights cutting through the dim light as the rain outside intensified. The house creaked ominously, the storm amplifying every sound.

"Bravo team," Rick said into his comm. "We're coming out. Clear the path to the transport."

"Copy," the Bravo lead responded. "Perimeter secure. Route is clear."

As they stepped into the living room, a faint noise made Rick pause. It was soft, almost imperceptible, but distinct—a shuffling sound coming from the far corner of the room.

"Hold up," Rick muttered, his hand raised to signal a stop. He set the feral down gently, his flashlight sweeping across the debris-strewn floor. The room seemed still, but the shuffling sound came again, this time accompanied by a faint growl.

Emma tensed, her tranquilizer gun raised. "Don't tell me there's another one."

Rick's jaw tightened. "Could be. Everyone stay sharp."

The growl grew louder, and a third feral emerged from the shadows, its movements slow and predatory. This one was different—larger, older, and clearly more experienced. Its glowing eyes locked onto the team, its lips curling back to reveal sharp teeth.

"Target spotted," Rick said into his comm. "Third feral. Ground floor."

The Bravo lead's voice crackled through the earpiece. "Need backup?"

"Negative," Rick replied. "We've got it."

The feral let out a guttural snarl, crouching low as if preparing to lunge. Rick raised his tranquilizer gun, his aim steady. "Easy," he said softly, his voice calm but firm. "You don't want to do this."

The feral lunged, a blur of motion in the dim room. Rick fired without hesitation, the dart embedding itself squarely in the creature's chest. It faltered but didn't stop. Before it could close the gap, Emma fired another dart. The second hit sent the feral crashing into the overturned coffee table, the splintering wood adding to the chaos before it collapsed in a heap.

Rick advanced cautiously, his weapon still trained on the feral's motionless form. "Emma, grab the restraints. Kyle—stay back," he said, his tone sharp but steady.

Kyle froze where he stood, his wide eyes glued to the fallen creature. "That thing was huge," he muttered, the disbelief clear in his voice.

"Older," Rick corrected as he crouched down, his gloved hand hovering just above the feral's chest to check its breathing. The creature's ribs rose and fell, slow but steady. "Stronger, too. Could've been leading the others."

Emma moved quickly, the heavy restraints clinking faintly in her hands as she secured the feral's wrists and ankles with practiced efficiency. Her expression was hard to read, her focus entirely on the task. "Makes sense. That explains why the first two were so aggressive—they were probably taking orders from this one."

Rick stood, brushing off his gloves as he glanced at Emma. "Yeah. Without it, the group dynamic falls apart. Let's move it before it wakes up—it's not staying down for long."

They worked together, lifting the unconscious feral and maneuvering it toward the door. The rain outside had intensified, the downpour pounding relentlessly against the house and vehicles. The sound was a constant backdrop, muffling the crunch of boots on wet gravel as they approached the waiting Bravo team.

The team stood near the transport cage, their weapons still at the ready as they scanned the surrounding darkness. Rick and Emma hauled the feral into the reinforced enclosure, the metal creaking under its weight as they secured it alongside the others.

Emma double-checked the restraints, tugging on the thick collar fastened to the cage wall. "These should hold, but we've seen what they can do," she said, her voice low.

Rick nodded, stepping back to let the vampires on the team inspect the setup. Their sharp eyes flicked over every detail, ensuring nothing was out of place.

Kyle lingered behind the group, his clipboard clutched tightly to his chest. He swallowed hard, his gaze darting between the transport cage and the still-dark perimeter. "This one was different," he said quietly. "Faster. Smarter, maybe?"

"Maybe," Rick replied, his tone neutral but thoughtful. "Doesn't matter now. It's secure." He gestured toward the Bravo team, his voice firm. "Keep an eye on it until we're back at the facility. If it even twitches, you let me know."

The rain continued to hammer down as Rick stepped back, his hands on his hips as he surveyed the scene. Emma secured the cage lock with a heavy clang, her hand lingering on it for a moment before she turned to Rick.

"We good?" she asked.

Rick nodded, his expression set. "Yeah. Mission complete. Let's move."

Kyle exhaled deeply, his shoulders sagging with relief as he climbed into the transport vehicle. Emma slid into the passenger seat, glancing at Rick as he settled behind the wheel.

"Well," she said with a faint grin. "That was fun."

Rick smirked, starting the engine. "If that's your idea of fun, you need a new hobby."

The vehicle rumbled to life, and the team pulled away from the house, leaving the storm and its secrets behind.

CHAPTER 8

As the transport vehicle rumbled through the sanctuary gates, Kyle couldn't tear his gaze away from the view outside. The towering walls stretched endlessly in both directions, their textured surfaces bathed in harsh, white spotlights that cut through the misty night. Shadows loomed long and jagged, like silent sentinels guarding the unknown. Beyond the gates, the compound was cloaked in an eerie stillness, broken only by the faint hum of distant machinery and the occasional, haunting call of ferals echoing through the sanctuary's forested depths.

Kyle shifted in his seat, the unease tightening his jaw. The silence pressed down on him, heavy and suffocating, until his curiosity finally bubbled over.

"So... what happens now? With them, I mean."

Rick eased the vehicle to a stop near the intake facility, the engine sputtering into silence. He turned slightly, fixing Kyle with a steady, neutral gaze that carried the weight of routine. "Now, they're evaluated."

Kyle's brow furrowed, his frown slight but unmistakable. "Evaluated how?"

Emma, lounging back in her seat as though they were discussing the weather, let a faint smirk tug at her lips. "Medically, behaviorally—you name it. Every feral that comes through these gates gets the full workup." She tilted her head toward the back of the vehicle, where the three ferals lay restrained and eerily still. "We check for injuries, diseases, malnutrition. Anything that might make them a risk to themselves or anyone else."

Kyle's eyes lingered on the cage, the harsh light from the intake building glinting off the reinforced metal. "And if they're… fine?" he asked, his voice quieter now, as though speaking too loudly might wake the beasts.

Rick stepped out of the vehicle, motioning for Kyle and Emma to follow. "If they're fine, they're released into the sanctuary," he said simply. "But it's not that straightforward."

Kyle hesitated as he climbed out, the cool night air hitting him. "What do you mean?"

Emma gestured toward the handlers already waiting to offload the ferals. "It's not just about their health. A feral might look fine physically, but if their behavior suggests they're a threat, they'll stay in containment. We don't release anyone until we're sure they can survive out there without causing chaos."

Kyle's brow furrowed as he watched the staff transfer the sedated ferals into portable units. "But isn't the sanctuary… chaotic by default?"

Rick gave a faint chuckle, crossing his arms as he leaned against the transport. "You could say that. But it's controlled chaos. The sanctuary's designed to give them space to exist without threatening anyone outside these walls."

Kyle's curiosity deepened as he followed Rick and Emma toward the intake facility. "What's it like in there? I mean, I know it's massive, but I've never really… gotten details."

Emma glanced at Rick, who nodded slightly, giving her the go-ahead. She turned to Kyle, her tone slipping into her usual matter-of-fact cadence. "Think of it like a national park, but with a wall around it. It's big—miles in every direction. Forests, rivers, caves—everything a feral would need to survive."

Kyle tilted his head, intrigued. "So… they just live out there? Like animals?"

"They live how they want," Rick said. "Some stay alone, some form groups. It depends on the feral. The sanctuary's designed to mimic their natural instincts. The more it feels like their environment, the less likely they are to cause problems."

Emma added, "We monitor them, of course. Drones, cameras, patrols—non-intrusive but enough to keep tabs on their behavior. If something goes wrong—a fight, an injury, or an escape attempt—we respond."

Kyle's eyes widened slightly. "Escape attempts? They can get out?"

Rick shook his head. "No one's ever made it over the wall. Not for lack of trying, though. But the sanctuary's built to handle that. The walls are high enough and reinforced enough that even the strongest feral can't break through. And if they dig, we've got seismic sensors to detect it."

Kyle whistled softly, impressed. "Sounds... intense."

Emma smirked. "It has to be. This place is the only reason the world outside hasn't descended into chaos. Without it, ferals would be everywhere."

Kyle watched as the handlers wheeled the containment units into the intake facility, disappearing through a set of heavy doors. "So... those three," he said, nodding toward the building. "They'll get checked out, and if they're fine, they'll just... walk out into the sanctuary?"

Rick nodded. "More or less. Once they're cleared, the staff releases them at one of the sanctuary's entry points. From there, it's up to them where they go."

"And if they're not cleared?" Kyle asked, his tone quieter.

Emma's expression darkened slightly. "Then they stay here. Containment, isolation—whatever's necessary to keep them and everyone else safe."

Kyle shivered slightly at the thought. "How many are... contained?"

Rick's gaze drifted toward the intake facility, his expression unreadable. "Not many. Most ferals adapt to the sanctuary. It's rare for one to be so unstable that they can't be released."

Emma placed a hand on Kyle's shoulder, her tone softening. "You'll get used to it, Kyle. The sanctuary's not perfect, but it works. It's better than the alternative."

Kyle nodded slowly, though the weight of what he'd learned still hung heavy in his mind. As they turned to head inside, he cast one last glance at the towering walls in the distance. The faint sound of feral growls echoed from the forest beyond, a chilling reminder of what lay within.

Rick, Emma, and Kyle stood on the gravel lot, rain-soaked jackets clinging to their shoulders as they watched the containment units being wheeled into the intake facility. The handlers moved efficiently, their reinforced suits reflecting the cold overhead lights as they secured the ferals for processing. Each movement was deliberate, practiced—every latch double-checked, every restraint tested.

Kyle's eyes were glued to the scene, his grip tightening on his clipboard. "They're so... calm about it," he muttered. "Like it's just another day."

"For them, it is," Emma replied, brushing a strand of wet hair from her face. "This isn't their first rodeo."

Rick didn't respond immediately, his gaze fixed on the ferals. The youngest of the three stirred briefly, letting out a low growl before slumping back into sedation. The sound seemed to echo in the still night, cutting through the hum of machinery.

"They have to be calm," Rick said finally, his tone low but firm. "The ferals can smell fear. If you panic, you lose control. You lose control, people get hurt."

Kyle swallowed hard, nodding slowly. His eyes darted toward one of the handlers, who was carefully adjusting the collar around the largest feral's neck. Even sedated, the creature's size was imposing, its muscular frame a reminder of the raw power it possessed.

Emma leaned closer to Kyle, her voice softer now. "Watch how they handle them. Every step matters. They're not just throwing these things in a cage—they're making sure the transition is smooth. Less stress means less risk when they wake up."

Kyle watched as the handlers wheeled the ferals into the intake facility, disappearing behind heavy, reinforced doors. A faint hiss sounded as the seals engaged, and the lights above the entrance turned from red to green.

"What happens in there?" Kyle asked, his curiosity overcoming his nerves.

"Standard procedure," Rick replied, gesturing toward the building. "Medical scans, bloodwork, behavioral assessments. They'll monitor their vitals, check for diseases, and record anything unusual. Once they're cleared, they'll be released into the sanctuary."

Kyle hesitated, then turned to Rick. "And if they're not cleared?"

Rick's gaze didn't waver. "Then they stay in containment. For as long as it takes."

Emma shifted her weight, nodding toward the observation tower nearby. "Come on, Kyle. You want to see what's inside the wall?"

Kyle blinked, his interest piqued. "We can see it?"

Emma smirked, already heading toward the tower. "Not up close, but close enough."

Rick followed without a word, his boots crunching against the gravel. The tower loomed overhead, its steel frame glistening with rain as they climbed the narrow staircase to the top. Kyle gripped the railing tightly, his heart pounding with each step.

At the top, a pair of binoculars hung from a metal hook, their lenses slightly fogged from the damp air. Emma grabbed them, wiping the lenses clean before handing them to Kyle. "Take a look."

Kyle hesitated for a moment, then pressed the binoculars to his eyes. The world beyond the wall came into sharp focus, and his breath caught in his throat.

The sanctuary stretched out like a vast wilderness, its dense forest canopy swaying gently in the breeze. Rivers wound through the landscape, their surfaces glinting faintly in the moonlight. In the distance, jagged cliffs rose like sentinels, casting long shadows across the terrain.

"Whoa," Kyle whispered, his voice barely audible.

Emma leaned against the railing, her expression softening as she watched him. "Impressive, isn't it?"

Kyle nodded, unable to tear his gaze away. "It's… massive. I didn't think it would look so… natural."

"That's the point," Rick said, his tone matter-of-fact. "The more natural it feels, the less likely the ferals are to try and escape. It's their world, not ours."

As Kyle scanned the sanctuary, a faint hum reached his ears. He adjusted the binoculars, spotting a Spearhead helicopter sweeping low over the trees. Its spotlight cut through the darkness, illuminating the forest floor as it patrolled the area.

"Is that… normal?" Kyle asked, nodding toward the helicopter.

"Routine patrol," Emma explained. "They're not looking

for trouble—they're just making sure everything's running smoothly. If there's a fight or an injury, they're the first to respond."

Kyle's gaze followed the helicopter as it disappeared behind the cliffs, its spotlight casting long beams of light across the terrain. "How do they monitor all of this? It's so... big."

"Drones, sensors, cameras," Rick said. "The walls are lined with tech that tracks movement and sound. The drones cover the areas the patrols can't reach. It's not perfect, but it works."

Emma chuckled softly. "And when it doesn't, that's when we get called in."

Kyle lowered the binoculars, his brow furrowed. "It's incredible, but... it feels like a prison."

Rick turned to him, his expression unreadable. "It is a prison. But it's also a second chance. For the ferals, and for everyone they might've hurt."

Kyle nodded slowly, the weight of Rick's words settling over him. As he handed the binoculars back to Emma, his gaze lingered on the towering walls below. The sanctuary was vast, but its purpose was clear—a place of containment, protection, and survival.

"Come on," Rick said, motioning toward the stairs. "Let's head back. Long night ahead."

Emma slung the binoculars over her shoulder, her smirk returning. "And you haven't even seen the fun parts yet, Kyle."

Kyle groaned softly, following them down the stairs. "Great. Can't wait."

CHAPTER 9

The rain hammered against the windshield, the wipers sweeping in slow, rhythmic arcs as the Spearhead vehicle cut through the dense darkness. The roads were slick, glistening under the sharp glare of the headlights, which carved narrow paths through the shadows stretching endlessly on either side. Inside the cabin, the silence weighed heavy, broken only by the steady hum of the engine—a sound that seemed louder than usual.

Kyle sat in the backseat, his gaze flicking between Rick and Emma, reading their body language like an open book. Something about this call was different. Rick's knuckles gripped the steering wheel tightly, the skin pale against the pressure. His jaw was locked, the muscle twitching subtly, his focus razor-sharp on the road ahead.

Beside him, Emma leaned forward in the passenger seat, her narrowed eyes fixed on the rain-slicked road, her fingers tapping out an erratic rhythm against her knee. The usual ease she carried was gone, replaced by something colder—sharper.

Kyle shifted uncomfortably, the tension curling in his chest until he couldn't take it anymore. He cleared his throat, the sound awkward in the heavy quiet. "So... what's the deal with this one? It's just a few ferals, right?"

Emma glanced back at him, her expression uncharacteristically serious. "Four young ones. Between three and four years old."

Kyle frowned. "Okay... and?"

Rick's voice was low, almost a growl. "No mother."

Kyle blinked, confused. "No mother? Isn't that... a good thing?"

Emma shook her head, her tone clipped. "Not even close. Baby ferals don't just wander off on their own. If the mother's not with them, it means one of two things: either she's dead... or she's nearby, watching."

"And if she's watching," Rick added, his tone sharp, "she'll tear us apart the second we get too close."

Kyle swallowed hard, the gravity of the situation sinking in. "But... what if she's not dead or nearby? What if they're just... abandoned?"

"Doesn't happen," Rick said firmly. "Ferals don't abandon their young. Ever."

Emma nodded, her gaze darkening. "If they're alone, something's seriously wrong. Either way, we're walking into a mess."

The radio crackled, cutting through the tension. "Dispatch to Spearhead Unit 4. You're approaching the location. Perimeter has been secured by Bravo team. No additional feral sightings reported."

Rick picked up the radio, his voice steady. "Copy that. ETA two minutes."

Kyle shifted in his seat, the weight of the situation pressing down on him. "So... what's the plan?"

"Standard containment," Rick replied, his eyes on the road. "We secure the young ones, assess the area, and get out. Fast."

"And if the mother shows up?" Kyle asked hesitantly.

Emma smirked faintly, though there was no humor in it. "Then we hope she's in a good mood."

The vehicle slowed as they approached the location—a small clearing at the edge of the forest, illuminated by the harsh beams of spotlights. Bravo team was already on-site, their figures silhouetted against the rain as they stood near a cluster of trees. The air was thick with the smell of damp earth and ozone, the storm still lingering overhead.

Rick parked the vehicle and stepped out, his boots crunching against the gravel. Emma and Kyle followed, the tension between them palpable as they approached the team.

"Status?" Rick asked, his tone sharp.

The Bravo lead, a tall vampire with sharp features, nodded toward the trees. "Four juveniles, just like the call said. They're huddled together near the roots of that oak. No sign of the mother or any other ferals in the area."

Rick's eyes narrowed as he scanned the scene, his hand resting on the tranquilizer gun at his hip. "How close did you get?"

"Close enough to confirm their condition," the Bravo lead replied. "They're scared, but not injured. No signs of aggression so far."

Emma crossed her arms, her gaze sweeping over the clearing. "Any tracks?"

The lead agent hesitated. "Nothing definitive. Rain's washed most of it away. But... there are a few faint impressions heading deeper into the forest. Could be the mother."

Rick exhaled slowly, his expression grim. "Alright. You hold the perimeter. We'll handle the containment."

Kyle blinked, his nerves spiking. "We're just... going in? What if she's out there?"

Emma gave him a sharp look. "You want to sit this one out, Kyle?"

Kyle shook his head quickly, gripping his flashlight tighter. "No, I'm good."

Rick didn't wait for further discussion, already moving toward the trees. Emma followed, her tranquilizer gun at the ready. Kyle trailed behind, his heart pounding as the shadows seemed to close in around them.

The young ferals came into view, their small forms barely visible beneath the gnarled roots of the oak tree. They were huddled together, their glowing eyes wide and frightened as they stared at the approaching figures. Their thin bodies were smeared with mud, and their movements were jittery, every sound making them flinch.

"Easy," Rick murmured, his voice low and steady. "We're not here to hurt you."

Emma moved to his side, her movements slow and deliberate. "They're not aggressive. Just scared."

Kyle stayed a few paces back, his flashlight trembling slightly as he watched. "They're so... small."

"Doesn't make them any less dangerous," Rick muttered. He crouched down slowly, keeping his tranquilizer gun at his side. "We need to get them into containment units before they bolt. Emma, get the restraints ready."

Emma nodded, pulling a set of small harnesses from her pack. She moved carefully, her gaze never leaving the ferals. "Rick, they're not going to like this."

"They don't have to," Rick replied. "They just have to stay put."

One of the ferals let out a low growl, its tiny claws digging into the mud. The others tensed, their glowing eyes darting between Rick and Emma.

Kyle took a step forward, his voice hesitant. "What do we do if they run?"

"They won't get far," Rick said firmly. "But let's make sure it doesn't come to that."

As Rick reached for the nearest feral, a faint rustling sound came from the trees behind them. Everyone froze, their eyes snapping toward the darkness. The growling started again, low and guttural, but this time it wasn't coming from the young ones.

Rick rose slowly, his hand tightening on his gun. "Bravo, report. You see anything?"

The radio crackled, but there was no response.

"Emma," Rick said quietly, his tone razor-sharp. "Stay with the juveniles. Kyle, back her up. I'm checking the perimeter."

Rick moved through the dense underbrush, his steps deliberate and soundless despite the rain-soaked terrain. The growling grew louder, interspersed with sharp snarls and the faint sound of scuffling. He tightened his grip on the tranquilizer gun, his sharp eyes scanning the dimly lit forest as he approached the commotion.

When he reached the edge of the clearing, the scene before him made his stomach tighten. Bravo team was spread out, their weapons trained on two large ferals—a male and a female. Both creatures were tall and sinewy, their bodies scarred from countless battles. They moved with a predatory grace, circling the team in erratic, aggressive motions.

But it wasn't just their size or ferocity that caught Rick's attention. The male feral was clutching something—a smaller, lifeless figure dangling from its clawed hand. It took Rick only a moment to recognize the broken body as another feral, her form smaller and less intimidating than the two holding her.

Rick's jaw tightened as he stepped forward, raising his voice over the din. "Status?"

The Bravo lead, a vampire with a steady but strained demeanor, glanced back at him. "They're not backing down. Every time we move, they lunge. The dead one's got them riled up."

Rick's gaze flicked to the lifeless feral, her body limp and marred with deep gashes. It was clear she'd been in a brutal fight before succumbing to her injuries. But it wasn't just her wounds that drew his attention—it was her size and the faint signs of maternal care he recognized in her form. Her teeth were worn in a way that indicated she'd scavenged for food, her claws dulled from frequent digging.

"She's the mother," Rick said quietly, more to himself than to anyone else.

Emma's voice crackled through his comm. "Rick, what's going on? Did you find Bravo?"

Rick raised the comm to his mouth, his voice low but urgent. "Found them. Two adults. One dead feral—the mother. Juveniles' mother. These two killed her."

A heavy silence followed on the other end. Then Emma's voice came back, colder this time. "So, what's their play?"

Rick's expression darkened as he watched the ferals snarl and pace. "Could be anything. Some ferals kill to take younglings —raise them as their own or use them to strengthen a pack. Others..." He trailed off, his tone hardening. "Others eat them."

Emma's response was sharp. "You're saying they came here for the kids?"

Rick nodded grimly, though she couldn't see him. "Looks like it."

The male feral growled deeply, a sound that seemed to reverberate through the trees, its glowing eyes fixed unrelentingly on Rick. It lifted the lifeless body of the mother higher, the broken form dangling limply in its claws, as though mocking them—taunting the line of agents. A guttural snarl ripped from its throat, raw and primal, the sound echoing into the surrounding darkness.

Beside it, the female feral crouched low, her claws digging into the mud as her muscles coiled like a spring, ready to launch.

Rick raised a hand, palm flat, signaling Bravo team to hold their fire. "Easy," he said, his voice cutting through the growing tension like a blade—calm, firm, and unyielding. "We don't need a bloodbath."

The lead agent, his rifle half-raised, spoke up, frustration bleeding into his tone. "They're not giving us much of a choice, Rick. Every time we move, they get more aggressive."

Rick took a measured step forward, his boots sinking slightly into the rain-softened earth. His movements were deliberate, controlled, his tranquilizer gun steady in his hands. "That's because they think they've won," he said, his tone quiet but edged with certainty. "They've got the mother, and they think the kids are next." He glanced briefly at the lead agent before turning his gaze back to the ferals. "We need to change the narrative."

"And how do you plan to do that?" the agent pressed, tension still thrumming in his voice.

Rick's smirk was faint, a mere flicker of determination. "By reminding them who's in charge."

Another step forward. The male feral's snarl deepened, its claws flexing instinctively around the mother's corpse. The creature's muscles tensed, its eyes narrowing, as though trying to decide whether Rick was predator or prey.

Rick didn't waver. His tranquilizer gun remained trained on the creature's chest, his gaze locked unshakably onto those glowing, feral eyes. "You think you've got the upper hand," Rick said, his words deliberate and steady, carrying no hint of fear. "But you don't."

The male feral screeched in response, a piercing sound that cut through the damp air like shattered glass. It bared its jagged teeth, hoisting the dead mother higher, its posturing desperate and aggressive—one last push for dominance.

Rick didn't blink. Didn't flinch. He stood his ground, letting the creature test him, waiting for its resolve to crack.

The moment broke.

The female feral moved first, a blur of speed and instinct as she darted toward Rick, her claws slicing through the air.

"Fire!" the lead agent barked. Bravo team sprang into action, their tranquilizer rifles hissing as a volley of darts struck the female in quick succession. She let out a choked snarl, stumbling mid-sprint, her momentum crumbling as the sedative surged through her veins. She staggered, her claws scraping the dirt before she finally collapsed in a heap.

Rick didn't hesitate. His finger squeezed the trigger, and his dart struck the male feral dead center in the chest.

The creature roared in fury, the sound a deafening mix of rage and desperation. Its grip on the mother's body tightened momentarily before its limbs began to tremble. A second dart from Bravo team buried itself into the side of its neck, and the feral let out one last guttural growl before its legs buckled. It collapsed backward, the mother's lifeless body slipping from its claws and landing with a dull thud.

Rick exhaled slowly, his tranquilizer gun still raised as he surveyed the scene. The forest felt unnaturally still for a moment, as though even the air was holding its breath.

"Targets down," Rick said finally, his voice calm and steady despite the lingering tension. He lowered his weapon, glancing toward the lead agent. "Secure them."

The Bravo team moved quickly, restraining the two ferals with reinforced cuffs and harnesses. Rick crouched beside the dead mother, his expression grim as he examined her injuries. It was clear she'd fought hard to protect her young, but against two larger, more experienced ferals, the odds had been impossible.

"She never stood a chance," Rick muttered, his voice low.

The lead agent nodded, his tone somber. "What about the juveniles?"

Rick straightened, his gaze hardening. "We secure them. We're not leaving them out here."

He turned back toward the direction of the oak tree, his comm crackling as Emma's voice came through. "Rick? What's going on?"

"Two hostiles secured," Rick replied. "Mother's dead. Kids are safe for now, but we're not out of the woods yet. Literally."

Emma sighed heavily, her frustration evident. "Great. And I thought tonight couldn't get worse."

Rick smirked faintly, his tone laced with dry humor. "Welcome to Spearhead."

CHAPTER 10

Rick wiped the rain from his face as he made his way back to the oak tree where Emma was crouched with the four feral younglings. The faint sound of the restrained adult ferals being loaded into the transport cage echoed in the distance, but his focus was now entirely on the little ones.

As he approached, Emma glanced up, her expression tight but relieved. "About time. How bad was it?"

Rick crouched down beside her, keeping his voice low. "Mother's dead. Two adults killed her—most likely trying to take the kids. Bravo team has them secured, but it's not pretty."

Emma let out a slow breath, her gaze flicking back to the younglings huddled together. "Figures. They've been like this since we got here. Scared out of their minds, but..." She trailed off, nodding toward the smallest of the group.

Rick followed her gaze. One of the younglings, no older than three, was curled up under a tattered blanket, her wide, glowing eyes darting between Rick and Emma. Despite her obvious fear, she kept her small body pressed tightly against her sisters, her arms spread protectively around them. She bared her teeth in a faint snarl, her claws clutching the edge of the blanket like it was her last line of defense.

"She's been guarding them the whole time," Emma said quietly. "Didn't let me get close until I brought the blanket. Even then, she hasn't let her guard down."

Rick studied the youngling, his expression unreadable. Her

movements were jittery, her breathing shallow but steady. She looked malnourished—ribs visible beneath her pale, mud-streaked skin—but her resolve was unshakable.

"She's the dominant one," Rick murmured. "Protective instinct kicked in when the mother was killed. She's doing everything she can to keep them safe."

Emma nodded, her tone softening. "She's got guts, I'll give her that. But it's not enough. They're too young to survive out there without help."

Rick shifted slightly, lowering himself to their eye level. The youngling's gaze snapped to him immediately, her small body tensing as she let out a low growl. Her sisters clung to her sides, their glowing eyes peeking out from behind her shoulders.

"Easy," Rick said gently, his voice calm but firm. "We're not here to hurt you."

The youngling didn't relax. If anything, her growl deepened, her tiny claws digging into the dirt as if preparing to lunge. Rick didn't move, his steady gaze meeting hers.

"She doesn't trust you," Emma said, not unkindly. "Can you blame her?"

"No," Rick replied, his tone measured. "But she's going to have to."

He reached into his jacket pocket, pulling out a small packet of dried meat. The faint scent caught the youngling's attention immediately, her growling faltering as her nose twitched. Her sisters stirred behind her, their own hunger overriding their fear for a brief moment.

Rick held the packet out, his movements slow and deliberate. "Here," he said quietly. "Take it. It's yours."

The youngling hesitated, her glowing eyes flicking between the packet and Rick's face. For a moment, she didn't move, her protective instincts warring with her need to eat. Then, cautiously, she reached out, her small claws snatching the packet from his hand.

"She's quick," Emma remarked, watching as the youngling tore into the meat, her sisters following suit as they crowded around her. "Smart, too. She knew it wasn't a threat."

Rick nodded, his gaze never leaving the younglings. "They'll need more than food to survive. They're going to need time. Stability. And a hell of a lot of patience."

Emma's brow furrowed. "You think they'll adapt?"

"They don't have a choice," Rick said simply, his tone carrying a quiet finality. "If we leave them like this, they'll die. Something out there will get to them, or their own instincts will tear them apart."

The younglings finished the packet of blood with desperate speed, the faint crinkle of the empty plastic breaking the stillness. When it was gone, their glowing eyes flicked back to Rick, sharp and wary, as if calculating whether he had more to give. The dominant one—small but fierce—remained in front, her frail frame squared protectively between her sisters and the strangers.

"Look at her," Rick murmured, nodding subtly toward the youngling. "She's already taking on the role of pack leader. She doesn't understand it yet, but it's there. Pure instinct."

Emma watched the youngling for a long moment, her sharp features softening just slightly. The girl's posture, the way her narrowed eyes tracked every move—they spoke of strength, but it was a fragile kind of strength, stretched thin by survival.

"She's tough," Emma said quietly. "But tough only gets you so far when you're that small."

Rick stood slowly, rising to his full height, his joints creaking faintly as he brushed dirt from his knees. "That's why we're here."

He turned his attention to Kyle, who had kept his distance, lingering several paces back like he wasn't sure if he was allowed to get any closer. His eyes were wide, filled with something between awe and apprehension, as he took in the scene.

"Kyle," Rick said, his tone snapping the younger man from his daze, "call in the handlers. We're bringing them back to the sanctuary."

Kyle blinked, startled, as though he hadn't expected that decision. "All four of them?"

"All four," Rick confirmed, his voice firm and unwavering. He glanced back at the younglings, the faintest hint of something unreadable flickering across his expression. "And tell them to bring containment units. Small ones. They'll need to stay together, but we can't risk them breaking out."

Kyle hesitated, his eyes shifting toward the younglings huddled together—small, fragile, but undeniably dangerous. After a brief pause, he nodded quickly, turning to pull his radio from his belt, as he relayed the instructions. Emma rose to her feet, stretching slightly as she glanced at Rick.

"You're taking this one personally, aren't you?" she asked, her tone light but knowing.

Rick didn't answer immediately, his gaze lingering on the younglings as they huddled together under the blanket. Finally, he sighed. "They've already lost everything. We can't let them lose each other."

Emma smiled faintly, her usual sharpness softening. "You've got a soft spot, Rick. Don't let the kids figure that out. They'll take advantage of it."

Rick smirked, his expression unreadable. "They'll have to earn it first."

As the handlers arrived, carrying the small containment units, the younglings huddled closer together, their fear returning. The dominant one growled again, her tiny body trembling as she positioned herself in front of her sisters.

Rick crouched down once more, his voice calm but firm. "It's okay," he said quietly. "We're going to keep you safe. I promise."

The youngling didn't respond, but her growling stopped. She watched him carefully as the handlers approached, her glowing eyes filled with both fear and determination.

Rick stood, his gaze hardening as he addressed the handlers. "Be careful with them. They're not just cargo."

The handlers nodded, moving with slow precision as they secured the younglings into the containment units. The dominant one resisted briefly, her small claws scrabbling against the restraints, but she eventually relented, her protective instincts unable to overcome the handlers' careful approach.

As the units were loaded into the transport, Rick and Emma exchanged a glance. "Think they'll make it?" Emma asked.

Rick's smirk returned, faint but determined. "We'll make sure they do."

The hum of the transport vehicle was subdued as Rick navigated the quiet roads back to the lab. The rain had stopped, leaving a faint mist clinging to the asphalt, illuminated by the vehicle's headlights. In the back, the four younglings lay in their containment units, their glowing eyes occasionally flickering open before shutting again, exhaustion overtaking them.

Kyle glanced toward the rear compartment, his clipboard resting on his lap. "You think they'll be okay in the lab? I mean... after everything?"

Rick kept his eyes on the road, his voice steady. "It's not about what we think. It's about what they need. And right now, they need safety."

Emma leaned against the passenger-side window, her gaze distant. "And space. If we crowd them too soon, it'll only make things worse."

Kyle nodded, though his nervous energy was still apparent. "Yeah, I get that. But they're so... small. It feels wrong to put them in a containment room."

Rick's grip on the wheel tightened briefly. "It's not containment. It's their space. Safe, secure, and designed to make them feel like they're not trapped."

Kyle didn't argue further, his eyes returning to the glowing dashboard as the lab's towering structure came into view. The facility was quiet at this hour, the usual hum of activity subdued in the aftermath of the long night.

Rick parked the vehicle in the loading bay, cutting the engine. He stepped out and stretched briefly, his muscles stiff from the drive. Emma followed, her sharp gaze scanning the area out of habit before moving toward the transport's rear compartment.

"Let's get them inside," Rick said, motioning to the handlers waiting nearby. "Carefully."

The handlers worked with practiced precision, lifting the containment units and carrying them toward the lab's interior. Rick, Emma, and Kyle followed, their boots echoing faintly against the sterile floors. The air inside was cool, the faint hum of machinery a constant backdrop.

They reached the designated room—a spacious, enclosed area with a reinforced glass front. Inside, the environment had been designed with the ferals' needs in mind. Soft, dim lighting illuminated the space, and the floor was covered in textured mats that mimicked natural terrain. Small alcoves and hideaways lined the walls, offering the younglings places to retreat and feel secure.

Emma stepped closer to the glass, her arms crossed as she inspected the room. "Looks good. Plenty of hiding spots, but open enough for observation."

Rick nodded, his gaze sweeping over the space. "They'll need time to adjust. For now, we just let them settle in."

The handlers carefully transferred the younglings from their containment units into the room. The dominant one, the smallest of the group, was the first to stir. Her glowing eyes blinked open, and she let out a faint growl, immediately positioning herself in front of her sisters.

Rick crouched near the glass, his movements slow and deliberate. "It's okay," he said quietly. "You're safe here."

The youngling didn't relax, her small body trembling as she watched him through the barrier. Her sisters huddled behind her, their wide eyes darting around the unfamiliar environment.

"They're scared," Kyle said softly, standing a few paces back. "Maybe we should give them some space."

Rick stood slowly, his gaze never leaving the younglings. "That's the plan. They need to feel like this is their territory. If we push too hard, they'll just see us as a threat."

Emma stepped closer, nodding toward the alcoves. "They'll probably claim one of those corners first. Ferals like to feel enclosed when they're scared."

Rick glanced at her, his smirk faint. "You've been paying attention."

"Somebody has to keep you in check," Emma replied, her tone light but teasing.

Kyle approached cautiously, his clipboard tucked under one arm. "So... what now?"

Rick turned to him, his expression calm but firm. "Now, we wait. Monitor them, but don't interfere unless it's absolutely necessary. Let them come to us on their own terms."

Kyle nodded, scribbling a few notes. "Got it."

The three of them watched as the younglings began to explore hesitantly. The dominant one led the way, sniffing at the mats and inspecting the alcoves with cautious curiosity. Her sisters followed closely, their movements slow and jittery.

"She's already taking charge," Emma observed. "Not surprising."

Rick nodded. "She's the protector. That instinct won't go away anytime soon."

Kyle frowned slightly, glancing at Rick. "Is that a good thing?"

"It can be," Rick said. "But it can also make things harder. If she sees us as a threat, she'll fight tooth and nail to keep her sisters safe."

Emma leaned against the glass, her arms crossed. "And we've seen how small ferals can fight. Don't let their size fool you, Kyle. They're faster and stronger than they look."

Kyle swallowed hard, his gaze returning to the younglings. "Noted."

The dominant youngling paused near one of the alcoves, her glowing eyes scanning the room before darting back to Rick and Emma. She let out a low growl, her small claws scratching at the mat as if to warn them to stay away.

Rick took a step back, his hands raised in a gesture of non-threat. "It's your space," he said quietly. "We're just here to help."

The youngling didn't respond, but her growling stopped. She turned back to her sisters, nudging them toward the alcove with a series of soft growls and chirps. They followed without hesitation, disappearing into the shadows.

Emma straightened, her expression thoughtful. "They're settling in faster than I expected."

Rick shrugged. "Survival instinct. They know they're safer in there than out here."

Kyle scribbled another note, glancing at Rick. "What happens when they do settle in? I mean, what's the next step?"

Rick's smirk returned, faint but resolute. "That depends on them. We'll take it slow—earn their trust one step at a time. But for now..." He glanced at the alcove where the younglings had disappeared. "For now, we let them rest."

Rick leaned against the counter in the break room, a steaming cup of coffee in his hand. Across from him, Emma sat with her feet propped up on another chair, her own mug balanced precariously on her knee. The faint hum of machinery from the lab filled the air, a background noise they had both grown used to over the years.

"So," Emma said, breaking the silence, "we're going to have to call them something eventually. Can't just keep saying 'the little ones.'"

Rick raised an eyebrow over the rim of his cup. "You're suggesting we name them?"

"Unless you want to start assigning them numbers," Emma quipped, taking a sip. "Might as well pick something that makes them sound less like a science project."

Rick exhaled through his nose, setting his mug down on the counter. "Alright. What do you have in mind?"

Emma tapped her chin, feigning deep thought. "Well, the dominant one... she's got that scrappy, protective vibe. Stubborn as hell, too. What about 'Raven'? Strong, sharp, and a bit brooding. Fits her."

Rick nodded slowly, considering it. "Raven works. What about the others?"

Emma tilted her head, her smirk returning. "The quiet one who keeps hiding behind Raven? Let's go with 'Willow.' Soft, but resilient."

Rick smirked faintly. "And the one who keeps fidgeting with everything? Always looking like she's about to bolt?"

"Skye," Emma said decisively. "She's got that restless energy."

Rick took another sip of his coffee, his gaze distant as he thought about the smallest one, who seemed to cling to Raven the most. "The littlest one… she's still holding onto everyone else. Keeps looking to them for reassurance."

Emma nodded thoughtfully. "Yeah, she's a little softer. What about 'Luna'? Has a quiet strength to it."

Rick repeated the names, testing them like pieces of a puzzle coming together. "Raven, Willow, Skye, and Luna." His voice was even, but something about the way he said it felt final. "Not bad."

Emma grinned, raising her mug in a mock toast, her expression smug. "See? Told you I'm good at this."

Rick opened his mouth for a retort, but the faint sound of approaching footsteps cut him off. Instinctively, he straightened, his posture shifting from relaxed to sharp, like a wire pulled taut. The door opened, and all the air in the room seemed to shift.

The leader of Spearhead stepped in, moving with the kind of grace that felt deliberate, every motion smooth and purposeful, as though time itself bent to her will. Tall and striking, she carried herself with a regal air that contrasted the quiet weight of her presence—a power so old it seemed to settle into the very air around her. Though she looked no older than her early thirties, her piercing gaze hinted at centuries of life, seeing through everything it landed on with unsettling clarity.

"Boss," Rick said, his tone respectful but easy, like he'd long grown accustomed to her intimidating aura. "Didn't expect you here tonight."

The ancient vampire's eyes swept the room in a single, assessing glance—Rick, Emma, the scattered paperwork—before settling on the observation room beyond the glass. For a moment, the hard edge of her features softened, if only slightly. "I heard about the younglings. Four of them, alive and together. That's... unusual."

Emma stood, setting her mug down carefully on the table, as though the presence of the Boss demanded even the smallest gesture be intentional. "Unusual is putting it lightly," she replied, her voice quieter, more reverent. She nodded toward the glass. "They're only alive because of their mother. Even after she died, they've managed to hold on."

The Boss's gaze lingered on the younglings beyond the glass, their faintly glowing eyes like pinpricks of light in the dim room. For a moment, she stood utterly still, her expression a perfect mask of neutrality. But beneath the surface, something flickered—curiosity, perhaps, or a deeper emotion carefully buried beneath centuries of composure.

Her eyes narrowed slightly as she stepped forward, the soft click of her heels punctuating the silence. She stopped just short of the glass, her presence commanding as she studied the little ones exploring their new space.

"It's rare," she said quietly, her voice low but carrying a weight that filled the room. "Almost unheard of." Her gaze tracked the dominant youngling as she nudged one of her sisters toward a quieter corner. "When a feral mother is killed, the younglings don't usually survive."

Her tone cooled, almost clinical, though the faintest edge of something mournful undercut her words. "The stress alone is often too much for them."

Rick leaned back against the counter, crossing his arms. "These ones are fighters. The dominant one—Raven—is already taking charge. She's keeping the others together."

"Raven?" the leader asked, arching an elegant brow.

"Just came up with names," Emma said with a faint smirk. "Makes it easier."

The leader hummed thoughtfully, her gaze not leaving the younglings. "Raven fits. She has that fire in her eyes. But don't mistake it for strength alone. That kind of protectiveness can be dangerous."

Rick nodded. "We're aware. She's got the instincts, but instincts aren't always enough. It'll take time to stabilize them."

The leader turned her sharp gaze to Rick. "Do you think it's possible? To stabilize them?"

Rick didn't hesitate. "Yes. It's not going to be easy, but they've already proven they can adapt. They've survived this long—they just need the right environment."

Emma chimed in, her tone lighter but firm. "And the right people watching out for them. Which, lucky for them, they've got."

The leader's lips curved into the faintest hint of a smile. "You've always had a soft spot for the difficult cases, Rick."

"Someone has to," Rick replied, his voice steady. "Better than giving up on them before we've even tried."

The leader nodded, her expression thoughtful as she returned her attention to the younglings. "They'll need more than just patience. If they survive, they'll be the exception, not the rule. And if they don't..."

"They will," Rick said firmly. "They're stronger than they look."

The leader studied him for a long moment before finally stepping back. "I hope you're right. For their sake, and for ours."

Emma exchanged a glance with Rick, her smirk softening into something more genuine. "No pressure, huh?"

Rick shook his head, picking up his coffee again. "Just another night at Spearhead."

The leader let out a soft chuckle, the sound rare but not unwelcome. "Keep me updated. I'll be watching their progress closely."

With that, she turned and strode out of the room, her footsteps fading into the quiet hum of the lab.

Emma leaned against the counter, exhaling deeply. "Well, that was... intense."

Rick shrugged. "She's got a point. These kids are an anomaly. If they make it, it'll change everything we thought we knew about ferals."

"And if they don't?" Emma asked, her tone quieter.

Rick's gaze returned to the observation room, where Raven was nudging her sisters toward a hiding spot near the corner. "Then we'll know we gave them the best shot they had."

CHAPTER 11

The lab hummed quietly through the night, its dimmed lights casting long shadows across the walls. Rain pattered softly against the reinforced windows, a soothing rhythm that blended with the ever-present sound of machines monitoring the younglings. It wasn't uncommon for the team to stay overnight—long shifts and unpredictable calls made the lab as much a home base as it was a workplace.

Rick leaned back in one of the break room chairs, his boots propped up on the table as he dozed lightly. His jacket was draped over his shoulders like a makeshift blanket, his breathing slow and even. Across the room, Emma sat cross-legged on a small couch, a datapad in her lap. The glow of the screen highlighted her focused expression as she reviewed reports, her attention occasionally flicking toward the observation room beyond the glass.

Kyle, however, was not so at ease.

He paced near the doorway, his arms crossed tightly over his chest. His eyes darted between the observation room and the sleeping Rick, his nerves plainly written across his face.

"Relax, Kyle," Emma said without looking up from her datapad. "They're not going to break through the glass."

Kyle stopped pacing, his eyes widening slightly. "That's not what I'm worried about."

Emma glanced at him, her smirk faint. "Then what? Afraid the coffee machine's going to malfunction?"

Kyle sighed, rubbing the back of his neck. "I don't know... It's just weird. Staying here. Sleeping here. This place feels... off."

"It's a lab," Emma replied, turning her attention back to the datapad. "It's supposed to feel off."

Rick stirred slightly, his voice cutting through the room without opening his eyes. "It feels like work. You'll get used to it."

Kyle glanced at Rick, his expression dubious. "Do you actually get used to it? Or do you just stop noticing how creepy it is?"

Rick opened one eye, his smirk barely visible in the dim light. "Both."

Emma chuckled softly, setting the datapad aside. "Kyle, you've got to learn how to compartmentalize. This place is what it needs to be. You want cozy? Go home. You want effective? Stay here."

Kyle sank into one of the chairs, his leg bouncing with nervous energy. "I just don't get how you two are so calm. We've got four ferals in there, and we're just... sitting around."

"They're kids," Rick said, his voice steady. "Scared, hungry, and exhausted kids. They're not a threat right now."

"But they *could* be," Kyle pressed. "If something sets them off—"

"They won't," Emma interrupted, her tone firm. "Not tonight, anyway. They're too busy trying to figure out if this place is safe."

Kyle exhaled sharply, shaking his head. "I don't know how you guys do this every night."

Rick sat up slowly, stretching his arms over his head. "Experience. And coffee."

Emma grinned. "Lots of coffee."

Kyle slumped back in his chair, staring at the ceiling. "So, this is normal for you? Sleeping in the lab, monitoring ferals, just...

waiting?"

"Pretty much," Emma said. "You'll get used to it."

Kyle muttered under his breath, "Not sure I want to."

The faint sound of growling drew all their attention to the observation room. Raven was awake, her glowing eyes scanning the space as she prowled near one of the alcoves. Her sisters were huddled together in the corner, their small forms barely visible in the shadows.

"She's still on edge," Emma observed, standing and moving closer to the glass. "Can't blame her, though. New environment, strangers everywhere—it's a lot for them to process."

Rick joined her at the glass, his gaze following Raven's movements. "She's testing the boundaries. Figuring out where she fits in this place."

Kyle hesitated, then moved to stand beside them. "You think she'll settle down?"

"She has to," Rick said simply. "If she doesn't, the others won't either."

Raven paused near the glass, her glowing eyes locking onto Rick's. She let out a low growl, her small body tense but not aggressive. It was more of a warning than a threat—a reminder that she wasn't ready to trust them yet.

Rick crouched slightly, meeting her gaze without flinching. "It's okay," he said softly, his voice steady. "You're safe here."

Raven didn't move, her growling tapering off into a faint rumble. After a moment, she turned and padded back to her sisters, curling up beside them in the corner.

"She's watching us," Kyle said quietly.

"They always are," Rick replied. "That's how they survive."

Emma leaned against the glass, her expression thoughtful. "She'll come around. Eventually."

Kyle glanced between Rick and Emma, his nerves settling slightly. "You two really do make it look easy."

Emma smirked. "That's because we've been doing it longer than you've been out of high school."

Rick chuckled softly, moving back to his chair. "Get some rest, Kyle. You'll need it."

Kyle hesitated, then finally nodded, settling into a nearby chair. The tension in the room eased as the quiet hum of the lab returned, broken only by the occasional sound of the younglings shifting in their sleep.

For Rick and Emma, it was just another night. For Kyle, it was a long step toward understanding the reality of their work.

The lab was silent except for the faint hum of machinery and the occasional crackle of static from a nearby monitor. Emma stirred on the couch, her datapad slipping from her lap onto the floor with a soft thud. She blinked groggily, brushing a hand through her hair as her sharp senses slowly returned. The dim light from the observation room caught her attention, drawing her gaze to the glass.

The younglings were restless.

Raven was prowling near the alcoves again, her small frame tense as she sniffed at the corners of the room. Her sisters remained huddled together, their glowing eyes watching her every move. The mats beneath them were crumpled and damp, evidence of the long night's unease.

Emma sighed, stretching as she stood. "Guess it's time for a refresh," she murmured, her voice barely above a whisper.

She grabbed a stack of clean, textured pads from a nearby

cabinet and made her way toward the observation room. The soft click of her boots echoed faintly in the quiet, a sound she knew would catch Raven's attention long before she reached the door.

Emma keyed in the access code, the lock disengaging with a soft hiss. She stepped inside carefully, the fresh pads balanced in her arms. The air was cooler here, designed to mimic an outdoor environment, and carried the faint scent of earth and rain from the mats.

Raven froze the moment Emma entered, her glowing eyes locking onto the vampire. A low growl rumbled from her throat, not loud but pointed. Her small body tensed, her claws gripping the textured surface beneath her.

"It's okay," Emma said softly, keeping her movements slow and deliberate. "I'm just here to clean up. You don't want to sleep on wet mats, do you?"

Raven didn't respond, of course, but her growl faded slightly. She watched Emma intently, every muscle in her tiny frame coiled and ready.

Emma crouched near the edge of the room, keeping her distance from the alcove where the others were huddled. She began swapping out the damp pads for fresh ones, her movements fluid and unthreatening. "See? Nothing to worry about. Just making things a little more comfortable."

One of the smaller younglings—Skye, Emma had decided—peeked out from behind Raven. Her glowing eyes were wide with curiosity, her small claws gripping the edge of the alcove. She chirped softly, a sound that caught both Raven and Emma's attention.

Emma glanced at her, a faint smile tugging at her lips. "You're braver than I thought."

Skye chirped again, stepping forward cautiously. Her

movements were jittery but curious, her nose twitching as she sniffed the air around Emma. Raven let out a faint rumble, but she didn't stop Skye from moving closer.

"That's right," Emma said softly. "Just checking things out, huh?"

She finished laying the fresh pads and backed away slowly, giving Skye room to explore. The little one sniffed at the new mats, her glowing eyes darting back to Emma as if seeking reassurance.

Raven growled again, stepping between Skye and Emma. Her protective instincts were still on high alert, and she nudged Skye back toward the alcove with a soft but firm gesture.

Emma didn't push further. She straightened slowly, brushing her hands against her jacket. "Alright, you win. I'll give you some space."

As she stepped back toward the door, she glanced over her shoulder. Raven was still watching her, but her growl had faded into a faint rumble. Skye peeked out again, curiosity flickering in her glowing eyes.

Emma smiled faintly. "You're a tough crowd, but I'll win you over eventually."

She stepped out of the room, the lock clicking back into place behind her. Rick was leaning against the wall nearby, his arms crossed and a knowing smirk on his face.

"Couldn't sleep?" he asked, his voice low.

Emma shrugged. "Mats were soaked. Figured they'd rest better if I swapped them out."

Rick nodded, glancing toward the observation room. "They let you get close?"

"Skye did," Emma said, a note of satisfaction in her tone. "Raven wasn't happy about it, though. She's got that whole 'pack leader' thing locked down."

Rick chuckled softly. "Sounds about right. You think they'll settle in?"

"They're getting there," Emma replied. "Slowly, but they are. Skye's already curious. That's a good sign."

Rick's smirk widened. "You're good at this, you know."

Emma rolled her eyes, brushing past him. "Don't get sappy on me, Rick. It's late."

He chuckled again, following her back to the break room. The night wore on quietly, but the faint sounds of the younglings shifting on their fresh mats carried a subtle sense of progress. It wasn't much, but it was a start.

CHAPTER 12

The morning light filtered weakly through the lab's reinforced windows, muted by layers of grime and the thick glass designed to withstand far worse than sunlight. Shadows stretched lazily across the observation room walls, shifting faintly with the hum of machinery and the soft, indistinct murmur of voices drifting in from the break room. It was a quiet morning—on the surface, at least.

Inside the younglings' enclosure, however, the quiet was deceptive. Something was happening.

Raven was at it again. The small but determined youngling moved with purpose, darting across the room like a shadow with glowing eyes. Overnight, she'd staked a claim on one of the alcoves in the corner—a tiny hollow carved out for herself. Now, she seemed intent on turning it into something more. Her claws scraped softly against the textured mats as she dragged one toward her chosen space, her movements deliberate, methodical.

Pausing only briefly, Raven lifted her head and let out a sharp chirp, the sound cutting through the stillness like a spark. It echoed off the walls, sending a ripple of motion through her sisters.

Skye was the first to react. The jittery youngling scrambled toward a crumpled pile of blankets in the corner, her claws snagging on the fabric as she tugged and pulled. The blanket caught stubbornly on one of the mats, but Skye refused to let go, her small frame straining with soft, determined grunts as she dragged it toward Raven's alcove.

Willow and Luna hung back at first, their glowing eyes darting between their sisters and the unfamiliar space that still felt too open, too exposed. Willow, quieter and more cautious, finally made her move. She crept forward on light, tentative steps, her head low as if expecting something to strike. Spotting a loose mat near the edge of the room, she grabbed it carefully with her teeth and began dragging it, her small movements precise and careful.

Luna, however, remained pressed against the wall, her small frame partially curled as though trying to disappear into the corner. Her wide eyes followed the others with quiet intensity, curiosity flickering behind her fear, but her instinct to stay hidden kept her frozen in place.

From the observation room, Rick and Emma stood side by side, mugs of coffee cradled in their hands, steam curling faintly in the chilled air. They watched in silence, the scene unfolding before them like an unscripted experiment.

"They're building a den," Emma said, breaking the quiet. Her tone carried a mix of amusement and curiosity, the faintest smile tugging at the corner of her mouth. "Classic feral behavior."

Rick nodded, his gaze steady. "Makes sense. They need a safe place to regroup, especially after everything they've been through."

"Raven's calling the shots," Emma added, gesturing toward the dominant youngling. "She's got them working like a team."

Rick's smirk was faint but approving. "She's got good instincts. Knows they need each other to survive."

Kyle joined them, yawning as he sipped from a steaming mug. He glanced through the glass, his brows furrowing. "What are they doing?"

"Instinct," Emma replied simply. "They're creating a den—a safe zone. Something to make this place feel like their own."

Kyle tilted his head, watching as Raven chirped again, nudging Skye to adjust the blankets. "It's... kind of impressive. They're so young, but they're already working together."

"Survival doesn't wait for age," Rick said. "They're scared, but they're adapting."

Inside the room, Raven stepped back to inspect their makeshift den. The alcove now had a crumpled mat as a floor, with the blankets piled around the entrance like a protective barrier. She chirped softly, nudging Skye and Willow into the space. Skye went willingly, curling up near the back, but Willow hesitated, her glowing eyes darting toward Luna.

Raven let out a sharp chirp, her tone almost scolding. Willow flinched but turned toward Luna, nudging her sister gently. Luna let out a faint whimper, her small claws scraping at the mat beneath her, but she didn't resist as Willow guided her toward the alcove.

"Look at that," Emma said, her voice softer now. "She's making sure they all stay together."

Kyle leaned closer to the glass, his interest piqued. "Is that normal? For them to... I don't know, act like a family?"

Emma shrugged. "Depends on the situation. Without their mother, they're relying on each other. Raven's stepping into that role because she has to. The others are following because it's their best shot."

Rick's gaze remained fixed on the younglings. "It's not just instinct. There's trust there, too. Even if they're scared, they know they're safer together."

Inside the room, Raven finally entered the alcove, settling herself at the entrance like a sentinel. Her glowing eyes scanned the room, her small body tense but calm. She let out a low rumble, a sound that seemed to reassure her sisters. The tension in the room eased slightly, the younglings huddling closer together in their makeshift den.

"They're settling in," Rick said quietly, taking another sip of his coffee. "Still a long way to go, but this is a start."

Emma nodded, her smirk faint. "Think they'll let us get close today?"

Rick's smirk mirrored hers. "One step at a time."

Kyle glanced between them, his expression skeptical. "You really think they'll trust us? After everything?"

"They don't have to trust us right away," Rick replied. "They just need to know we're not a threat. Trust comes later."

Emma tapped the glass lightly, drawing Raven's attention. The youngling's glowing eyes locked onto her, unblinking and cautious. Emma smiled faintly, her voice soft. "Good job, kid. Keep them safe."

Raven didn't respond, of course, but her gaze lingered for a moment before she turned back to her sisters, curling around them protectively.

Kyle let out a low whistle, shaking his head. "That's… something else."

"It's survival," Rick said simply. "And they're damn good at it."

As the three of them watched, the younglings settled deeper into their den, their small bodies finally relaxing as exhaustion took over. The room was quiet again, save for the soft sound of their breathing and the faint hum of the lab.

For the first time since their arrival, they seemed at peace.

As the morning wore on, the lab settled into its usual rhythm. Rick, Emma, and Kyle continued their work in the observation area, reviewing data and keeping a close eye on the younglings. The makeshift den they'd created in the alcove became their central point, with Raven still acting as the protector, her sharp gaze monitoring every corner of the room.

Kyle leaned against the counter, flipping through a stack of reports with a distracted expression. "So, what's the next step? Just... watch them all day?"

"Observation is the first step," Emma replied, not looking up from her datapad. "They've only just started to settle. If we try to push anything too soon, we'll lose whatever progress we've made."

Kyle frowned. "What kind of progress? They're hiding in a pile of blankets."

Emma arched an eyebrow at him. "And yesterday, they were clawing at the glass and growling at us like we were the enemy. Now they're starting to see this place as safe. That's progress."

Rick smirked faintly, sipping his coffee as he leaned back in his chair. "It's about small wins, Kyle. You're not going to see a feral flip a switch and suddenly act like a normal vampire. It's a process."

Kyle muttered something under his breath, flipping another page of the report. "I guess I just don't see how we go from 'hiding in blankets' to... whatever it is you're hoping for."

"You'll see," Rick said, his tone calm but firm. "If you're patient."

The faint sound of movement drew their attention back to the observation room. Skye had emerged from the den, her small form moving cautiously across the mats. Her glowing eyes scanned the room, her nose twitching as she sniffed at the air.

"She's curious," Emma murmured, stepping closer to the glass. "That's a good sign."

Raven chirped from the den, a sharp sound that made Skye

pause. The dominant youngling peered out from the alcove, watching her sister with a mixture of caution and command.

"She doesn't want her wandering too far," Rick observed. "Typical pack behavior. The leader sets the boundaries."

Skye hesitated, glancing back at Raven before continuing her exploration. She sniffed at the edges of the mats, her tiny claws scraping against the surface as she tested her surroundings. Willow peeked out from the den, her glowing eyes wide as she watched Skye's movements. Luna remained curled up near the back, her small body still pressed tightly against the blankets.

Kyle leaned closer to the glass, his curiosity piqued. "Why's she so interested in the mats? They're just... mats."

"To you," Emma said with a smirk. "To her, they're part of her environment. Ferals rely on their senses—smell, touch, sound. She's learning everything she can about this space."

Rick nodded. "She's figuring out if it's safe. If the mats smell like danger, she'll bolt. If they smell neutral or familiar, she'll relax."

Skye paused near the corner of the room, her glowing eyes darting toward the glass. She let out a soft chirp, her small claws tapping against the mat as she shifted her weight. Raven chirped back from the den, the sound sharper this time, almost scolding.

"She's calling her back," Emma said. "Doesn't want her too far from the group."

Skye hesitated, her gaze flicking between the glass and the den. Finally, she turned and scampered back, her small body moving with jittery but determined energy. She curled up next to Willow, her chirps softening into faint rumbles as she nestled into the blankets.

"Raven's keeping tight control," Rick said, his tone thoughtful. "She's not just protecting them—she's training them. Teaching them to stay close, to follow her lead."

Kyle shook his head, his expression one of amazement. "They're just kids, but they're already acting like... I don't know, soldiers."

Emma smirked. "Welcome to the world of ferals. Instinct runs deep."

Rick stepped away from the glass, setting his coffee cup down on the counter. "Alright, let's give them some space. They've done enough for one morning."

Emma followed him, her datapad tucked under her arm. "You think we'll be able to start "Interactions soon?" Kyle asked, his voice edged with equal parts curiosity and apprehension.

"Maybe," Rick replied cautiously, his eyes fixed on the observation room. "Raven's still on edge, but the others are starting to relax. If she starts seeing us as part of the environment instead of a threat, we'll have a better shot."

Kyle frowned, glancing at the younglings through the glass. "And if she doesn't?"

Rick's smirk was faint but brimming with confidence. "Then we keep trying. Patience, remember?"

Emma chuckled softly as they turned toward the break room, her footsteps light against the tile floor. "You should've put that on your resume, Rick. *Professional patience expert.*"

Rick raised an eyebrow at her, his smirk twisting into something drier. "If I had to deal with you every day, patience wasn't optional."

Emma rolled her eyes, though the grin tugging at her lips betrayed her amusement. "You're lucky I'm not a feral. You wouldn't last a day."

Kyle muttered under his breath, his gaze lingering on the observation room even as he followed them. "Sometimes I think I'm the only one here who remembers how dangerous they are."

Emma's smirk softened, fading just slightly. She glanced at Kyle, her voice quieter but firm. "Trust me, Kyle. We haven't forgotten. That's *why* we're doing this—to figure out if there's another way."

Rick's expression turned serious, his gaze steady as he looked back at the younglings through the glass. "And the fact that they're still here, still fighting to survive? That's proof enough that we have to try, too."

The hum of the lab was almost soothing, broken only by the occasional soft beep of machinery. Overhead, the lights inside the observation room had shifted subtly, warming to mimic the gentle glow of a mid-morning sun. The soft light pooled across the mats and alcoves, creating a faint illusion of natural warmth.

Inside the enclosure, movement stirred. Raven poked her head out of the den first, her glowing eyes slicing through the light as she scanned the room with sharp, calculating caution. Her small body was tense, coiled tight like a spring as she sniffed at the air, testing for any change in the atmosphere. Each subtle motion seemed deliberate—wary, but not panicked.

From the break room, Rick and Emma sat at the long counter facing the glass, stacks of datapads, reports, and hastily scribbled notes spread haphazardly across the surface. A pot of coffee sat nearby, steam curling lazily from its spout, the rich aroma mixing with the faint, sterile scent of antiseptic that clung stubbornly to the air.

"They're testing the waters," Emma said, her tone thoughtful as her pen tapped absently against the corner of her pad. She didn't look up, her sharp gaze catching every twitch of movement beyond the glass. "Raven's doing recon."

Rick smirked faintly, scrolling through a report on his datapad. "She's cautious. Smart, but cautious."

"She has to be," Emma replied. "If they wander too far and

something happens, she's the one responsible."

Inside the room, Raven took a tentative step out of the alcove, her small claws clicking softly against the mats. She sniffed the air again, her glowing eyes darting between the corners of the space. Satisfied for the moment, she let out a soft chirp, the sound drawing her sisters closer to the den's entrance.

Skye was the first to respond, her jittery energy propelling her forward. She darted out a few steps, her tiny form vibrating with curiosity, before retreating back to the safety of the den. Willow followed more cautiously, her movements deliberate as she sniffed at the mats and edges of the room.

Luna remained at the edge of the den, her small body pressed against the blankets. She chirped softly, her wide eyes watching her sisters with a mixture of hesitation and longing.

Rick's gaze shifted from the datapad to the younglings. "She's still hanging back."

Emma glanced up, following his gaze. "Luna? Yeah. She's the shy one."

"Think Raven will pull her out?" Rick asked, setting his datapad aside.

"Maybe," Emma said. "But it'll be on Luna's terms. Raven's protective, not pushy."

Inside the room, Skye ventured a little further, her small claws scraping against the edge of a mat. She sniffed at the glass barrier, her nose pressing against the surface as she peered into the lab beyond. Her glowing eyes locked onto Rick and Emma, curiosity flickering behind her cautious demeanor.

"Skye's bold," Emma said with a smirk. "She's going to be trouble."

"She's already trouble," Rick replied, watching as the youngling chirped at the glass. "But bold's not bad. She's the one who'll explore first and figure out what's safe."

Willow had followed Skye's lead, her quiet movements almost blending into the room's stillness. She clawed at a loose mat, nudging it with her nose before retreating slightly. Raven let out another chirp, the sound sharp but not aggressive, her gaze flicking between her sisters and the den.

"She's keeping the leash tight," Emma murmured. "Won't let them get too far before pulling them back."

Sure enough, after a few more seconds of tentative exploration, Raven chirped again, the sound more insistent this time. Skye paused mid-step, glancing back at her sister before reluctantly scurrying toward the alcove. Willow followed without hesitation, her small body blending into the shadows near the den.

Rick leaned back in his chair, crossing his arms. "They're retreating faster than I expected."

"They're still figuring it out," Emma replied, jotting down a quick note. "It's the push-and-pull of instinct. Explore too far, and you're vulnerable. Stay too close, and you don't learn. Raven's balancing it."

Luna chirped again, her soft voice barely audible through the glass. She peeked out of the den but didn't move further, her small frame trembling slightly.

"She's the one we'll need to watch," Rick said quietly. "If she doesn't start exploring soon, she'll fall behind."

Emma nodded. "It's a risk. But she's got Raven. If anyone can pull her out, it's her."

As if on cue, Raven turned back toward Luna, her glowing eyes narrowing slightly. She let out a low, rumbling chirp, the sound carrying a clear command. Luna flinched but didn't move, her tiny claws gripping the edge of the blanket.

"Come on, kid," Emma murmured, her gaze fixed on the youngling. "You can do it."

Raven chirped again, more insistent this time. Luna let out a soft whimper, her wide eyes flicking between her sister and the rest of the room. Finally, with a trembling step, she crept forward, her small body low to the ground.

"There we go," Rick said, his tone calm but approving. "She's trying."

Luna moved slowly, her movements cautious and deliberate. She paused near the edge of the mats, her glowing eyes darting toward the glass. Her sisters had already returned to the den, their tiny forms huddled together in the shadows. Raven stood at the entrance, her gaze fixed on Luna, as if willing her to take another step.

"She'll get there," Emma said softly, her smirk faint. "She just needs time."

Rick nodded, his gaze steady. "They all do."

The younglings repeated the pattern throughout the morning —venturing out a few steps at a time before retreating back to the safety of the den. Each cycle seemed to carry a little more confidence, their movements less hesitant and more curious. By the time the lab's lighting shifted to mimic midday, even Luna had managed to venture a few steps further than before.

Emma tapped her pen against the datapad, her expression thoughtful. "They're making progress. Slow, but steady."

Rick smirked, picking up his coffee cup. "That's all we need."

CHAPTER 13

The soft hum of the lab's systems continued into the evening as the scent of warmed blood and cooked meat filled the air. It was feeding time for the younglings, and the team gathered in the observation room to monitor the process. The handlers had just finished placing the trays inside the enclosure, careful not to linger too long to avoid triggering any territorial reactions from Raven.

The four younglings emerged cautiously from their den, their glowing eyes darting between the trays and the humans behind the glass. Raven led the way, her small body moving with purpose as she approached the nearest tray. She sniffed it briefly before letting out a sharp chirp, signaling the others.

Skye was the first to respond, darting forward with jittery energy to grab a piece of meat. She retreated quickly to a corner, her movements erratic as she began to eat. Willow followed more cautiously, sticking close to Raven as she picked at the tray. Luna hung back near the alcove, her glowing eyes wide as she watched her sisters.

Kyle leaned against the counter, his arms crossed as he observed the scene. "So... what's the deal with them? I mean, besides Raven being the boss and Luna being scared out of her mind. What's the difference between them?"

Emma glanced at him, her smirk faint. "You mean why they all act so differently?"

"Yeah," Kyle said, gesturing toward the younglings. "I mean, look at them. Raven's acting like she owns the place, Skye's bouncing off the walls, Willow's glued to Raven, and Luna... well, she's barely moved."

Rick leaned back in his chair, sipping his coffee as he watched the younglings. "They're individuals, Kyle. Just because they're ferals doesn't mean they don't have their own personalities."

Kyle frowned, his gaze returning to the enclosure. "But when they're exploring, it doesn't even look like a pack. It's so... unorganized. Like they're just doing whatever they want."

Emma chuckled softly. "Welcome to the world of feral younglings. They're not a pack yet—not in the way you're thinking. They're still figuring it out."

Rick nodded, setting his mug down with a quiet clink. "Raven's the leader, yeah, but she's not running a tight ship. She's keeping them alive—that's her priority. The rest? That's just instinct. They're acting on what they feel, not on some big coordinated plan."

Kyle tilted his head, his gaze following Skye as she darted back to the tray for a second piece of meat. She moved fast, narrowly avoiding a sharp nip from Raven. "So... they don't really work together?"

"They do," Emma said, her tone thoughtful as she leaned against the counter, arms crossed. "But not like adult packs. With older ferals, there's structure—clear roles, rules, an understanding of where they fit. These kids? They're still figuring that out. Raven's trying, but she's young, too. She doesn't know what she's doing—she just knows she has to protect them."

Kyle shifted his weight, his eyes narrowing as Willow nudged a small chunk of meat toward Luna, who hesitated before taking it with a cautious glance toward the others. "And the others? What's their deal?"

"Skye's the bold one," Rick said with a faint smirk. "First to grab food, first to explore, first to test boundaries. She's impulsive, but that's what makes her useful. She's the one who figures out if something's safe—or dangerous."

"Willow's the quiet one," Emma added, her voice softer now. "She sticks close to Raven, follows her lead, and keeps the peace. She's not the type to make waves, but she's solid. Reliable."

Kyle's gaze flicked to the smallest of the group, Luna, who was still nibbling cautiously on her piece of meat, her wide eyes darting between her sisters. "And Luna?" he asked, his tone curious.

Rick's expression softened just slightly, his posture easing. "Luna's the heart. She's scared, yeah, but she's also the glue. She's the one they'll protect, the one who reminds them why they stick together. Packs need someone like that."

Kyle leaned closer to the glass, his brows furrowed as he watched the subtle movements inside the enclosure. The younglings weren't coordinated, but there was a quiet rhythm to their interactions, a chaotic unity. "So... they're all important. Even if it looks like a mess."

"Exactly," Emma said with a faint smile. "It's messy now, but give them time. They'll figure it out. They'll find their rhythm."

Rick chuckled softly, shaking his head as he glanced at Kyle. "You sound surprised."

Kyle shrugged, still watching the younglings. "I guess I just didn't expect to see... I don't know. Something like this."

Rick's gaze returned to the glass, his tone quiet but firm. "There's more to them than claws and instincts. If you watch closely, they'll show you."

Inside the enclosure, Raven finished her meal and let out a sharp chirp, signaling the others to retreat. Skye grabbed one last piece of meat before darting back to the alcove, her jittery movements making Kyle chuckle softly.

"She's like a little ball of chaos," he said.

Rick nodded, his smirk widening. "And that chaos is what's going to keep them alive."

As the younglings settled back into their den, Kyle leaned against the counter, his expression thoughtful. "You think they'll figure it out? Become a real pack?"

Rick exchanged a glance with Emma before replying. "They're already on their way. They just don't know it yet."

As the younglings retreated into their den, the lab fell quiet again, save for the hum of the monitors and the occasional scratching sounds from inside the enclosure. Raven positioned herself at the entrance of the alcove, her glowing eyes scanning the room as her sisters huddled together in the back. The faint sound of Skye's restless movements was punctuated by Willow's soft chirps, a calming rhythm that seemed to settle Luna.

Kyle leaned back against the counter, his pen scratching against the clipboard as he jotted down notes. "It's weird watching them. They're not... predictable. One minute they're moving like a pack, and the next, it's every kid for themselves."

"That's because they're still figuring it out," Emma said, her eyes scanning the datapad in her hands. "They're unpredictable because they're not fully developed—mentally, physically, or emotionally. Everything they're doing is trial and error."

"Raven's doing what she can," Rick added, his gaze fixed on the enclosure. "She's setting boundaries, but she's not experienced enough to enforce them all the time. The others are testing her, testing each other, and testing us."

Kyle frowned, glancing back at the glass. "So this is normal for feral younglings? All this chaos?"

Emma smirked. "Chaos is their normal. But it's not just random. Watch closely—there's a pattern. Skye pushes the boundaries,

Willow keeps things steady, and Luna..." She gestured toward the alcove. "Luna reminds them why they're a group in the first place."

Rick leaned forward slightly, resting his elbows on the counter. "It's instinct layered over survival. Skye takes risks because someone has to. Willow supports Raven because it keeps things stable. And Luna? She's the reason they don't all just scatter. She keeps them grounded."

Kyle scribbled a few more notes, his expression skeptical. "I don't know... It still seems like a mess to me."

"That's because you're looking for structure," Emma said. "They don't have structure—not yet. They have instincts, and instincts don't always look neat."

Rick's smirk deepened. "It's like watching a team of rookies trying to play without a coach. They've got the raw talent, but they haven't figured out how to use it."

Inside the enclosure, Raven let out a sharp chirp, her glowing eyes narrowing as she scanned the room. Skye, who had been pacing near the edge of the mats, froze mid-step. She tilted her head, chirping back softly before retreating toward the den. Willow followed silently, her movements deliberate and cautious.

"They're resetting," Emma said, her tone thoughtful. "Raven's pulling them back in—probably to regroup."

Kyle tilted his head, watching as the younglings settled back into the alcove. "You think she knows what she's doing?"

"She knows enough," Rick said. "She's keeping them alive. That's all that matters right now."

Kyle tapped his pen against the clipboard, his gaze distant. "It's just... weird. They're not like the ferals we deal with out in the field. Those ones are..." He hesitated, searching for the right word.

"Dangerous?" Emma offered, her tone dry.

"Yeah," Kyle said. "These kids—they're not like that."

"They could be," Rick said evenly. "Give them the wrong environment, push them too far, and they'll turn out just like the others. That's why we're here—to stop that from happening."

Emma leaned back in her chair, crossing her arms. "It's a thin line, Kyle. Ferals are ferals because they've been forced into it—by their environment, by their circumstances, by whatever mess made them what they are. These kids? They're still on the edge. They haven't crossed that line yet."

Kyle let out a slow breath, his grip tightening on the clipboard. "So... what happens if we screw it up? If they don't... I don't know, adapt?"

Rick's gaze darkened slightly, the lines of his face hardening. "Then we've failed them," he said, his voice low and unyielding. "And we don't let that happen."

The weight of his words hung in the air, heavy and undeniable. Inside the enclosure, the younglings had fallen silent, their small forms huddled together in the comfort of their den. Raven, ever watchful, had finally begun to relax, her glowing eyes blinking slower and slower as sleep crept over her. The soft rise and fall of their breaths was the only sound, a fragile rhythm that seemed to steady the room.

Emma broke the silence with a quiet sigh, her gaze softening as she watched the younglings. "It's not just about adapting, Kyle. It's about giving them a chance. If we do our part, they'll figure out the rest."

Rick nodded, his eyes still fixed on the den. "They're tougher than they look. We just have to give them time."

Kyle stared at the enclosure, his expression conflicted. The faint glow of the younglings' eyes, now half-hidden as they drifted into sleep, seemed smaller, less threatening. "Time, huh?" he murmured. "Guess we've got plenty of that."

Emma smirked faintly, leaning back against the counter. "Welcome to Spearhead, kid. Patience isn't just part of the job—it's the job."

Kyle chuckled softly, his tension easing slightly. "Yeah, I'm starting to figure that out."

The three of them returned to their work, the quiet hum of the lab resuming as the younglings settled into their den. Outside, the rain began to fall again, a steady rhythm that seemed to echo the slow but steady progress being made within the glass walls.

The lab had settled into its usual rhythm as the evening wore on, but inside the observation room, the younglings were anything but calm. Emma stood near the secured entry with a tray loaded with fresh, pre-cut meat and a blood bag for each of the four. The moment the scent hit the air, all four younglings were up, their glowing eyes locked onto the tray like predators stalking their prey.

"Oh boy," Emma muttered under her breath, eyeing the small flurry of movement as they scurried toward the glass. "Looks like I've got their attention."

Raven was already at the forefront, her sharp claws tapping against the glass as she let out a demanding chirp. Behind her, Skye bounced on her feet, her jittery energy making her look like she might pounce on the food through sheer willpower. Willow and Luna stayed closer to the alcove, but even they couldn't hide their growing excitement. Luna whimpered softly, her glowing eyes darting between the tray and her sisters, while Willow nudged her as if urging her to stay calm.

Emma rolled her eyes as she keyed in the access code, the lock disengaging with a soft hiss. "Alright, kids, dinner's served. Try not to lose your minds."

Rick leaned against the counter, sipping his coffee as he watched her carry the tray inside. "You're braver than I am. They look like they'd eat you if they had the chance."

Emma smirked, balancing the tray carefully as she stepped into the room. "Oh, please. I've dealt with worse than a pack of hungry kids. At least these ones don't talk back."

Kyle, standing a few steps behind Rick, watched nervously as Emma placed the tray on the floor. "Are you sure about this? They look... kind of feral."

Rick arched an eyebrow at him. "Kyle, they *are* feral. That's kind of the point."

Inside the enclosure, Raven wasted no time darting forward, her claws scraping against the mat as she reached the tray. She sniffed it briefly before letting out a sharp chirp, signaling the others. Skye was next, practically diving at the food with an energy that made Emma step back quickly to avoid getting caught in the chaos.

"Easy, Skye," Emma said, her tone firm but calm. "There's plenty to go around."

Willow approached more cautiously, her movements deliberate as she grabbed a piece of meat and retreated to a corner. Luna lingered near the alcove, her small frame trembling slightly as she watched her sisters devour their portions.

"Come on, Luna," Emma said softly, crouching slightly to meet the youngling's gaze. "It's okay. You can have some too."

Luna hesitated, her glowing eyes flicking between Emma and the tray. Raven chirped sharply, her gaze snapping toward her youngest sister. The sound made Luna flinch, but it also spurred her into action. She crept forward slowly, her claws scraping lightly against the mat as she grabbed a small piece of meat and scurried back to the safety of the alcove.

"There we go," Emma murmured, standing up and brushing her hands off. "She's getting braver."

Rick chuckled from behind the glass. "Or hungrier."

The feeding quickly turned into a frenzied display of feral instincts. Raven stood guard near the tray, snapping at Skye whenever her younger sister tried to grab too much at once. Skye chirped in protest, darting around Raven to snatch another piece of meat before retreating to her corner.

"Skye's going to get herself in trouble," Kyle muttered, watching the youngling with wide eyes.

"She's testing Raven's limits," Rick replied. "It's how they figure out the hierarchy. Raven won't let it slide, but she won't overreact either. She knows they need to eat."

Willow stayed out of the conflict entirely, eating quietly in her corner as she watched her sisters with a calm, steady gaze. Luna nibbled on her piece of meat, still keeping close to the alcove but glancing toward the tray every so often.

Emma stepped back toward the door, her sharp eyes watching the younglings' every move. "They're still figuring it out, but they're getting there. The chaos is a little more controlled than it was this morning."

Rick smirked. "That's not saying much."

Kyle scribbled a note on his clipboard, his brow furrowed. "So this is normal? The snapping, the growling, the… whatever you call what Skye's doing?"

"Completely normal," Emma said. "They're ferals, Kyle. Instinct is their first language. This is just how they communicate."

"And how they learn," Rick added. "They're not just eating. They're testing boundaries, reinforcing roles, and figuring out how to survive as a group."

Kyle glanced at the tray, now nearly empty except for a few scraps. "And when the food's gone?"

Emma arched an eyebrow. "Then they'll go back to the den, lick their wounds, and start the whole process over again tomorrow."

As if on cue, Raven let out a sharp chirp, signaling the end of the meal. Skye chirped back in protest, but one look from Raven sent her scampering back to her corner. Willow followed quietly, nudging Luna back toward the alcove with a soft but firm gesture.

"Raven's keeping the peace," Rick said, his tone approving. "She's got a good balance. Enough authority to control them but not so much that they resent her."

Emma stepped out of the room, the lock clicking shut behind her. "She's got potential, that's for sure. If we can stabilize her, the others will follow."

Kyle scribbled another note, his expression thoughtful. "So... this is progress?"

Rick nodded, his smirk faint but confident. "This is progress."

After dinner, Rick carried a small, durable ball into the observation room. It was about the size of an orange, made of reinforced materials designed to withstand even the strongest feral claws and teeth. He rolled it thoughtfully between his hands as he approached the glass, watching the younglings settle back into their den.

"They're full," Emma remarked, leaning against the counter as she sipped her coffee. "Perfect time to give them something new to chew on."

"Literally," Kyle muttered, still fidgeting with his clipboard. "You think they'll know what to do with it?"

"They'll figure it out," Rick replied, a faint smirk tugging at his lips. "That's kind of the point."

Inside the enclosure, Raven was already watching him, her glowing eyes narrowing as he stepped closer. She let out a low chirp, a sound that made the others stir slightly in their alcove. Skye poked her head out first, her jittery energy propelling her closer to the glass.

Rick placed the ball on the floor near the edge of the enclosure and gave it a small push, sending it rolling gently toward the center of the room. Skye's glowing eyes widened, her head tilting curiously as she chirped softly. Raven growled low in her throat, a warning for Skye to stay back, but the younger sibling couldn't resist.

"She's going to touch it," Emma said, her tone amused.

Skye darted forward, her claws clicking against the mats as she pounced on the ball. She batted it with her front claws, chirping excitedly as it rolled away. She let out a delighted screech when the ball bounced slightly after hitting a mat edge.

"Looks like we've got a winner," Rick said, his smirk widening.

Skye chased the ball across the room, her movements erratic but filled with energy. She swiped at it with her claws, nudged it with her nose, and even tried to bite down on it, her small fangs scraping uselessly against the reinforced surface.

Willow and Luna crept out of the den, their glowing eyes fixed on Skye as she played. Willow approached cautiously, her movements deliberate as she sniffed at the ball when it rolled toward her. She clawed at it gently, testing its weight and texture before giving it a tentative push back toward Skye.

"They're testing it," Emma said, her voice thoughtful as she watched the younglings. "Figuring out what it is and what it can do."

Kyle leaned closer to the glass, his clipboard momentarily forgotten. "It's just a ball. What's there to figure out?"

"Everything," Rick replied, his tone calm but deliberate. "It's unfamiliar. New. They're not just playing—they're experimenting. Learning how it works, what it can do, and what it can't."

Inside the enclosure, Raven finally stepped out of the alcove, her glowing eyes locked on the ball. Her movements were deliberate, her sharp claws clicking softly against the mats as she approached. Skye chirped excitedly, nudging the ball toward her older sister, but Raven didn't react right away. She paused, lowering her head to sniff the object, circling it once with slow, measured steps before tapping it gently with a claw.

"She's assessing," Emma murmured, her tone carrying a hint of admiration. "Classic leadership behavior. She won't engage fully until she's sure it's safe."

Raven let out a soft chirp, her claws gripping the ball as she rolled it toward Luna. The smallest youngling flinched at the unexpected movement, her glowing eyes darting nervously toward Raven. After a brief hesitation, Luna reached out cautiously, her tiny claw tapping the ball lightly. It wobbled and rolled back toward her, prompting a faint, questioning chirp.

"She's encouraging Luna," Rick said quietly, his gaze steady. "Giving her space to engage without pressure. That's instinct—teaching without forcing."

Kyle frowned slightly, leaning closer. "You think she's doing that on purpose?"

Rick smirked faintly. "Doesn't matter if it's deliberate or instinct. The result's the same. She's giving Luna confidence."

Kyle watched in amazement as the younglings began to interact more confidently with the ball. Skye chased it across the room with unrestrained energy, while Willow and Raven took turns nudging it back and forth with calculated movements. Even Luna joined in, her small frame darting forward to push the ball before retreating to the safety of the alcove.

"They're working together," Emma said, her voice soft. "It's not just random anymore. They're learning from each other."

Rick nodded. "And from the ball. Watch how they're testing its limits—pushing, biting, even rolling it in different directions."

Inside the enclosure, Skye let out an excited screech as she batted the ball against the wall, sending it bouncing back toward the center of the room. Willow nudged it toward Raven, who stopped it with her claw and chirped softly, as if issuing instructions.

Kyle shook his head, his expression one of disbelief. "They're communicating. About a ball."

"It's not just a ball to them," Emma replied. "It's a problem to solve, a tool to understand. And they're doing it together."

Rick leaned back in his chair, his smirk faint but approving. "This is why we're here, Kyle. To see what they're capable of when they're given the chance."

As the younglings continued to play, their chirps and growls filling the air with a strange, harmonious rhythm, the team watched in silence. For the first time, the chaotic energy of the enclosure seemed to have a purpose—a focus that brought the younglings together in a way that felt almost… natural.

"They're smart," Kyle said finally, his voice quiet. "Really smart."

Emma glanced at him, her smirk softening into a genuine smile. "That's what we've been trying to tell you."

Rick stood, stretching slightly as he gestured toward the break room. "Let's give them some space. They'll figure the rest out on their own."

ROBERT W WILSON

As the team stepped away from the glass, the younglings' playful chirps and excited screeches continued to echo through the lab, a testament to their resilience and growing potential.

CHAPTER 14

The lab's lights dimmed to simulate nighttime, casting a soft glow over the observation room. Rick entered the enclosure carrying a brightly colored shape-sorting toy—one often found in playrooms for human toddlers. The cube-shaped toy had various cutouts on its sides, designed for children to fit differently shaped pieces into the corresponding holes. He held it up for a moment, observing the younglings as they stirred in their den.

"They're not going to eat that, are they?" Kyle asked, watching nervously from the other side of the glass.

Emma chuckled, leaning against the counter with her arms crossed. "Only one way to find out."

Rick knelt near the edge of the enclosure and placed the toy on the mat, just out of reach of the alcove. He added a small pile of the corresponding shapes beside it, arranging them so they were easily visible.

"Alright, kids," he murmured under his breath. "Let's see what you've got."

Raven, as usual, was the first to emerge. Her glowing eyes narrowed as she sniffed at the air, her attention immediately locking onto the brightly colored object. She let out a low chirp, signaling her sisters to follow.

Skye darted forward eagerly, her jittery energy propelling her straight to the toy. She clawed at it curiously, her claws clicking against the hard surface as she tilted her head to inspect it. Willow followed more cautiously, circling the cube while sniffing at the edges. Luna stayed closer to the alcove, her wide eyes fixed on the toy as if it were some alien object.

"They're curious," Emma said softly, her gaze fixed on the younglings. "That's a good start."

Inside the enclosure, Skye batted the cube with her claw, sending it tumbling a few inches across the mat. She chirped excitedly, as she chased after it. Willow picked up one of the loose shapes in her mouth, her glowing eyes narrowing as she examined it closely.

"Skye's going to make a mess of it," Kyle muttered, shaking his head. "She's just playing."

"Not quite," Rick said, his tone thoughtful. "She's testing it. Figuring out what it does."

Raven chirped sharply, silencing Skye's chaotic exploration. The dominant youngling padded forward, nudging the cube with her nose as if trying to understand its purpose. She turned her gaze toward the shapes scattered nearby, then back to the cube.

"She's making a connection," Emma murmured. "Look at her. She knows the shapes go with the cube."

Raven picked up one of the shapes—a red triangle—in her claws. She turned it over several times, her glowing eyes scanning the cube's surface. After a few moments, she nudged the cube with her claw, tilting it to reveal the triangular cutout. With a deliberate motion, she placed the shape near the hole and tried to push it in.

The shape didn't fit perfectly on the first attempt, but Raven didn't give up. She adjusted her grip, chirping softly as she tried again. This time, the triangle slid into place with a satisfying click.

"Did she just...?" Kyle started, his voice trailing off in disbelief.

"She did," Emma said, her tone laced with awe. "She figured it out."

Inside the enclosure, Raven let out a triumphant chirp, nudging the cube toward her sisters. Skye was next, grabbing a square shape and inspecting it closely. She moved with less precision than Raven, but after a few attempts, she managed to fit the square into the correct hole.

Willow joined in next, her movements careful and deliberate. She selected a circular shape, nudging it toward the cube with her nose before using her claws to guide it into place.

Even Luna, the most hesitant of the group, crept forward to observe. She let out a soft chirp, her glowing eyes darting between her sisters and the remaining shapes. With gentle encouragement from Willow, she picked up a star-shaped piece and carried it to the cube. Her first few attempts were clumsy, but she persisted, chirping softly with each adjustment.

"She's doing it," Emma said quietly, her eyes wide with amazement. "They're all doing it."

Rick leaned against the glass, his expression thoughtful. "This isn't just instinct. This is problem-solving. They're analyzing, adapting... learning."

Kyle stared at the scene, his clipboard forgotten in his hands. "But... how? They're ferals. They're not supposed to be this... smart."

Emma glanced at him, her smirk faint. "You keep saying 'feral' like it's a limitation. It's not. These kids are survivors. That takes intelligence."

Inside the enclosure, the younglings worked together to fit the remaining shapes into the cube. Skye and Willow chirped excitedly as they completed each side, while Raven kept a watchful eye on their progress. Even Luna seemed more confident, her chirps blending into the harmonious rhythm of her sisters' teamwork.

When the last shape clicked into place, Raven let out a sharp chirp of triumph. She nudged the cube toward the center of the room, circling it as if inspecting their completed work.

"They just solved a puzzle," Kyle said, his voice filled with disbelief. "Like... an actual puzzle."

Rick nodded, his gaze steady. "And they did it together."

Emma leaned closer to the glass, her expression softening. "They're not just surviving anymore. They're thriving."

The younglings settled back into their alcove, their energy finally beginning to wane as exhaustion crept over them. Raven curled up near the entrance, her glowing eyes scanning the room one last time before closing.

Rick turned away from the glass, his expression unreadable. "This changes things," he said quietly.

Emma raised an eyebrow at him. "How so?"

"If they're this smart now," Rick said, his tone thoughtful, "imagine what they could become."

As the night deepened, the lab grew quieter, the hum of the equipment becoming a steady backdrop. Rick, Emma, and Kyle sat in the observation room, their attention lingering on the younglings, who had finally settled into their den. The completed shape-sorting cube sat near the center of the enclosure, a silent testament to their unexpected problem-solving skills.

Emma broke the silence first, her voice low but curious. "You know, I've worked with ferals for years, but I've never seen anything like that."

Rick leaned back in his chair, crossing his arms as he watched the younglings through the glass. "Me neither. It's rare to even see them cooperate, let alone tackle something that complex."

Kyle glanced between the two of them, his expression torn between amazement and skepticism. "But how is this possible? I mean, they're ferals. Aren't they supposed to be more… animalistic?"

"Instinct and intelligence aren't mutually exclusive," Emma replied, sipping her coffee. "Just because they act on instinct doesn't mean they can't think. These kids are showing us that survival is more than just reacting—it's adapting."

Rick nodded, his gaze steady. "They're young. That's part of it. Their minds are still developing, still flexible enough to learn. If they were older, this would be a lot harder."

Kyle frowned, tapping his pen against his clipboard. "So, what are you saying? That we can… teach them?"

"That's exactly what I'm saying," Rick replied, his tone firm. "It won't be easy, and it won't be quick. But if they can solve a puzzle like that, they can learn other things too. Basic communication, boundaries, even trust."

Emma smirked faintly, leaning back in her chair. "That's a hell of a leap, Rick. Teaching ferals? You really think it's possible?"

Rick met her gaze, his smirk just as faint. "I wouldn't still be here if I didn't."

Kyle looked back at the enclosure, his brows furrowed. "So what's the next step? Do we just… keep giving them puzzles?"

"Not just puzzles," Emma said. "They need stimulation, challenges that push their instincts and intelligence. The more they learn, the more they'll grow."

Rick stood, stretching slightly as he glanced at the clock. "First, they need rest. Tomorrow, we'll take it up a notch. Something more interactive."

Kyle tilted his head, curious. "Like what?"

Rick smirked faintly, his tone teasing. "You'll see."

The conversation shifted to paperwork and logs, the hours ticking by until the lab's quiet hum was interrupted by the soft chirps and growls of the younglings stirring again. Raven was the first to emerge, her glowing eyes scanning the room as if checking for threats. Satisfied that all was calm, she padded toward the cube, nudging it with her nose.

"She's not done with it," Emma murmured, leaning forward slightly. "She wants more."

Skye bounded out of the den, her jittery energy propelling her toward Raven. She chirped excitedly, clawing at the cube as if trying to open it. Willow followed more cautiously, her movements deliberate as she joined her sisters.

Even Luna crept forward, her small frame moving with hesitant curiosity. She sniffed at the cube, her glowing eyes darting between her sisters as if waiting for permission to engage.

"They're still working," Rick said quietly, his tone filled with admiration. "Even after they've solved it, they're still learning."

Emma nodded. "They're testing its limits. Seeing if there's more to discover."

Kyle watched in silence, his skepticism giving way to quiet awe. "Maybe they're smarter than we've been giving them credit for."

Rick glanced at him, his smirk faint. "Maybe we've been underestimating all of them."

Inside the enclosure, the younglings chirped and growled softly, their movements filled with purpose as they continued to interact with the cube. It was a small moment, but it carried the weight of something much larger—something that hinted at a future none of them had dared to imagine.

For the first time, Rick felt a flicker of hope. These younglings weren't just surviving—they were evolving. And maybe, just maybe, they could learn to thrive.

Rick leaned against the counter, his arms crossed as he watched the younglings interact. The quiet hum of the lab surrounded him, but his focus was razor-sharp, fixed entirely on the four small figures in the enclosure. Raven, ever the leader, was nudging the cube toward Luna, encouraging the smallest of the group to engage while Skye buzzed with excitement, darting around like a whirlwind. Willow, steady and calm, observed from a few steps back, her glowing eyes tracking every movement.

Rick's mind churned with possibilities. This wasn't just a moment—it was an opportunity. He had seen ferals exhibit flashes of intelligence before, moments of problem-solving and adaptability, but nothing quite like this. The girls weren't just surviving; they were thriving, working together, and learning from one another.

Emma noticed the look on his face and raised an eyebrow. "You've got that look, Rick. The one that means you're about to start something."

Rick smirked faintly, not taking his eyes off the younglings. "This is it, Emma. This is the chance I've been waiting for."

Emma tilted her head, curious. "What do you mean?"

Rick gestured toward the enclosure, his tone calm but determined. "Look at them. They're young, adaptable, and smarter than anyone gives them credit for. If there's ever going to be a chance to prove that ferals can be more than just animals, it's with them."

Kyle, sitting nearby with his clipboard, frowned slightly. "You're talking about integrating ferals into society? You really think that's possible?"

Rick turned to face him, his expression serious. "I think it's worth trying. They're showing us that they're capable of learning, of working together. If we can build on that, teach them, guide them... who's to say what they can achieve?"

Emma crossed her arms, leaning against the counter. "It's a bold idea, Rick. But it's not just about proving they can learn. You'd have to convince the rest of the world that they're not a threat."

Rick nodded, his gaze steady. "I know. And I know it's not going to be easy. But if we don't try, we'll never know. These girls—they're the closest we've ever come to understanding what ferals are capable of. If we can show that they can adapt, that they can integrate, it could change everything."

Kyle glanced at the enclosure, his skepticism still lingering. "And what if it doesn't work? What if they revert or prove too dangerous to trust?"

Rick's smirk was faint but confident. "Then we'll know. But until then, I'm not giving up on them. They've got potential, Kyle. More than anyone's ever given them credit for."

Emma tapped her finger against her datapad, her expression thoughtful. "If you're serious about this, you're going to need a plan. It's not just about teaching them to follow commands or solve puzzles. You'd have to show that they can live alongside people, that they can control their instincts."

Rick nodded. "It starts here. Small steps. We teach them to trust us, to communicate, to interact without aggression. If we can build that foundation, the rest will follow."

Inside the enclosure, Raven chirped softly, nudging the cube toward Luna. The smallest youngling hesitated for a moment before reaching out with her claw, mimicking the movements she had seen from her sisters. When the cube rolled slightly, she chirped back, a faint but excited sound that made Skye dart over to join her.

"They're testing it," Emma said, her voice thoughtful as she watched the younglings. "Figuring out what it is and what it can do."

Kyle leaned closer to the glass, his clipboard momentarily forgotten. "It's just a ball. What's there to figure out?"

"Everything," Rick replied, his tone calm but deliberate. "It's unfamiliar. New. They're not just playing—they're experimenting. Learning how it works, what it can do, and what it can't."

Inside the enclosure, Raven finally stepped out of the alcove, her glowing eyes locked on the ball. Her movements were deliberate, her sharp claws clicking softly against the mats as she approached. Skye chirped excitedly, nudging the ball toward her older sister, but Raven didn't react right away. She paused, lowering her head to sniff the object, circling it once with slow, measured steps before tapping it gently with a claw.

"She's assessing," Emma murmured, her tone carrying a hint of admiration. "Classic leadership behavior. She won't engage fully until she's sure it's safe."

Raven let out a soft chirp, her claws gripping the ball as she rolled it toward Luna. The smallest youngling flinched at the unexpected movement, her glowing eyes darting nervously toward Raven. After a brief hesitation, Luna reached out cautiously, her tiny claw tapping the ball lightly. It wobbled and rolled back toward her, prompting a faint, questioning chirp.

"She's encouraging Luna," Rick said quietly, his gaze steady. "Giving her space to engage without pressure. That's instinct—teaching without forcing."

Kyle frowned slightly, leaning closer. "You think she's doing that on purpose?"

Rick smirked faintly. "Doesn't matter if it's deliberate or instinct.

ROBERT W WILSON

The result's the same. She's giving Luna confidence."

CHAPTER 15

The following morning, Rick and Emma stood in the boss's office, a room as imposing as its occupant. The space was a blend of ancient and modern—a desk crafted from dark, polished wood sat alongside sleek, glowing monitors that displayed Spearhead's latest reports. The walls were lined with bookshelves, their contents a mix of old tomes and digital archives, all testaments to the centuries of knowledge the organization had accumulated.

Behind the desk sat their boss, an ancient vampire who, despite her youthful appearance, exuded an air of timeless authority. She leaned back in her chair, her sharp eyes studying Rick and Emma with quiet intensity as they explained their idea.

"You're serious about this?" she asked, her voice calm but laced with intrigue.

Rick nodded, his stance firm. "Completely. The girls are showing potential—more than any ferals I've ever worked with. This could be our chance to prove that integration is possible."

Emma leaned forward slightly, her tone passionate but measured. "They're young, adaptable, and already demonstrating problem-solving skills. If we can guide them, teach them, they could become the foundation for something much bigger."

Their boss tapped her fingers lightly against the desk, her gaze flicking to the monitor displaying a live feed of the younglings in their enclosure. Raven was already up and about, chirping softly as she nudged her sisters awake. Skye bounded around the room with her usual jittery energy, while Willow stretched and moved with deliberate calm. Luna lingered near the den, her wide eyes fixed on her more confident siblings.

"And you believe these four can serve as proof?" their boss asked, her tone thoughtful. "Proof that ferals can not only be rehabilitated but integrated into society?"

"That's the goal," Rick said. "It's not going to be easy, and it's not going to happen overnight. But if we can show that these girls can learn and adapt, it could change everything we know about ferals."

The vampire leaned forward, resting her elbows on the desk as she studied them. "You understand the risks, of course. If this fails, it won't just reflect poorly on you—it could undermine everything we've worked for."

Rick met her gaze, unflinching. "I know. But I believe it's worth the risk. These girls deserve a chance."

A faint smile tugged at the corners of the vampire's lips. "You've always been ambitious, Rick. It's one of the reasons I tolerate your stubbornness."

Emma smirked, unable to resist a quip. "He's stubborn, alright. But he's got a point. This isn't just about proving something to the world—it's about understanding ferals on a level we never have before."

The boss glanced back at the monitor, her sharp eyes narrowing slightly. "They're different, I'll give you that. Most ferals their age wouldn't have survived without their mother, let alone demonstrated this level of intelligence and cooperation."

"That's exactly why we need to do this," Rick said. "They're a unique case, and if we don't take this chance, we might never get another one like it."

The vampire's gaze lingered on the screen for a long moment

before she finally leaned back in her chair. "Very well. You have my approval. But understand this—if things start to spiral out of control, I will shut this down immediately. Do I make myself clear?"

"Crystal," Rick replied, his tone steady.

Emma nodded, her expression serious. "We won't let it get to that point."

The vampire's faint smile returned, her tone softening slightly. "Good. Because as much as I value order, I find myself curious about this... experiment of yours. Prove to me that these girls are more than just ferals. Show me that they're capable of something greater."

Rick and Emma exchanged a brief glance, a shared sense of determination passing between them. "We will," Rick said firmly.

The vampire gestured toward the door, her tone signaling the end of the meeting. "Then go. I expect regular updates. And, Rick?"

He paused, turning back to face her. "Yes?"

Her smile widened, just enough to show a hint of fang. "Don't make me regret giving you this chance."

Rick smirked faintly. "I wouldn't dream of it."

As they left the office, Emma let out a low whistle. "Well, that went better than I expected. I thought she was going to rip us apart for even suggesting it."

Rick chuckled, his stride confident as they walked down the corridor. "She's tough, but she's not unreasonable. Besides, she's just as curious as we are."

Emma nodded, her expression thoughtful. "Alright, so we've got the green light. What's next?"

Rick's smirk widened. "Now we start putting the plan into action. It's time to see just how much these kids can handle."

Rick and Emma returned to the lab with renewed determination, the gravity of their new mission settling over them like a quiet storm. The younglings were awake and active, chirping and growling softly as they explored their enclosure. Raven, as always, kept a watchful eye on her sisters, her movements purposeful as she nudged Skye away from the glass.

Kyle was already there, perched awkwardly on a stool with his clipboard in hand. He looked up as they entered, his expression curious. "So, what's the verdict? Are we doing this?"

Rick smirked, shrugging off his jacket. "We're doing it. Boss gave us the green light."

Kyle blinked, his eyes widening slightly. "Seriously? She's okay with it?"

Emma rolled her eyes, grabbing a datapad from the counter. "Don't sound so surprised, Kyle. She's a lot of things, but she's not blind to potential."

Kyle glanced toward the enclosure, where the younglings were now huddled together near the cube from the previous night. "So... what's the first step?"

Rick leaned against the counter, his gaze fixed on the younglings. "We start small. Build trust, encourage learning, and test their limits. It's not just about teaching them—it's about seeing what they're capable of."

Emma nodded. "We'll need a controlled environment and structured tasks. Something that challenges them without overwhelming them."

Kyle frowned, tapping his pen against his clipboard. "Like... puzzles?"

"Puzzles, games, interactive exercises," Emma said. "Anything that pushes their instincts and intelligence."

Rick's smirk returned. "And eventually, we'll start introducing basic communication. Words, gestures, cues. If they can understand us, even on a rudimentary level, it'll be a game-changer."

Kyle tilted his head, his skepticism evident. "You really think they can learn to… I don't know, talk?"

"They don't need to talk," Rick replied. "They just need to understand. Ferals communicate with each other through sounds and body language. If we can tap into that, we can start bridging the gap."

Emma raised an eyebrow. "And if they don't respond?"

Rick's expression turned serious. "Then we try again. And again. We're not giving up on them."

Inside the enclosure, Raven let out a sharp chirp, drawing the attention of her sisters. Skye darted toward the cube, her jittery energy propelling her forward, while Willow followed with quiet precision. Luna lingered at the edge of the alcove, her small frame trembling slightly as she watched the others.

"They're curious," Emma observed. "That's a good sign. Curiosity means they're open to new experiences."

Rick nodded. "Then let's give them something new."

He grabbed a small metal tray from the counter, carefully arranging a series of brightly colored blocks on its surface. Each block was marked with a simple symbol—circle, square, triangle, star—and designed to stack neatly when aligned correctly. He carried the tray to the enclosure's access hatch, placing it just inside the glass barrier.

The younglings froze at the sound, their glowing eyes snapping toward the tray. Raven was the first to move, her sharp gaze scanning the blocks as she sniffed cautiously at the air.

Emma crossed her arms, her tone thoughtful. "Think they'll figure it out?"

"They will," Rick said confidently. "It's just a matter of time."

Raven approached the tray slowly, her movements deliberate. She nudged one of the blocks with her nose, tilting her head as it rolled slightly. Skye chirped excitedly, bounding forward to grab a block in her claws. She swiped at it, sending it tumbling across the mat before chasing after it.

"She's not helping," Kyle muttered.

"She's learning," Rick countered. "Even if it looks like chaos, she's processing what the blocks can do."

Willow picked up a block next, her quiet focus evident as she turned it over in her claws. She chirped softly, nudging it toward Raven, who inspected it briefly before setting it aside.

Luna remained at the edge of the den, her glowing eyes darting between her sisters and the tray. She whimpered softly, her small frame trembling with hesitation.

"Come on, Luna," Emma murmured, her gaze softening. "You've got this."

Raven let out a low chirp, glancing toward Luna. The youngest youngling flinched but took a tentative step forward, her movements slow and careful. When she reached the tray, she hesitated, sniffing at one of the blocks before nudging it lightly with her claw.

"There we go," Rick said quietly, a faint smile tugging at his lips. "She's starting to trust the environment."

The younglings continued to interact with the blocks, their chirps and growls filling the air as they experimented with stacking and sorting. Raven maintained her role as the leader, guiding her sisters with sharp, deliberate sounds that kept the chaos in check.

"They're working together," Emma said, her tone laced with admiration. "It's not perfect, but it's progress."

Rick leaned against the glass, his gaze steady. "It's more than progress—it's potential. If they can do this, they can do so much more."

As the hours passed, the younglings' initial caution gave way to an energy that could only be described as playful chaos. The blocks Rick had introduced had quickly become the center of their attention, not just as tools for learning but as a source of amusement. Skye, as always, was the most animated, darting around the room with a block clutched in her claws, chirping triumphantly as she evaded her sisters.

Raven let out a sharp chirp, her glowing eyes narrowing as she tracked Skye's erratic movements. When Skye paused to inspect her prize, Raven pounced, swiping the block from her and retreating to the center of the room. She placed it deliberately near the others she had collected, letting out a low, rumbling growl that made Skye freeze in her tracks.

"She's organizing," Emma observed, leaning closer to the glass, her eyes fixed on Raven's deliberate movements. "She doesn't want Skye messing it up."

"Classic Raven," Rick said, a smirk tugging at his lips. "She's all about control."

Willow approached cautiously, her steps measured and deliberate. She chirped softly at Raven, her small frame low as if seeking permission. Raven growled again, a low rumble of authority, but made no move to stop her. With slow precision, Willow nudged one of the blocks, flipping it over with her claws before stacking it neatly atop another.

"They're cooperating," Emma said, her tone laced with approval. "Well, sort of."

"It's not just cooperation," Rick added, his smirk fading into something more thoughtful. "It's teaching."

Inside the enclosure, Skye crept closer at last, her jittery energy momentarily subdued by curiosity. Her glowing eyes darted between the growing stack of blocks and Willow's deliberate movements. Tentatively, she reached out with her claws, mimicking Willow's tilt-and-place technique. When her block wobbled precariously, Skye chirped in frustration, her gaze flicking to Willow for reassurance.

Willow responded with a soft, almost melodic chirp, nudging Skye's block back into place before retreating slightly. Her movements were calm, deliberate—encouraging without overwhelming.

Raven watched from her perch, her sharp eyes flicking between her sisters as if silently enforcing her unspoken rules. She remained still, exuding a quiet authority that kept the fragile harmony intact.

"It's like watching siblings figure out how to share," Kyle muttered, breaking the silence. He scribbled furiously on his clipboard, his gaze darting between the younglings. "Raven's the enforcer, Willow's the teacher, and Skye's... well, Skye."

Rick chuckled softly, folding his arms across his chest. "Not a bad analysis, kid. Just don't forget Luna."

Kyle frowned, glancing toward the smallest youngling, who lingered at the edge of the alcove. Her glowing eyes peeked out warily as she watched her sisters, her small frame curled tightly against the den wall.

"She's the observer," Emma said gently, her tone warm. "She's watching, learning. She'll join when she's ready."

"She's the chaos," Emma said with a chuckle. "But chaos has its place."

Luna remained near the alcove, her small frame pressed against the blankets as she watched her sisters. Her glowing eyes darted between the stack of blocks and the tray, a faint whimper escaping her as if she wanted to join but couldn't quite find the courage.

"Come on, kid," Rick murmured, his voice soft. "You can do it."

Raven seemed to sense Luna's hesitation. She let out a sharp chirp, her gaze snapping toward the youngest youngling. Luna flinched but didn't retreat. Instead, she took a hesitant step forward, her claws clicking softly against the mat.

"She's trying," Emma said, her tone hopeful. "Raven's pushing her."

Luna crept closer, her movements slow and cautious. When she reached the pile of blocks, she froze, her glowing eyes fixed on the stack. Raven chirped again, nudging a loose block toward her with surprising gentleness.

"She's teaching her," Rick said quietly. "Just like Willow did with Skye."

Luna hesitated, her small claws trembling as she picked up the block. She turned it over clumsily, letting out a soft chirp as she glanced toward Raven. The older youngling growled low, her tone almost encouraging. Luna placed the block on the stack, her first attempt shaky but earnest.

"She's doing it," Emma said, her smile widening. "And Raven's letting her."

Luna chirped softly, her confidence growing as she adjusted the block. When it finally stayed in place, she let out a high-pitched screech of excitement, her glowing eyes darting toward her sisters as if seeking approval.

Skye bounded over immediately, chirping loudly as she nudged Luna playfully with her nose. Willow followed more calmly, letting out a soft, soothing chirp as she added another block to the stack. Raven stood back, her gaze steady but approving as her sisters worked together.

"They're not just learning," Rick said, his tone filled with admiration. "They're sharing knowledge. Helping each other grow."

Kyle leaned closer to the glass, his expression a mix of awe and disbelief. "It's like... teamwork. Real teamwork."

"It is," Emma agreed. "And it's all instinct. They're not just surviving—they're thriving."

Inside the enclosure, the younglings continued to play and build, their chirps and growls blending into a harmonious rhythm. For the first time, even Luna seemed fully engaged, her small frame moving with surprising confidence as she added another block to the growing stack.

Rick leaned against the counter, his smirk faint but satisfied. "They're proving it, Emma. Every step, every move—they're proving it."

Emma nodded, her gaze fixed on the younglings. "Yeah. They really are."

As the morning sun began to filter through the high, reinforced windows of the lab, the younglings were still engrossed in their activities. The block tower they had built stood surprisingly tall for something constructed by small claws and inexperience. Skye circled it proudly, chirping with excitement, while Willow adjusted one of the blocks near the base to ensure it remained steady.

Luna sat nearby, nibbling on a leftover piece of meat from breakfast, but her glowing eyes stayed fixed on her sisters as if absorbing everything they did. Raven, ever the leader, perched near the top of the alcove, her gaze sweeping over the room like a sentinel. She chirped occasionally, a low sound that seemed to keep the others in line.

Rick and Emma stood side by side in the observation room, sipping their morning coffee as they watched the younglings. Kyle had taken up his usual spot on a stool, his clipboard resting on his lap as he furiously scribbled notes.

"I have to admit," Kyle said, breaking the silence, "I didn't think they'd take to that block set so quickly. It's… impressive."

"It's more than impressive," Emma replied, her voice soft with awe. "It's borderline remarkable. They're not just playing—they're strategizing."

Rick nodded, his gaze steady on the enclosure. "Raven's clearly the brain of the operation, but they're all contributing in their own way. Even Luna's stepping up."

Kyle glanced at him, his brow furrowed. "You think they realize what they're doing? Or is it just instinct?"

Rick tilted his head thoughtfully. "It starts as instinct, sure. But what we're seeing here… this is something else. They're learning, adapting, and building trust—not just with each other, but with us."

Inside the enclosure, Raven let out a sharp chirp, signaling the end of their play. Skye pouted slightly, batting the air with her claws in protest, but a single growl from Raven sent her scampering back to the alcove. Willow followed more quietly, nudging Luna along as the youngest youngling hesitated near the stack of blocks.

"They're tired," Emma observed. "Raven's calling it for now."

"Smart move," Rick said. "They've had a busy morning. Let them rest, and we'll see what they're ready for this afternoon."

As the younglings settled into the alcove, their small bodies curling together for warmth, Rick turned to Emma and Kyle. "Alright, let's get to work. If we're going to keep pushing their limits, we need a plan."

Emma raised an eyebrow. "You've got something in mind?"

Rick smirked faintly. "Always. Let's introduce them to something interactive—something that requires more coordination. A task they can't complete alone."

Kyle frowned slightly, tapping his pen against his clipboard. "Like what? Another puzzle?"

"Not exactly," Rick replied. "Something physical. A challenge that forces them to rely on each other."

Emma nodded slowly, her expression thoughtful. "You're thinking about building teamwork."

"Exactly," Rick said. "It's one thing for them to stack blocks or teach each other. It's another for them to tackle something that requires real cooperation."

Kyle scribbled a note, his curiosity evident. "What kind of task are we talking about?"

Rick leaned against the counter, his tone calm but determined. "We'll set up an obstacle course in the enclosure—something simple but engaging. Barriers to climb over, gaps to jump across, maybe even a few items they have to carry from one point to another."

Emma's smirk widened. "You want to turn them into little soldiers."

"Not soldiers," Rick corrected. "Problem-solvers. If they can learn to navigate challenges as a group, it'll show us just how far they can go."

Kyle raised an eyebrow, his skepticism clear. "And if they don't figure it out?"

Rick shrugged. "Then we reassess and try again. This isn't about rushing results—it's about giving them the tools to succeed."

Emma set down her coffee, her excitement evident. "Alright, let's make it happen. Kyle, grab the materials for the course. Rick and I will map out the layout."

Kyle groaned softly, but there was a hint of amusement in his tone. "Fine. But if one of them claws me through the glass, I'm blaming you."

Emma laughed, nudging him playfully. "Deal."

As the team got to work, the younglings remained curled together in their alcove, their soft chirps and growls fading into the quiet hum of the lab. It was a moment of calm, but Rick knew it wouldn't last long. The next step in their journey was about to begin, and he was determined to see just how far these younglings could go.

By early afternoon, the enclosure had been transformed. The once-open space now featured a series of simple obstacles: low ramps made of reinforced metal, small walls for climbing, and gaps that required careful coordination to cross. At the far end of the enclosure, Rick had placed a bright, durable ball as the goal, its familiar shape meant to encourage the younglings to engage with the task.

Emma stood outside the enclosure with her arms crossed, surveying their handiwork. "Not bad for a first try," she said, smirking. "Think they'll figure it out?"

"They will," Rick replied, his tone confident. "It might take them some time, but that's the point. We're not just testing their intelligence—we're testing their ability to work as a team."

Kyle adjusted his clipboard, glancing nervously at the younglings, who were beginning to stir in their alcove. "You're really throwing them into the deep end, huh?"

"They'll adapt," Emma said. "They always do."

Inside the enclosure, Raven was the first to emerge, as expected. She stretched her lean frame, her glowing eyes scanning the altered space with sharp curiosity. Skye bounded out behind her, chirping excitedly as she darted toward the nearest ramp. Willow followed more cautiously, her movements deliberate as she observed her surroundings. Luna lingered at the edge of the alcove, her small frame trembling slightly as she watched her sisters.

"They've noticed the changes," Rick said, nodding toward Raven. "Let's see how they handle it."

Raven padded toward the first ramp, her claws clicking softly against the mat as she sniffed at the unfamiliar structure. She nudged it with her nose, testing its stability before placing a cautious claw on the incline. When the ramp held steady, she climbed to the top and let out a sharp chirp, signaling her sisters.

Skye immediately bolted toward the ramp, her energy sending her bounding up the incline without hesitation. She chirped triumphantly at the top before leaping down the other side, with excitement.

"She's enthusiastic," Emma said, smirking as she watched Skye dart toward the ramp. "Not exactly graceful, but she gets the job done."

Skye bounded up the incline with jittery energy, her glowing eyes wide with excitement. Her claws scraped against the mat as she scrambled upward, nearly losing her balance before reaching the top. Without pausing, she flung herself down the other side, landing in an awkward tumble but chirping triumphantly as she straightened herself out.

Willow approached next, her movements slower, deliberate, and precise. She placed one claw on the ramp, testing its sturdiness before ascending with careful precision. At the top, she paused briefly, her glowing eyes scanning her surroundings as if assessing her options, before descending with smooth, practiced steps.

Luna lingered at the edge of the alcove, her small frame pressed against the wall. Her glowing eyes were wide, her soft whimpering barely audible over the faint hum of the lab.

"Come on, Luna," Rick murmured, his gaze steady on the youngest youngling. "You've got this."

Raven, perched nearby, let out a low chirp, her sharp gaze shifting toward Luna. The youngest hesitated, her small claws flexing nervously against the mat. Then, cautiously, she crept forward, her movements hesitant and jerky.

"She's testing it," Emma observed, her tone thoughtful. "Smart move."

Luna sniffed at the ramp, her nose twitching as she assessed the strange surface. Slowly, she placed one claw on the incline, then another, her tiny frame trembling as she climbed. Each step was deliberate, her glowing eyes darting toward her sisters for reassurance.

Raven chirped again, the sound firm yet encouraging. Luna paused at the top, her small body quivering, but the noise seemed to steady her. With a soft exhale, she descended the ramp one step at a time. When she reached the bottom, she let out a faint chirp of triumph, her small chest puffing slightly as if proud of her accomplishment.

"They're learning to trust each other," Rick said quietly, his voice tinged with admiration. "That's progress."

The younglings turned their attention to the next challenge: a low wall that required climbing. Raven approached first, her sharp claws gripping the edges as she hoisted herself upward with practiced ease. She balanced at the top for a brief moment, her glowing eyes scanning the room, before leaping gracefully to the other side. Her landing was smooth and controlled, her posture exuding authority.

Skye darted forward next, her boundless energy propelling her up the wall in a chaotic scramble. She slipped near the top, her claws scraping against the surface as she struggled for purchase. With a determined chirp, she recovered quickly, flinging herself over the edge and landing in a heap beside Raven. She let out an excited trill, shaking herself off before standing proudly.

Willow followed with her usual calm precision, her movements steady and deliberate. When she reached the other side, she turned to chirp softly at Luna, who was once again hesitating near the edge of the alcove.

"Luna's cautious," Emma observed. "She doesn't jump into things like the others."

"And that's not a bad thing," Rick replied. "She's learning by watching them."

Raven let out a sharp chirp, her gaze fixed on Luna. The youngest youngling hesitated but finally crept forward, her small frame trembling slightly as she approached the wall. She placed her claws on the edge, testing the surface before attempting to climb.

"She's struggling," Kyle said, his tone nervous. "Should we help her?"

"No," Rick said firmly. "She needs to figure it out on her own. If we interfere, she won't learn."

Luna slipped slightly on her first attempt, letting out a soft whimper as she scrambled for footing. Raven chirped again, her tone sharper this time, and Luna tried again, her movements more deliberate. When she finally reached the top, she paused, her glowing eyes wide with a mix of fear and triumph.

"She did it," Emma said softly, a faint smile tugging at her lips. "She's braver than she looks."

The younglings continued to navigate the course, their chirps and growls blending into a harmonious rhythm as they worked together. Raven led with sharp precision, while Skye provided energy and enthusiasm. Willow acted as the steadying force, guiding Luna through each challenge with quiet encouragement.

When they finally reached the ball at the end of the course, Raven batted it gently toward her sisters, letting out a low, triumphant chirp. Skye pounced on it immediately, chirping excitedly as she rolled it across the mat. Willow and Luna joined in, their small chirps blending into the joyful cacophony.

"They did it," Rick said, his voice filled with quiet pride. "They figured it out."

"And they did it together," Emma added, her gaze softening as she watched the younglings play. "That's the real win."

Rick leaned against the glass, his smirk faint but satisfied. "This is just the beginning. If they can handle this, there's no telling what they're capable of."

As the younglings continued to play with the ball, their chirps and growls filled the lab with an almost musical rhythm. It was a moment of unguarded joy, a stark contrast to the tension and uncertainty that usually defined their lives. Rick leaned back in his chair, arms crossed, watching them closely.

"They're adapting faster than I thought," he said, his tone thoughtful.

Emma nodded, her gaze fixed on the younglings. "Raven especially. She's not just leading them—she's guiding them. That's a level of social intelligence you don't see in older ferals."

Kyle, still perched on his stool with his ever-present clipboard, frowned slightly. "It's impressive, sure. But... do you think it's enough? I mean, they're still ferals. What happens when they outgrow this enclosure?"

Rick's smirk was faint but confident. "That's what we're here to figure out, Kyle. They're learning, evolving. If we can guide them through this stage, there's no reason they can't handle more."

The younglings had now transitioned from playing to what looked like a form of teaching. Skye was chirping excitedly at Luna, batting the ball toward her with an exaggerated motion as if encouraging her to mimic the action. Luna hesitated for a moment, then tentatively swiped at the ball, her small claws making contact and sending it rolling back toward Skye.

"She's teaching her," Emma said, her tone laced with admiration. "They're not just following Raven's lead—they're learning from each other."

"It's instinct," Rick said, his voice thoughtful. "But it's also intelligence. They're recognizing patterns, adapting their behavior. That's the foundation of everything we're trying to prove."

Kyle scribbled a note, his brow furrowed. "So what's the next step? Do we keep them in this enclosure forever? Or do we give them more freedom?"

Rick's smirk widened slightly. "Freedom isn't something you give—it's something they earn. They're not ready for the outside world yet, but we can start preparing them."

Emma raised an eyebrow. "And how do you propose we do that?"

Rick leaned forward, his gaze steady. "We start small. Introduce them to controlled environments outside the enclosure. Let them experience new stimuli, new challenges. If they can handle that, we move to the next step."

Kyle tapped his pen against the clipboard, his skepticism clear.

"And what happens if they don't handle it? What if they can't adapt?"

Rick met his gaze, unflinching. "Then we reassess. But I'm not giving up on them, Kyle. Not now, not ever."

Inside the enclosure, Raven let out a sharp chirp, signaling the end of playtime. The other younglings immediately responded, gathering near the alcove with a surprising level of order. Even Skye, despite her usual chaotic energy, settled down quickly, her glowing eyes fixed on her older sister.

"They're ready for the next step," Emma said, her tone decisive. "You can see it in the way they're behaving. They're not just reacting anymore—they're thinking."

Rick nodded. "Then let's give them a chance to prove it."

CHAPTER 16

When feeding time arrived, the team prepared the usual assortment of fresh, pre-cut meat and blood bags, arranging the trays with careful precision before sliding them into the feeding slots of the enclosure. Inside, the younglings perked up immediately, their glowing eyes locking onto the food. Their noses twitched, sniffing the air as soft, expectant chirps filled the space.

Rick stood by the observation glass, arms crossed, his steady gaze tracking their movements. "Alright," he murmured. "Let's see what they've learned."

Raven moved first, as she always did. Her sharp claws clicked softly against the mat as she stepped forward, her posture confident and commanding. Her sisters stirred behind her, their chirps rising in anticipation, but none dared to approach until Raven made the first move. She paused near the trays, her glowing eyes sweeping over the offerings before glancing back at her sisters.

"She's really taken to this leadership role," Emma observed, leaning against the counter, her tone a mix of fascination and approval. "Look at her. She's not just leading—she's managing them."

Rick nodded, his expression unreadable but clearly focused. "It's instinct, sure, but there's more to it. She's creating order, showing them how to wait their turn. She's teaching without even realizing it."

Raven let out a low, deliberate chirp, the sound sharp enough to command attention. Skye reacted instantly, her jittery energy tempered by her older sister's presence. She darted forward, snatched a piece of meat, and retreated to her corner with a triumphant chirp, settling down to eat.

Willow moved next, her steps measured and deliberate. She approached the tray cautiously, her glowing eyes scanning the food as if weighing her options. After selecting a smaller piece of meat, she returned to her corner without incident, her movements calm and unhurried.

In the alcove, Luna lingered, her small body pressed low against the mat as she watched her sisters. Her glowing eyes flicked nervously between the tray and Raven. A sharp chirp from the eldest made her flinch, but she didn't retreat.

"Come on, Luna," Rick murmured, his voice low but firm. "You've got this."

Luna crept forward hesitantly, her small claws clicking faintly against the mat. She paused near the tray, her nose twitching as she sniffed at the food. Her wide eyes darted toward Raven, seeking silent permission. When Raven gave a softer, approving chirp, Luna reached out tentatively, selecting the smallest piece of meat before retreating quickly to her corner.

"They're getting better," Kyle said, breaking the silence. His voice carried a note of surprise as he scribbled something on his clipboard. "No fighting, no chaos… it's almost organized."

"That's all Raven," Emma replied, her gaze never leaving the enclosure. "She's setting the tone, and they're following her lead."

Inside the enclosure, the younglings ate quietly, their soft chirps and occasional growls blending into a harmonious rhythm. Raven finished her portion first, her sharp gaze scanning the room with practiced authority. She watched her sisters for a moment before moving back to the tray, her movements deliberate and precise.

Skye, now emboldened, darted toward the tray again, her chirps quick and excited. But before she could grab another piece, Raven stepped in, a sharp growl escaping her throat. The sound froze Skye mid-step, her body tensing as she backed away with a subdued chirp.

"She's keeping order," Rick said, a faint note of admiration in his voice. "She knows they need structure, even if they don't."

Skye retreated to her corner, her energy visibly dampened but not defeated. Raven, meanwhile, selected another piece of meat. Instead of keeping it for herself, she carried it toward Luna, nudging the youngest youngling gently with her nose before retreating.

"Did she just... share?" Kyle asked, his disbelief evident.

Emma blinked, her brow furrowing slightly. "It looks like it. That's... not normal."

Rick's smirk was faint but approving. "It's more than sharing. She's reinforcing the group dynamic. Luna's the weakest, so Raven's making sure she gets enough to eat. It's survival, but it's also care."

Inside the enclosure, Luna chirped softly, nudging the piece of meat with her nose before eating it cautiously. Willow and Skye finished their portions without incident, their glowing eyes flicking toward Raven occasionally as if waiting for further instructions.

"They're becoming a unit," Emma said quietly. "Not just siblings —something more. They're learning to function together."

Rick nodded. "And it's all because of Raven. She's setting the example, and the others are following."

When the trays were finally empty, the younglings retreated to their alcove, their movements calm and deliberate. Even Skye, despite her usual energy, settled down quickly, her small frame curling up next to Willow. Raven stood near the entrance, her sharp gaze scanning the room one last time before settling into her spot.

"They're getting better," Rick said, his voice filled with quiet pride. "Every day, they're showing us what they're capable of."

Emma smirked, leaning against the counter. "You're not wrong. If they keep this up, we might just pull this off."

Kyle scribbled a final note on his clipboard, his expression thoughtful. "So what's next? More training?"

Rick's smirk widened. "Something bigger. They're ready for the next step."

While the girls ate quietly in their enclosure, Emma sat at her workstation, her eyes fixed on her monitor as she sifted through the reports. Each file she opened added another layer to the story, piecing together a fragmented history that was both fascinating and heartbreaking. She leaned closer to the screen, a frown forming as she reviewed the details of the mother's last moments.

Rick leaned against the counter nearby, sipping his coffee as he kept an eye on the younglings. "You're still digging into her file?" he asked.

Emma nodded, not looking away. "There's a lot to go through. The more I read, the more I realize just how extraordinary she was."

Rick set his mug down, moving to stand beside her. "She kept those kids alive against impossible odds. I don't think 'extraordinary' even covers it."

Emma pulled up a report that included a blurry image of the feral mother's body. She was sprawled in the middle of a clearing, her frame still and bloodied, surrounded by signs of a violent struggle. Claw marks and broken branches painted a clear picture of the chaos that had unfolded.

"She died fighting," Emma said quietly. "The team reported that the wounds matched those of other ferals. She was overwhelmed."

Rick's jaw tightened as he stared at the screen. "I remember. I was there. When we found the girls hiding, I knew right away they were hers. She must've fought to the death to keep the others away from them."

Emma pulled up another image, this one of the younglings huddled together when they were first discovered. Their small frames were covered in dirt and scratches, their glowing eyes wide with fear. Even in the photo, Raven was standing slightly in front of her sisters, her protective instincts already apparent.

"She must've known the end was coming," Emma said. "Everything about the scene points to her putting them somewhere safe before she turned to face the others."

Rick nodded, his gaze distant as he remembered the moment they'd found the girls. "She did everything right. Gave them a fighting chance. It's not her fault those bastards came for her."

Emma sighed, leaning back in her chair. "The way she fought... it wasn't just instinct. There was strategy there. The reports describe her luring the attacking ferals away from where the younglings were hiding. That takes more than just courage—it takes intelligence."

"She was smart," Rick agreed, his tone grim. "And she passed that on to her kids. Look at them now—they're not just surviving. They're learning, adapting. That's her legacy."

Emma turned back to the screen, pulling up earlier records of the mother's encounters with Spearhead teams. "She was spotted dozens of times over the years. Always one step ahead, always outsmarting the trackers. It's rare to see a feral exhibit that level of intelligence."

Rick frowned, leaning closer. "But even with all that, they couldn't catch her."

Emma shook her head. "She never let herself get cornered. She'd set traps, double back, even use the terrain to her advantage. There's a note here about a team that spent three days chasing her, only to end up right back where they started."

Rick smirked faintly. "Sounds like she was running circles around them."

"She was," Emma said. "But this... this wasn't just survival. It was strategy. She was calculating."

Rick's gaze shifted back to the enclosure, where the girls had finished eating and were now settling into their alcove. Raven nudged Luna gently, guiding the youngest youngling into the safest corner before curling up beside her. Skye chirped softly as she nestled against Willow, her jittery energy finally giving way to rest.

"Raven's the same way," Rick said. "She's not just looking out for herself—she's leading them. Teaching them."

Emma nodded. "She's her mother's daughter, no doubt about it. And the others have inherited it too, in their own ways. Skye's energy, Willow's focus, Luna's cautiousness—it's all part of the bigger picture."

Rick's expression darkened slightly. "But their mother's gone. She gave everything to keep them safe, and now it's up to us to make sure her sacrifice wasn't for nothing."

Emma leaned forward, her tone thoughtful. "She passed on more than just her genes, Rick. She passed on her determination, her intelligence, her instincts. These girls are a testament to her strength."

Rick nodded slowly, his voice steady. "And we owe it to her to give them a chance. She died protecting them, and now it's on us to make sure they don't just survive—but thrive."

The room fell into a quiet stillness, the weight of their conversation hanging in the air. Inside the enclosure, the younglings chirped softly as they curled into one another, their small bodies a tangle of warmth and trust. Raven's sharp gaze lingered on the glass, her glowing eyes locking briefly with Rick's before she finally closed them, her protective stance giving way to rest.

"She didn't just save them," Emma said softly. "She gave them a future. And they're proving every day that she was right to fight for them."

Rick leaned back against the counter, his smirk faint but determined. "Then let's make sure that future is everything she hoped for."

Later that afternoon, the younglings were engrossed in their puzzles, the colorful pieces scattered across the mat in their enclosure. The atmosphere was calm yet filled with a quiet energy as each of them tackled the challenge in their own unique way. Skye was, as usual, the most animated—her jittery movements making the pieces clatter softly as she shuffled them around. Willow worked methodically, her glowing eyes scanning each piece before fitting it carefully into place. Luna sat close to Willow, mimicking her actions with a cautious curiosity.

Raven, however, was observing more than participating. She watched her sisters with a discerning gaze, occasionally nudging a piece toward them or chirping softly to offer guidance. It was clear she was not just a participant but also a mentor, ensuring that the group remained focused.

Kyle stood outside the enclosure, his clipboard in hand but his attention fixed on the younglings. A puzzled expression crossed his face as he noticed a recurring behavior. "Why do they keep putting the puzzle pieces in their mouths?" he wondered aloud.

Emma glanced up from her notes, following his gaze. Sure enough, Skye had just popped a piece into her mouth, chewing on it thoughtfully before pulling it out and placing it on the puzzle board. Luna did the same, hesitating before lightly gnawing on an edge.

"It's a way for them to explore," Emma explained. "They're using all their senses to understand the objects."

Kyle raised an eyebrow. "By chewing on them?"

"Think about it," Rick interjected, joining the conversation. "For ferals, especially young ones, taste and texture are as important as sight and touch. They don't have the same learning experiences as human children. Putting things in their mouths helps them gather information."

Emma nodded. "It's similar to how human toddlers explore the world. They haven't been taught not to, so it's a natural behavior."

Kyle tilted his head, considering this. "I guess that makes sense. But aren't we worried about them swallowing something they shouldn't?"

Rick shook his head. "We've designed all their tools and toys to be safe for them. Non-toxic, no small parts that could be a choking hazard. We anticipated this kind of behavior."

Inside the enclosure, Skye chirped excitedly as she finally found where the piece she'd been chewing on fit into the puzzle. She tapped it into place with her claw, with satisfaction. Willow glanced over and offered a soft chirp of approval, while Luna watched with wide eyes, slowly trying to replicate the action.

Raven moved closer to her sisters, picking up a piece and examining it closely. Instead of putting it in her mouth, she turned it over in her claws, her glowing eyes narrowing as she studied its shape. With deliberate precision, she placed it where it belonged, then looked up at the observation window, her gaze meeting Kyle's.

"Look at that," Emma said softly. "She's aware we're watching."

"More than that," Rick added. "I think she's trying to understand us as much as we're trying to understand them."

Kyle felt a slight shiver run down his spine. "It's a bit eerie, isn't it? They're so... aware."

"That's what makes this project so important," Emma replied. "They're not just animals reacting on instinct. There's a level of intelligence here that challenges everything we thought we knew about ferals."

Raven broke eye contact with Kyle and nudged a puzzle piece toward Luna, chirping softly. Luna picked it up, hesitated, and then placed it in her mouth for a brief moment before pulling it out and fitting it into the puzzle. Raven chirped again, a sound that seemed approving.

"See how she's guiding them?" Rick pointed out. "She's teaching them the most efficient ways to solve the problem."

Kyle nodded slowly. "I suppose the mouth thing is just part of their learning process."

"Exactly," Emma affirmed. "It's a phase. As they develop and learn new methods, you'll probably see less of it."

Skye, apparently bored with the puzzle, began to stack the remaining pieces into a precarious tower. Willow watched for a moment before adding a piece to stabilize the structure. The two exchanged chirps, a playful banter that filled the enclosure with a lighthearted atmosphere.

Luna, encouraged by Raven's guidance, focused intently on her puzzle. Her movements were less hesitant now, more confident. She picked up a piece, examined it carefully—this time without putting it in her mouth—and fitted it into place. She let out a soft chirp of delight, glancing up at Raven, who responded with a gentle nudge.

"They're growing," Rick said quietly. "Not just physically, but mentally and emotionally. They're becoming more confident, more collaborative."

"And less reliant on oral exploration," Emma added with a smile. "See, Kyle? It's just a matter of time."

Kyle chuckled. "Alright, alright. I get it. They're like any kids, really—just with a few more quirks."

"Quirks we'll help them navigate," Rick said. "That's our job, after all."

As the afternoon light began to wane, the younglings started to wind down. Raven gathered her sisters, leading them back toward their alcove. Skye stretched extravagantly before bounding after her, while Willow and Luna tidied up the puzzle pieces, a behavior that didn't go unnoticed by the observers.

"Did they just clean up after themselves?" Kyle asked incredulously.

Emma laughed softly. "It appears so. Another sign of their developing social structure."

Rick glanced at the clock. "Let's call it a day. They've made good progress, and so have we."

The team began to pack up their materials, but not before taking one last look at the younglings, now nestled together and drifting into sleep. Raven's eyes remained open a fraction longer, casting a final, thoughtful gaze toward the observation window before she too closed her eyes.

"Goodnight, girls," Emma whispered.

CHAPTER 17

The next morning, the lab was buzzing with its usual quiet activity. Rick arrived early, a cup of coffee in hand, as he entered the observation room. The younglings were already awake, their glowing eyes darting around the enclosure as they explored their environment. Raven, as usual, was perched near the alcove, observing her sisters with a calm yet watchful demeanor.

Skye darted around the room, chirping excitedly as she chased an imaginary target. Willow, on the other hand, was more measured, carefully inspecting the toy blocks scattered around the enclosure. Luna lingered near the alcove, her small frame trembling slightly as she watched the others.

Rick leaned against the counter, sipping his coffee as Emma entered the room. She had a tablet in hand, her sharp eyes scanning the data. "They're up early," she remarked, glancing at the younglings.

"Raven probably got them moving," Rick replied. "She doesn't let them slack off."

Emma smirked. "She's more disciplined than most recruits."

Kyle arrived shortly after, rubbing the sleep from his eyes as he joined them. "Morning," he mumbled, stifling a yawn. "What's on the agenda today?"

Rick set his coffee down, his expression thoughtful. "I was thinking about introducing a new challenge—something that pushes their boundaries a bit."

Emma raised an eyebrow. "You've got something specific in

mind?"

Rick nodded, his gaze fixed on the younglings. "We've been focusing on their problem-solving skills and teamwork. But I want to see how they handle a scenario that requires quick thinking and adaptability."

Kyle frowned slightly. "You mean like an obstacle course?"

"Something like that," Rick replied. "But with a twist. I want to simulate a situation where they have to react to changing conditions."

Emma tapped her tablet thoughtfully. "We could set up a course with moving parts—ramps that tilt, barriers that shift positions. It would force them to adapt in real time."

Rick smirked. "Exactly. And it'll give us a better sense of their cognitive flexibility."

Kyle scribbled a note on his clipboard, his brow furrowed. "And if they can't figure it out?"

Rick glanced at him, his tone calm but firm. "Then we learn what their limits are and work from there. This isn't about failure—it's about growth."

Emma nodded. "Alright, let's make it happen. Kyle, start gathering the materials. Rick and I will map out the layout."

Kyle groaned softly but got to work, muttering under his breath about being the team's unofficial gopher. Emma chuckled, glancing at Rick. "Think they're ready for this?"

Rick's smirk widened. "They're more ready than we think. Let's give them the chance to prove it."

Inside the enclosure, Raven watched as the team began setting up the course. Her sharp gaze tracked their movements, her head tilting slightly as she observed the changes being made to her environment. Skye chirped excitedly, darting toward the glass as if eager to see what was happening. Willow and Luna remained near the alcove, their curiosity evident but their caution keeping them in place.

By the time the course was ready, it spanned the entire length of the enclosure. Moving ramps, shifting barriers, and dangling ropes created a maze of challenges designed to test the younglings' adaptability. At the far end, a small platform held a brightly colored ball—their ultimate goal.

Emma stood back, hands on her hips as she surveyed their work. "It's a bit chaotic, but that's the point."

Rick nodded, his gaze steady. "They'll figure it out. Let's see how they handle it."

The team opened the enclosure door, allowing the younglings access to the new setup. Raven was the first to move, as always, her cautious steps bringing her closer to the nearest ramp. She sniffed at it, her glowing eyes narrowing as she studied its movement.

Skye bounded forward, chirping loudly as she leaped onto the ramp without hesitation. The ramp tilted under her weight, sending her sliding back to the ground with a startled chirp. She shook herself off, as she tried again.

"She's persistent," Emma remarked. "But not exactly strategic."

"That's what Raven's for," Rick said. "Watch."

Sure enough, Raven let out a sharp chirp, stopping Skye mid-leap. The older youngling stepped onto the ramp herself, moving cautiously as she tested its balance. When she reached the top, she chirped back at Skye, signaling her to follow.

"She's guiding her," Kyle said, his tone filled with quiet amazement.

Willow and Luna remained near the starting point, observing their sisters. Willow seemed to be analyzing the course, her glowing eyes scanning the obstacles with a measured focus. Luna, as usual, lingered behind, her small frame trembling slightly as she watched.

"Come on, Luna," Rick murmured, his voice soft but encouraging. "You've got this."

Raven let out another chirp, this one directed at Willow. The calmer youngling moved forward, her steps deliberate as she approached the ramp. She climbed it with ease, pausing at the top to chirp softly at Luna.

The youngest youngling hesitated but finally stepped forward, her movements slow and tentative. When she reached the ramp, she sniffed at it cautiously before placing a single claw on the incline.

"She's learning by watching," Emma said. "That's a good sign."

Rick nodded. "She's cautious, but she's not afraid to try. That's progress."

Luna slipped slightly on her first attempt, letting out a soft whimper. Raven chirped sharply, her gaze fixed on the youngest. Luna tried again, her movements more deliberate this time. When she reached the top, she chirped softly, her glowing eyes darting toward her sisters as if seeking approval.

Raven nudged her gently before moving on to the next obstacle, a shifting barrier that required careful timing to pass. The younglings worked together, their chirps and growls blending into a harmonious rhythm as they navigated the course.

"They're getting it," Rick said, his tone filled with quiet pride. "They're adapting."

"And they're doing it as a team," Emma added, her gaze softening. "That's the real breakthrough."

As the younglings finished navigating the obstacle course, the atmosphere in the lab began to relax. The team had taken a break from observation, allowing the girls some unstructured time to explore the enclosure and decompress. That's when the chaos began.

Skye, ever the ball of energy, had discovered the dangling ropes near the course and decided they were the most fascinating thing she'd ever seen. She chirped excitedly, leaping up to grab one with her claws. The rope swung wildly as she hung from it.

"She looks like she's auditioning for a circus," Emma said, smirking as she leaned against the counter.

Rick chuckled. "Skye doesn't need an audition. She's the whole show."

Skye let go of the rope mid-swing, landing in an exaggerated sprawl that earned a startled chirp from Willow, who had been quietly inspecting one of the ramps. Willow glared at her sister, letting out a low growl as if to say, *Really?*

"Oh, come on, Willow," Kyle said from his stool, grinning. "Live a little."

Willow, ever the composed one, showed annoyance before returning to her task, methodically nudging a puzzle piece into place. Skye, meanwhile, had moved on to the dangling ropes again, determined to master them.

The next moment of hilarity came courtesy of Raven. Always the serious leader, she had found herself a perch atop the highest platform in the enclosure, surveying her domain like a queen on her throne. But her regal demeanor was interrupted when Skye, in one of her exuberant leaps, accidentally bumped into the platform's base. The slight jolt caused Raven to lose her balance, and she slid down the side with an indignant chirp, landing in an undignified heap.

Emma burst out laughing, covering her mouth with her hand. "Well, that's a first. Raven looks genuinely annoyed."

Rick shook his head, smirking. "She'll be fine. Her pride might take a hit, though."

Raven stood up, shaking herself off before glaring at Skye, who was already halfway across the enclosure, chirping as if nothing had happened. Willow and Luna exchanged soft growls that sounded suspiciously like laughter.

The most unexpected moment of the day, however, came from Luna. The youngest and most timid of the group, she had been watching her sisters' antics from the safety of the alcove. But when she noticed Raven's attention was elsewhere, Luna made her move. She darted forward, snagged the ball from the center of the enclosure, and bolted back to the alcove with surprising speed.

"Did she just steal the ball?" Kyle asked, his voice filled with disbelief.

"She sure did," Rick replied with a grin. "And look at her—she's proud of it."

Inside the alcove, Luna crouched protectively over her prize, letting out soft chirps as her sisters began to take notice. Skye bounded toward her, chirping loudly in protest, but Luna responded with a low, determined growl. Her small frame puffed up with defiance, every inch of her radiating resolve.

"She's staking her claim," Emma said with a laugh. "I didn't think Luna had it in her."

Raven approached next, her sharp gaze assessing rather than aggressive. She let out a soft chirp, tilting her head slightly as if trying to reason with Luna. The youngest hesitated, her growl softening into a whimper before she reluctantly nudged the ball toward Raven.

"She gave it back," Kyle said, his voice tinged with relief. "I thought for sure there'd be a fight."

"That's Raven's influence," Rick said, his tone steady. "She knows how to handle them."

As the younglings settled back into their usual dynamic, the team couldn't help but smile. Even amid the chaos, the girls were proving themselves to be more than just ferals—they were individuals with distinct personalities, quirks, and a budding sense of humor.

"They keep surprising us," Emma said softly, her tone warm. "And honestly? I'm okay with that."

Rick nodded, his smirk faint but genuine. "Surprises are part of the job. Keeps things interesting."

Kyle shook his head, still grinning. "I'll say this much—I'll never get bored working with them."

Inside the enclosure, Raven nudged the ball toward Skye, who chirped with excitement and darted off like an overzealous puppy. Luna chirped softly from her spot in the alcove, her wide eyes gleaming with a mix of curiosity and mischief. Meanwhile, Willow resumed her meticulous inspection of the puzzle pieces, her movements deliberate and focused.

For a brief moment, the lab was alive with laughter—not just from the observing team, but from the younglings themselves. Their playful chirps and growls blended into a cheerful symphony, a rare glimpse of unrestrained joy.

Later that afternoon, the younglings discovered a new source of entertainment: a small, sturdy crate that had been left in the enclosure. Its intended purpose was simple—storage for puzzle pieces and other toys—but it quickly became the centerpiece of their latest adventure.

Skye was the first to approach the crate, her nose twitching as she sniffed around it with an air of curious determination. She chirped excitedly, clawing at the edges as if trying to unlock its secrets. Willow wandered over moments later, her glowing eyes narrowing in quiet concentration as she examined the box with a more calculated approach.

"What are they up to now?" Kyle asked, his tone laced with amusement as he watched from the observation room.

"Trying to break into a crate, apparently," Emma replied with a smirk.

"Of course they are," Rick said, his tone dry but tinged with amusement. "It was only a matter of time."

Inside the enclosure, Raven finally approached the crate. Her commanding presence silenced her sisters' playful chirps almost immediately. She circled the box once, her head tilting as she studied it from every angle. After a moment, she let out a low chirp, prompting Willow to step forward.

"They're plotting," Rick said, leaning forward with interest. "Watch this."

Willow obediently began clawing at the crate's edge, her sharp claws scraping audibly against the surface. Skye, brimming with restless energy, bounced around her, chirping loudly as if offering enthusiastic encouragement. Raven stood back, observing the effort with a watchful gaze, her body language radiating authority. Luna, meanwhile, hung back in the alcove, her small frame trembling with equal parts excitement and trepidation, unwilling to leave her safe spot but clearly captivated by the action.

After a few moments of effort, Willow let out a frustrated growl, her claws catching on the crate's latch but failing to pry it open. Skye chirped again, bounding forward to take her turn. She clawed at the latch with wild energy, but her erratic movements only made the crate wobble.

"They're not giving up," Emma observed. "They're determined to figure it out."

Raven finally intervened, letting out a sharp chirp that froze her sisters in place. She approached the crate and nudged the latch with her nose, testing its resistance. Then, in a surprising display of problem-solving, she used her claws to lift the edge of the latch while simultaneously pushing the lid with her head.

The crate popped open with a satisfying click, revealing a pile of small foam balls inside. Skye let out an excited screech, immediately diving into the crate and scattering the balls across the enclosure.

"She did it," Kyle said, sounding impressed. "Raven actually figured it out."

"And now Skye's turning it into a party," Emma added with a laugh.

The younglings quickly turned the foam balls into a game, batting them across the enclosure with chirps and growls of excitement. Skye darted around like a whirlwind, chasing after multiple balls at once, while Willow carefully lined up a few in one corner, arranging them as if planning a strategy. Luna, emboldened by the playful atmosphere, ventured out of the alcove and began nudging a ball timidly with her nose.

Raven, true to form, stayed slightly apart from the chaos, watching her sisters with a mix of amusement and patience. When one of the balls rolled toward her, she batted it lightly back to Luna, who chirped happily and continued her game.

"They're like a pack," Emma said softly. "Each one has a role, but they work together. Even in play, there's a bond."

Skye suddenly attempted to balance on top of the overturned crate, her small claws scrabbling against the surface as she tried to keep her footing. The crate wobbled precariously, and Skye let out a startled chirp as she toppled off, landing in a clumsy heap. Willow growled softly, a sound that seemed suspiciously like laughter.

"Skye's enthusiasm is unmatched," Rick said, shaking his head. "Even when it gets her into trouble."

The funniest moment came when Luna, still experimenting with her ball, accidentally rolled it into the shallow water feature at the far end of the enclosure. She let out a startled chirp, hopping back as if the water had personally offended her. Skye bounded over immediately, chirping excitedly as she splashed into the water to retrieve the ball.

The two sisters spent the next several minutes splashing around, their chirps and growls filling the air. Willow eventually joined them, stepping into the water with cautious precision and carefully scooping out a few of the balls. Raven stayed at the edge, watching the chaos with an air of bemused authority.

"They're making a mess," Kyle said, though he was clearly amused.

"It's not a mess," Rick replied. "It's teamwork."

Inside the enclosure, the younglings had shifted their focus to moving the balls back into the crate. Raven took charge, chirping sharply to organize her sisters. Skye was tasked with chasing down the scattered balls, while Willow lined them up near the crate. Luna, still hesitant but eager to contribute, nudged the balls closer with her nose.

When the last ball was finally back in the crate, Raven chirped triumphantly, prompting her sisters to gather around her. They chirped softly in unison, a sound that was almost celebratory.

"They're proud of themselves," Emma said, her tone filled with quiet admiration. "And honestly? They should be."

Rick nodded. "They're more than just a group of younglings. They're a team. And that bond? That's what's going to make all the difference."

CHAPTER 18

A few weeks had passed, and the younglings had outgrown their current enclosure—not in size, but in spirit. Their boundless curiosity and restless energy had begun to exceed the limitations of the room, leaving no doubt they needed more space to grow, explore, and develop. Rick and Emma had spent days overseeing the preparations for a larger, more enriching environment—a carefully designed space meant to mimic natural elements while maintaining the safety and control of the lab.

The new enclosure was nearly double the size of the original. Artificial trees and rocks dotted the area, creating a sense of wilderness. A shallow stream wound through the center, its soft trickle adding a soothing ambiance. Along one wall, small alcoves offered secure hiding spots, while the open spaces encouraged movement and play. The glass observation wall remained, allowing the team to monitor the younglings' behavior without interfering, but the overall design was far less confining.

As moving day arrived, Rick stood near the glass of the old enclosure, arms crossed as he watched the younglings chirp and growl softly among themselves. Raven, as expected, perched slightly apart from her sisters, her sharp gaze sweeping over the group. She maintained her usual air of quiet authority, though her attention occasionally flicked toward the shifting movements of the lab team.

"You think they're ready for this?" Emma asked, stepping up beside Rick with a tablet in hand. Her eyes scanned the enclosure, taking in the younglings' behavior.

Rick didn't look away from the glass. "They don't have a choice," he replied evenly. "They need more room to grow, and this is the next step."

Emma nodded, her tone thoughtful. "It'll also give us a chance to start building trust. In a bigger space, they might feel less cornered—less defensive."

"Maybe," Rick said. "But it's going to take time. They're still ferals, Emma. Trust doesn't come easy to them."

Emma smirked faintly. "It doesn't come easy to you either."

Rick didn't argue, his smirk mirroring hers for a brief moment before he turned back to the younglings. "Let's get started."

The transition began carefully. The team opened the old enclosure door, allowing the younglings access to a secure, enclosed hallway leading to their new room. Raven was the first to approach, her movements cautious as she sniffed the air. She let out a low chirp, signaling her sisters to stay back as she investigated.

Skye, as expected, didn't wait long. She darted past Raven, chirping excitedly as she explored the unfamiliar space. Willow followed more carefully, her glowing eyes scanning the hallway as she moved. Luna lingered near the old enclosure, her small frame trembling slightly as she watched her sisters venture ahead.

"Come on, Luna," Emma murmured, her voice soft. "You can do it."

Raven turned back, letting out a sharp chirp that seemed to snap Luna out of her hesitation. The youngest youngling crept forward, her movements slow and tentative. Raven waited for her, nudging her gently with her shoulder before leading her down the hallway.

When the younglings finally stepped into the new room, their reactions were immediate. Skye let out a loud, excited chirp and bolted toward the stream, splashing into the shallow water with reckless abandon. Willow sniffed at one of the artificial trees, tilting her head as she inspected its texture. Luna clung to Raven's side, her glowing eyes wide as she took in the unfamiliar surroundings.

"They're curious," Emma observed, her tone filled with quiet amusement. "That's a good sign."

"Curious is good," Rick agreed. "But it's trust we're after. And that's going to take work."

Over the next several days, Rick and Emma began a deliberate effort to gain the younglings' trust. It started with simple gestures—spending more time near the glass, speaking in calm, measured tones, and offering small treats through the feeding slots. At first, the younglings were wary, especially Raven, who watched every movement with a sharp, calculating gaze.

"She's sizing us up," Rick said one evening as he sat near the observation glass, holding a small piece of meat in his hand. "Trying to figure out if we're a threat or an ally."

Emma sat beside him, her tone thoughtful. "She's smart. But even the smartest ferals have limits. If we're consistent—if we show them we're not here to hurt them—they'll come around."

Rick smirked faintly. "That's the plan."

Raven was the first to approach, her movements slow and deliberate as she sniffed at the meat Rick held out. She didn't take it immediately, instead studying him with her glowing eyes as if trying to read his intentions. After several tense moments, she finally snatched the meat from his hand, retreating quickly to a safe distance.

"She's testing you," Emma said, her tone amused.

"And she'll keep testing me," Rick replied. "That's how trust works. You don't get it all at once—you earn it, piece by piece."

Skye was the next to approach, her usual enthusiasm tempered slightly by her sister's caution. She chirped loudly, sniffing at the treat before taking it from Rick's hand. Willow followed soon after, her movements calm and deliberate. Luna, however, remained at a distance, her small frame curled into one of the alcoves.

"She's the hardest nut to crack," Rick said, glancing toward the youngest youngling. "But she'll come around. Eventually."

Emma smiled faintly. "If anyone can get through to her, it's you."

By the end of the week, the younglings were beginning to relax in their new environment. They explored the space more freely, chirping and growling softly as they interacted with one another. Raven continued to lead, her protective instincts guiding her sisters as they adapted to their surroundings.

One evening, as Rick and Emma sat near the glass, Raven approached the observation wall. She stood there for a moment, her glowing eyes locking onto Rick's. Slowly, cautiously, she placed a single hand against the glass, chirping softly.

Rick leaned forward, his voice low and calm. "We're getting there," he murmured. "Little by little, we're getting there."

Over the following days, Rick became increasingly focused on building a connection with Raven. She was the leader—there was no doubt about that. Her sisters followed her cues in everything, from when to explore to when to retreat to their alcove. If Rick could gain her trust, the others would naturally follow.

He started by spending more time near the enclosure, always in Raven's line of sight. He avoided sudden movements, keeping his demeanor calm and steady. Every action was deliberate, designed to show her he wasn't a threat. She watched him with those sharp, glowing eyes, her expression unreadable but attentive.

"She's analyzing you," Emma remarked one evening as she joined Rick by the glass. "Every move you make, she's filing it away."

"Good," Rick replied, his tone low. "Let her. The more she understands me, the less reason she'll have to see me as a threat."

Emma leaned against the counter, studying Raven. The youngling was perched near the stream, her sisters gathered behind her in their usual positions. Skye darted back and forth, playing with a piece of moss she'd pulled from the water. Willow crouched beside her, her movements precise as she inspected a smooth stone. Luna stayed close to Raven, chirping softly as she nuzzled against her side.

"You think she's the key, don't you?" Emma asked.

Rick nodded. "She is. If I can get through to her, the rest will follow. But if she doesn't trust me, it doesn't matter what I do with the others."

One afternoon, Rick decided to take a calculated risk. He brought a piece of fresh meat into the observation area, placing it near the feeding slot. Instead of simply dropping it into the enclosure as usual, he crouched near the glass, holding the meat in his hand where Raven could see it.

She noticed immediately, her head tilting slightly as she observed him. Her sisters stayed behind her, chirping softly but not moving forward. Raven let out a low growl—not aggressive, but cautious. Rick didn't react, keeping his posture relaxed as he met her gaze.

"Come on, Raven," he murmured. "I know you're the smart one. You've figured out I'm not here to hurt you. This is yours if you want it."

Raven took a slow step forward, her glowing eyes locked onto the meat. She sniffed the air, her movements deliberate as she closed the distance between them. When she reached the glass, she hesitated, her claws tapping softly against the surface.

Rick waited, his hand steady. "It's alright. You've got nothing to lose here."

After a long moment, Raven reached through the slot, her claws brushing against his hand as she took the meat. She pulled back quickly, retreating a few steps before crouching to eat. Her sisters chirped softly, inching closer to her as she began to eat.

"That's progress," Emma said, her voice filled with quiet admiration.

Rick nodded, a faint smirk tugging at his lips. "Piece by piece, Emma. Piece by piece."

Over the next few days, Rick repeated the process. Each time, Raven approached a little faster, her movements less hesitant. She no longer growled when he held out the meat, and once, she even paused after taking it, glancing back at him with an expression that almost resembled curiosity.

Skye was the first of the sisters to follow Raven's lead. She bounded forward one afternoon, chirping excitedly as she reached through the slot to grab her own piece of meat. Willow followed soon after, her movements calm and deliberate as always. Luna remained hesitant, staying close to Raven and only approaching when her older sister nudged her forward with a soft chirp.

"She's the glue that holds them together," Emma observed as she watched the interaction. "If Raven's comfortable, the others feel safe."

"That's what I'm counting on," Rick replied. "But it's not just about food. I need her to see me as more than just a source of meals."

One evening, Rick decided to push things further. He brought a durable rubber ball into the observation area, one of the girls' favorite toys. Instead of placing it in the enclosure, he rolled it gently along the floor near the glass, stopping it within Raven's reach.

She watched the ball roll, her glowing eyes narrowing as she considered it. Her sisters chirped softly behind her, their curiosity evident, but they didn't move until she did.

Raven stepped forward cautiously, her claws clicking softly against the floor as she approached the ball. She nudged it with her nose, letting out a quiet chirp. When Rick rolled it back to her, she tilted her head, her curiosity deepening.

"That's it," Rick murmured. "You figure it out. This isn't a trap—it's just a game."

Raven batted the ball with her claws, sending it rolling toward her sisters. Skye pounced on it immediately, chirping loudly as she played. Willow joined in soon after, nudging the ball toward Luna, who hesitated before giving it a tentative push.

"They're following her lead," Emma said, smiling. "Like always."

Rick smirked. "She's the boss. They trust her, and if she starts to trust me, they will too."

That night, as Rick sat near the observation glass, Raven approached on her own. She stood there for a long moment, her gaze meeting his through the glass. Then, slowly, she placed a single hand against the surface, her claws resting lightly against the glass.

Rick leaned forward, his voice low and calm. "We're getting there, Raven. One step at a time."

Raven chirped softly, her glowing eyes holding his for a moment longer before she turned back to her sisters. Rick watched her go, a faint smile on his face.

"She's starting to trust you," Emma said, her tone filled with quiet pride.

Rick nodded. "It's a start. And with her on board, the others won't be far behind."

While Rick focused on building trust with Raven through actions, Emma had a different plan in mind—one that would test the younglings' intelligence and adaptability. She wanted to teach them something entirely new: communication through pictures.

In the early stages of her experiment, Emma prepared a set of cards, each featuring a simple, brightly colored image: food, water, a ball, and even a generic image of their enclosure to signify "home." Her goal was straightforward—to help the younglings understand that pointing to a specific image could result in receiving the associated item. It was a rudimentary form of language, but for the ferals, it was a monumental step.

The first trial began the day after the younglings had settled into their larger enclosure. Emma sat on the floor outside the observation glass, the cards spread out in front of her. She placed a piece of raw meat near the card with the picture of food and waited.

Inside the enclosure, Raven watched her with a familiar, calculating gaze. Skye bounded forward, her energy undiminished, while Willow and Luna lingered near the back.

"Alright, girls," Emma murmured softly, keeping her tone calm. "Let's see what you make of this."

Skye was the first to approach the glass, her chirps loud and curious as she eyed the piece of meat. Emma pointed to the card and then to the meat, repeating the motion several times. Skye tilted her head, her glowing eyes darting between the card and the food. Then, without hesitation, she clawed at the glass where the meat was.

"Not quite," Emma said with a small smile. "But good try."

Skye chirped again, more insistently this time, and clawed at the glass harder. Raven let out a low growl from behind her, causing Skye to retreat slightly. Emma noted the interaction—Raven wasn't discouraging Skye, but she clearly wanted her sister to think before acting.

"Raven's watching," Rick said from his position nearby, his voice low. "She's trying to figure out what you're up to."

"That's the idea," Emma replied. "If I can get her interested, she'll guide the others."

The trials continued throughout the week, with Emma refining her approach each day. At first, the younglings seemed more interested in the food itself than the card, often clawing at the glass or chirping loudly in frustration when their efforts didn't yield results. But Emma remained patient, repeating the process over and over.

On the third day, Skye made the first breakthrough. After Emma pointed to the food card several times, Skye tentatively touched her claw to the glass in front of the card. Emma immediately rewarded her by placing a small piece of meat in the feeding slot.

"There you go!" Emma exclaimed, her tone filled with genuine excitement. "You did it, Skye!"

Skye chirped loudly, darting back to show her sisters the treat. Willow and Luna chirped softly, inching closer to the glass, while Raven remained in her usual spot, her sharp gaze fixed on Emma.

"You see that, Raven?" Emma said, holding up the card again. "That's how it works."

Raven didn't move, but her eyes flicked to the card briefly before returning to Emma's face. It was a small reaction, but Emma noted it with satisfaction.

By the end of the first week, Willow had joined Skye in touching the food card during trials. Her approach was slower and more methodical, her claw movements deliberate as she tapped the glass in front of the image. Emma rewarded her with equal enthusiasm, offering small pieces of meat through the slot.

"Two down," Emma said to Rick as they observed the younglings that evening. "Raven's going to take more time, but I think Luna might surprise us."

Rick smirked. "Luna's cautious, but she watches everything. If she sees enough success, she'll want to try it."

Emma nodded. "That's what I'm counting on."

The turning point came on the tenth day of trials. Emma decided to up the challenge by introducing two cards at once: one with the image of food and another with the image of water. She placed a small bowl of water near the corresponding card and a piece of meat near the food card, then waited.

Skye bounded forward as usual, her chirps loud and enthusiastic. She clawed at the food card, receiving her treat, and then turned to the water card, her glowing eyes bright with curiosity. After a moment's hesitation, she tapped the glass in front of the water card and was immediately rewarded with the bowl of water.

"That's my girl!" Emma said, clapping her hands softly. "You're getting it."

Willow followed suit, her movements measured as she touched the water card and lapped at the bowl Emma provided. Luna watched from a distance, her small frame trembling slightly, but her glowing eyes were fixed on the cards.

Then, to Emma's surprise, Raven stood and approached the glass. She moved slowly, her gaze shifting between the cards and her sisters. When she reached the glass, she hesitated, her claws resting lightly against the surface. Emma waited, her heart pounding slightly.

"Come on, Raven," Emma murmured, her tone encouraging. "You've got this."

Raven glanced at her, glowing eyes narrowing slightly in cautious calculation. Then, with deliberate precision, she extended a claw and tapped the food card.

Emma's smile widened as she placed a piece of meat into the feeding slot. "That's it! Good girl, Raven!"

Raven took the meat and retreated to the back of the enclosure, where her sisters chirped softly, crowding around her as if seeking approval. She didn't growl or push them away—another small but significant sign of trust.

By the end of the second week, even Luna had begun participating in the trials. Her movements were still hesitant, but with Raven's guidance, she managed to tap the food card during one session. Emma rewarded her immediately, offering words of encouragement as Luna took the treat back to her alcove.

"They're getting it," Rick said one evening as they watched the younglings interact. "It's slow, but it's progress."

Emma smiled, her tone filled with quiet pride. "And it's not just about the cards. It's about showing them that they can communicate with us—that we're willing to listen."

Rick nodded. "Trust works both ways. And thanks to you, they're starting to see that."

The progress with the cards was steady but not without its challenges. While Skye and Willow eagerly participated in the trials, Raven remained discerning, and Luna's caution continued to hold her back. However, the successes were undeniable. Each day brought small victories, whether it was Luna hesitantly tapping the water card or Raven guiding her sisters with subtle cues.

One afternoon, Emma decided to introduce a new layer to the experiment. Alongside the usual food and water cards, she added a card featuring an image of the ball they often played with. This time, the reward wasn't something they could eat or drink—it was the ball itself.

"This should be interesting," Emma remarked as she set the cards on the table. "Let's see if they understand the connection when the reward isn't immediately satisfying hunger or thirst."

Rick, leaning against the counter, raised an eyebrow. "You're testing their curiosity now. Bold move."

"They're smart," Emma replied. "It's time to push their limits a little."

Inside the enclosure, the younglings gathered as usual. Raven was at the front, her posture alert, while Skye bounced on the balls of her feet, her sharp claws clicking softly against the floor. Willow stood calmly, her gaze flicking between the cards and Emma, while Luna lingered at the back, her glowing eyes wide with curiosity.

Emma tapped the glass lightly to get their attention, then held up the ball. She rolled it across the table and placed it near the card with the ball image. "This is your new option," she said softly. "Let's see what you make of it."

Skye was the first to approach, as always, her movements quick and eager. She glanced at the cards, then at the ball, her glowing eyes narrowing slightly as she considered the setup. With a chirp of determination, she tapped the food card, earning a piece of meat.

"Good choice," Emma said with a small smile. "But what about this one?" She gestured toward the ball card.

Skye tilted her head, her curiosity piqued. After a moment's hesitation, she tapped the ball card. Emma immediately rolled the ball through the slot, watching as it landed in the enclosure. Skye let out an excited chirp and pounced on the ball, batting it around with obvious delight.

"Well, that's one way to motivate her," Rick said, smirking.

Willow followed next, her movements as deliberate as always. She tapped the water card first, sipping from the bowl Emma provided, then carefully tested the ball card. When the ball rolled into the enclosure, she sniffed it briefly before pushing it toward Skye, who chirped loudly in thanks.

"She's practical," Emma remarked, jotting down a quick note. "But she still engages with the game."

Raven stayed motionless, her glowing eyes fixed intently on Emma. She remained silent until Luna began to creep forward, her small frame trembling slightly as she inched closer to the glass. Raven let out a low chirp, prompting Luna to pause. It wasn't a warning—it was encouragement.

"Come on, Luna," Emma murmured softly. "You can do this."

Luna hesitated for a long moment before finally reaching out with one clawed hand. She tapped the food card first, then glanced back at Raven as if seeking approval. When Raven chirped again, Luna tentatively touched the ball card.

Emma rolled the ball into the enclosure, watching as Luna darted back to her alcove. But instead of hiding, she peeked out cautiously, her glowing eyes fixed on the ball as Skye and Willow batted it around. After a few moments, Luna crept closer, her movements slow but determined. When the ball rolled near her, she nudged it gently, earning a delighted chirp from Skye.

"She's warming up," Rick said, his tone thoughtful. "It's slow, but it's progress."

"And Raven's the key," Emma replied. "Her encouragement makes all the difference."

As the weeks went on, the younglings' understanding of the cards deepened. They began to use them not just during trials but in their own way. One evening, Rick and Emma observed as Raven tapped one of the feeding slots lightly, then turned to Willow and chirped softly. Willow immediately approached the card setup, tapping the water card. When Emma provided the bowl, Raven allowed her sisters to drink first before taking her turn.

"They're using the cards to communicate with each other," Emma said, her voice filled with quiet awe. "It's more than I expected."

Rick nodded, a faint smirk tugging at his lips. "They're smarter than we give them credit for. And they're proving it every day."

One particularly humorous moment came when Skye decided to test the system. During a trial, she tapped the food card, received her treat, and then immediately tapped the water card. After lapping at the water, she tapped the ball card, chirping loudly as the ball rolled into the enclosure.

"She's working the system," Kyle said from his position near the back of the room, shaking his head in disbelief. "She's figured out how to get everything she wants."

Rick chuckled. "She's not wrong. The system works."

Emma laughed as well. "Skye might be impulsive, but she's not stupid. If anything, she's teaching us more about their problem-solving abilities than we ever planned."

Inside the enclosure, Skye batted the ball toward Luna, who chirped softly and nudged it back. Willow joined in, her movements precise as she guided the ball toward Raven. The leader of the group paused briefly before nudging the ball forward, completing the circle.

"They're a team," Emma said softly. "Even in play, they work together."

CHAPTER 19

Later that evening, as the lab settled into its usual nighttime calm, the younglings adjusted to their new enclosure. The team gathered around the observation window, their expressions a mix of curiosity and quiet admiration.

Inside, the girls huddled together in their den, their soft chirps and low growls weaving into an almost conversational rhythm. At the edge of the group, Raven perched like a sentinel, her sharp eyes scanning the enclosure while her sisters rested under her watchful gaze.

Kyle leaned against the counter, his brow furrowed in thought. "I've been meaning to ask," he began, breaking the silence. "Why are they so... advanced? I mean, these girls can solve puzzles, recognize patterns, and even cooperate better than most adults I've seen. But they're what—three, maybe four years old? A human child that age can barely read, let alone do half of what they're doing."

Emma glanced at Rick before setting her tablet down, her expression thoughtful. "That's a good question," she said, her tone measured. "The answer lies in how ferals adapt to their environment."

Kyle tilted his head, curiosity sparking in his eyes. "Adapted how?"

Emma adjusted her position, folding her arms as she leaned back slightly. "Let's start with the basics. Ferals are vampires, biologically speaking, but they've diverged significantly from what you'd call a 'normal' vampire. Their biology is optimized for survival in extreme conditions—harsh environments, constant threats, and scarcity of resources. To survive, they had to develop not just physical adaptations, but cognitive ones as well."

Rick smirked faintly. "In other words, they don't have the luxury of a slow childhood."

"Exactly," Emma continued. "For human children, the first few years of life are about learning foundational skills—walking, talking, basic communication. Humans have the benefit of stable environments and caretakers who provide for them during this slow development period. Ferals, on the other hand, don't have that luxury. Their survival depends on rapid development, both physically and mentally."

Kyle nodded slowly. "So, you're saying they're born knowing more?"

"Not quite," Emma replied. "They're not born with knowledge, but their brains are hardwired for accelerated learning. Their neuroplasticity—the brain's ability to form new connections—is off the charts compared to humans or even normal vampires. It's a survival mechanism. Within weeks of being born, they're already moving, hunting, and recognizing threats."

Rick leaned against the counter, his voice steady as he added, "Think of it this way: in the wild, a feral youngling doesn't get years to figure out how to fend for itself. If it can't learn fast—how to find food, avoid predators, and navigate its environment—it's not going to make it. The ones who survive pass on those traits to the next generation."

Kyle scribbled a few notes on his clipboard, his brow furrowing. "Okay, but how does that translate to things like problem-solving? I mean, figuring out those puzzle toys or using the cards—that's not just instinct."

Emma nodded, her expression brightening as she delved deeper.

"You're right—it's not just instinct. Their problem-solving skills are a byproduct of their environment. Imagine a feral youngling in the wild. It might encounter situations where food is trapped behind a barrier, or where it needs to cross a dangerous area to reach safety. Over generations, the ferals who could think creatively and adapt to new challenges were the ones who survived."

She paused, tapping her chin thoughtfully. "There's also a biological component to this. Ferals have an unusually high density of neural connections in their prefrontal cortex—the part of the brain associated with decision-making, planning, and complex problem-solving. It's not just about intelligence; it's about adaptability. They're wired to analyze their surroundings and find solutions quickly."

Kyle glanced back at the girls, who were now chirping softly as Raven nudged one of the puzzle toys toward Luna. "That explains their brains. But what about their bodies? They move so fast, and their coordination is insane for their age."

"That's another survival adaptation," Emma explained. "Ferals grow faster than humans or even normal vampires. Their skeletal structure, muscle density, and reflex pathways develop at an accelerated rate. By the time they're a few months old, they're already capable of climbing, running, and even hunting. Their physical development complements their cognitive abilities—it's all designed to keep them alive."

Rick leaned forward slightly, his smirk faint but genuine. "And don't forget the claws and fangs. They're not just for show. Those are tools for survival, just like their minds."

Kyle scratched the back of his head, still processing the information. "So, basically, everything about them is about surviving as quickly as possible. But... doesn't that take a toll? I mean, growing up that fast has to have some kind of downside, right?"

Emma's expression turned more serious. "It does. Rapid development comes at a cost. For one, their lifespan is significantly shorter than a normal vampire's. Their bodies burn through resources at an incredible rate, which is why they're constantly hungry. And then there's the psychological toll. Ferals don't have the luxury of a stable, nurturing environment. They live in a constant state of fight-or-flight, and that shapes how they see the world."

Rick added, his tone grim, "It's also why trust is so hard for them. From the moment they're born, their world teaches them one thing: survive at all costs. That mindset doesn't leave a lot of room for anything else."

Kyle nodded slowly, his gaze returning to the younglings. "That's... a lot to take in. But it makes sense. They're not like human kids—or even like vampires. They're something entirely their own."

Emma smiled faintly. "Exactly. And that's what makes them so fascinating. They're not just survivors—they're innovators. And if we can find a way to bridge the gap between their world and ours, there's so much we could learn from them."

Rick straightened, his expression firm but thoughtful. "That's the goal, Kyle. To understand them. To show them there's more to life than just surviving."

Inside the enclosure, Raven chirped softly, nudging the puzzle toy toward Luna again. The youngest youngling hesitated, her glowing eyes wide as she studied the pieces. Then, slowly, she began to fit them together, her sisters chirping their quiet encouragement.

Kyle watched the scene, a faint smile tugging at his lips. "Well, they're already proving one thing."

"What's that?" Emma asked.

"That even when the odds are stacked against them, they find a way to keep going."

Rick nodded. "That's ferals for you. Survivors, through and through."

As the conversation continued, Kyle leaned forward, resting his elbows on the counter. His curiosity only deepened, each new detail adding fuel to his questions. "Okay, so their brains are more adaptive, and their bodies grow faster. But what about their senses?" he asked, his brow furrowing slightly. "They seem... heightened, like they're always on edge."

Emma nodded, clearly pleased by his observation. "You're absolutely right. Their sensory systems are another critical part of their survival toolkit. Ferals have heightened senses of sight, hearing, and smell—far beyond what even normal vampires possess. Let's break it down."

She tapped a few buttons on her tablet, pulling up a diagram of a vampire brain and sensory system on the screen. "First, their vision. Ferals have an increased density of photoreceptor cells in their retinas, particularly the rods, which are responsible for low-light vision. This gives them exceptional night vision, allowing them to navigate and hunt in near-total darkness."

Rick added, "It's not just about seeing in the dark, though. Their eyes are tuned for motion detection. If something moves—even slightly—they'll notice it immediately."

Kyle glanced at the girls, who were quietly resting in their den. "And the glowing eyes?"

"That's a byproduct of their retinal structure," Emma explained. "The tapetum lucidum—a reflective layer in the back of their eyes—enhances their ability to see in low light by reflecting light back through the retina. It's similar to what you'd see in nocturnal animals, but far more advanced."

Kyle whistled softly. "So they're built for the dark. What about their hearing?"

"Another evolutionary masterpiece," Emma said with a small smile. "The structure of their inner ear is incredibly sensitive, with a wider range of frequency detection than humans or normal vampires. They can pick up sounds that are far beyond our range—subtle movements, distant footsteps, even the vibrations of a heartbeat."

Rick smirked. "It's why you don't sneak up on a feral. You'll never get close enough."

Kyle laughed nervously. "Good to know. And smell?"

Emma's smile faded slightly, her tone becoming more clinical. "Their olfactory system is highly developed. The number of olfactory receptors in their nasal passages is staggering—easily ten times that of a human. They can distinguish individual scents with incredible precision. That's why they're so good at tracking. Once they pick up a scent, they can follow it for miles."

Rick leaned forward, his voice low. "And it's not just about tracking prey. That sense of smell also helps them identify threats, including other ferals. It's one of the reasons their territories rarely overlap—if a stronger feral is nearby, they'll either leave or prepare to fight."

Kyle frowned, his brow furrowing as another thought occurred to him. "You mentioned their territories. Does that mean they have some kind of social structure, like packs or tribes?"

"Not exactly," Emma said, shaking her head. "Ferals are primarily solitary by nature, especially as they get older. Their social interactions are limited and often antagonistic—territorial disputes, competition for resources, things like that. But younglings are different. They rely on their siblings or their mother for survival, forming temporary bonds during their early development."

Rick added, "Those bonds don't last long, though. Once they're old enough to fend for themselves, they go their separate ways. The only exception is when you get an alpha—a feral strong enough to dominate a group. They're rare, but when they show up, they can control entire territories."

"Alpha?" Kyle asked, raising an eyebrow. "Like a leader?"

"More like a tyrant," Rick replied. "An alpha doesn't lead through loyalty or trust—it's pure dominance. The other ferals follow because they're too scared to do anything else."

Emma nodded. "And that dominance isn't just physical. Alphas tend to have higher intelligence as well, making them more dangerous. They can strategize, coordinate attacks, and even manipulate weaker ferals into doing their bidding."

Kyle shivered. "That's… unsettling."

"It is," Rick agreed. "But it's also rare. Most ferals don't have the capacity—or the desire—to form groups like that. They're survivors, first and foremost. Trust doesn't come naturally to them."

Emma turned the tablet toward Kyle, showing a close-up image of a feral's claw. "Speaking of survival," she said, "let's talk about their weapons. Their claws and fangs are perfectly designed for hunting and self-defense."

Kyle studied the image, noting the razor-sharp edges of the claw. "They're like knives."

"Better than knives," Emma said. "The claws are made of keratin, just like human nails or hair, but they're reinforced with a unique protein structure that makes them incredibly durable. They can cut through bone if needed."

Rick smirked. "Trust me, I've seen it."

"And their fangs?" Kyle asked.

"Equally impressive," Emma replied. "They're designed for puncturing and tearing, allowing ferals to take down prey quickly. But they're not just tools for feeding—they're also a deterrent. A single bite from a feral can cause massive trauma, even to another vampire."

Kyle leaned back, his expression a mix of awe and unease. "So, everything about them—their senses, their bodies, their minds—it's all geared toward survival."

Emma nodded. "Exactly. They're not just predators—they're apex predators. Their entire biology is optimized for one purpose: to survive in a world that's constantly trying to kill them."

Rick's expression hardened slightly. "And that's why they're so dangerous. But it's also what makes them incredible. If we can tap into that potential—if we can find a way to work with them instead of against them—we might be able to bridge the gap."

Kyle glanced back at the girls, who were now stirring slightly in their den. Raven stretched, her sharp claws glinting in the dim light, before settling back down. "It's a lot to take in," he said softly. "But I think I'm starting to understand."

Rick smirked faintly. "Good. Because if you're going to work with them, you'd better respect what they're capable of."

Kyle nodded, his gaze fixed on the younglings. "Trust me—I do."

The younglings stirred restlessly in their den as the team continued their observations. Raven stretched out first, her glowing eyes briefly scanning the room before nudging Luna with a gentle tap of her claw. Luna let out a soft chirp but didn't move, prompting Willow to step in, nipping lightly at her younger sister's arm. Skye, already up and pacing, circled the den impatiently.

"They're restless," Kyle noted, watching as Raven finally stepped out, followed by the others. "Is that normal?"

Rick glanced at Emma, then back at Kyle. "For them? Yes. Ferals are naturally hyper-aware. They're not used to staying in one place for too long—it goes against their instincts. Movement is survival."

Emma tapped her pen against her clipboard. "It's a combination of energy and vigilance. Ferals are built to operate in high-stress environments, constantly moving, constantly scanning for threats. Even when they're safe, their brains are wired to assume danger is just around the corner."

"So they can never really relax?" Kyle asked, his brow furrowing.

"Not fully," Emma replied. "Even when they rest, their alertness doesn't completely shut off. Think of it like a predator in the wild—they may sleep, but they're ready to bolt or fight at the first sign of danger."

Skye let out a sharp chirp, bounding toward the water feature in the enclosure. She splashed in enthusiastically, her claws scraping against the shallow pool's edge as she batted at the water. Willow followed, moving more gracefully but still joining in the activity. Luna lingered behind, watching from the safety of the alcove, while Raven remained at the den's entrance, her sharp eyes fixed on her sisters.

Rick observed Raven with a faint smirk. "And there's your leader again. She's not just sitting back because she's lazy—she's guarding the others."

Kyle frowned. "Guarding them? From what?"

Rick shrugged. "It's instinct. Even if there's no immediate threat, she's taking responsibility for their safety. That's why she's so important. If we're going to make progress with these girls, it starts with her."

The team's discussion shifted as Emma set her clipboard aside, pulling up a holographic model on the lab's central table. The image displayed a cross-section of a feral's nervous system, highlighting the spinal cord and the intricate web of nerve pathways extending through the body.

"I've been thinking about what you said earlier, Kyle," Emma began. "About why ferals develop so quickly compared to humans or vampires. There's another piece to the puzzle: their nervous system."

Kyle leaned closer, studying the model. "What about it?"

Emma pointed to the glowing lines that represented nerve pathways. "Ferals have an incredibly efficient nervous system. Their reflex arcs—the pathways that control automatic responses—are faster and more direct than anything we've seen in humans or normal vampires. This allows them to react to stimuli almost instantaneously."

Rick chimed in, his tone matter-of-fact. "It's why they seem so fast in a fight. They're not just moving quickly—they're reacting before you've even finished your first move."

Kyle scratched his head, trying to process the information. "So their bodies and brains are always... what, primed for action?"

"Exactly," Emma said. "But it goes deeper than that. Their nervous system isn't just fast—it's adaptable. If they encounter a new threat or challenge, their brains can rewire themselves to respond more effectively next time. It's called neuroplasticity, and ferals have it in spades."

"That explains a lot," Kyle said, glancing back at the girls. "But wouldn't that kind of constant rewiring burn them out?"

"It does," Emma admitted, her tone somber. "That's one of the reasons ferals have such a high caloric requirement. Their brains and bodies are always working at full capacity, and they need fuel to sustain that. Without enough food, their systems start to shut down—first cognitively, then physically."

As if on cue, Raven let out a low growl, her glowing eyes shifting toward the feeding slot. She chirped softly, prompting the others to gather around her. Skye was the first to chirp back, followed by Willow and Luna.

"They're asking for food," Rick said, pushing off the counter and heading toward the feeding station. "And when Raven asks, we listen."

Kyle watched as Rick prepared the food, carefully portioning out meat and placing it in the slots. The younglings approached cautiously at first, with Raven taking the lead. She sniffed at the offering, then chirped sharply, signaling her approval. The others followed quickly, each taking their share under Raven's watchful eye.

"You've noticed how they eat, right?" Emma asked, turning to Kyle.

Kyle nodded. "Yeah. Raven eats first, and the others wait for her signal."

"It's a survival strategy," Emma explained. "In the wild, the leader ensures the food is safe before the rest of the group eats. It's another way Raven maintains her authority."

"And if she doesn't approve?" Kyle asked.

"Then no one eats," Rick said, his tone flat. "But that's rare. Raven's smart enough to know when food is scarce, and she won't waste a resource unless it's truly dangerous."

As the girls finished their meal, Kyle leaned back against the counter, his curiosity still buzzing. "One last question," he said, glancing between Rick and Emma. "If ferals are so advanced—so perfectly adapted—why haven't they taken over? I mean, it sounds like they're the ultimate predators."

Rick exchanged a look with Emma, then folded his arms. "Because survival comes at a cost."

Emma nodded, picking up the explanation. "Ferals are built for survival, not domination. Their adaptations make them incredible in the short term, but those same traits limit them in the long run. They burn through resources quickly, their lifespans are shorter, and their social structures are fragile. They're not designed to thrive—they're designed to endure."

Kyle frowned. "So they're powerful, but... unsustainable?"

"Exactly," Emma said. "And that's why they're so fascinating. They're a glimpse into what evolution can do under extreme pressure. But they're also a reminder of the balance nature requires. For all their strengths, ferals are just as vulnerable as they are dangerous."

Rick smirked faintly. "And that's why they need us. Not to control them, but to find a way to help them survive without burning out."

Kyle nodded slowly, his gaze returning to the girls. "I think I'm starting to understand. They're not just animals. They're something more."

"They're survivors," Emma said softly. "And that's what makes them extraordinary."

CHAPTER 20

Later that evening, Emma sat at her desk, poring over a stack of reports on feral biology and behavior. The soft glow of her desk lamp illuminated the pages, casting long, shifting shadows across the walls of the lab. Despite the quiet hum of the machinery in the background, her focus remained unbroken. Each report, filled with data and field notes, painted a vivid picture of just how extraordinary ferals truly were.

She flipped through the pages methodically, her sharp eyes scanning graphs, annotations, and detailed observations. One line caught her attention, halting her progress. She leaned closer, her finger tracing the text as she read aloud under her breath:

"Newborn ferals exhibit immediate motor function, achieving full mobility within hours of birth."

She leaned back in her chair, her gaze drifting toward the observation enclosure where the younglings rested. It was hard to fathom—imagine a human or even a vampire infant being born and, within hours, running alongside their mother, navigating dangerous terrain, and evading predators. Yet, for ferals, this was the norm.

Rick approached from the other side of the lab, holding a steaming mug of coffee. "You've got that look again," he said, setting the mug down beside her. "What's on your mind?"

Emma gestured to the report, her tone thoughtful. "I'm just marveling at how ferals develop. Did you know that within hours of being born, they're already running? Not crawling, not stumbling—running. On all fours, no less."

Rick smirked, taking a sip of his own coffee. "Yeah, I've seen the footage. A feral mother gives birth, and before you know it, the youngling is up and moving, keeping pace like it's been doing it for years."

Emma shook her head, her expression a mix of awe and disbelief. "It's not just movement, Rick. It's coordination, speed, agility—all fully functional within hours. A human baby can't even hold its head up for weeks, and even a normal vampire infant takes months to master basic motor skills. But ferals? They hit the ground running—literally."

Rick leaned against the counter, his smirk fading into something more thoughtful. "Makes sense when you think about it. A feral youngling that can't keep up is a liability. And in their world, liabilities don't survive."

Emma tapped her pen against the table, her tone growing more animated. "But it's not just about survival—it's about efficiency. Their entire developmental process is condensed into weeks or months, compared to years for humans or vampires. And it's not just physical—it's cognitive, too. They learn how to navigate their environment, identify threats, and even hunt, all within an incredibly short timeframe."

Rick nodded. "It's evolution at its most brutal. The ones that don't adapt fast enough? They don't make it."

Emma pulled up a series of videos on her tablet, showing various field observations of feral mothers with their newborns. In one clip, a feral mother crouched low in a dense forest, her sharp claws gripping the ground as she scanned her surroundings. Behind her, a tiny youngling—barely the size of a large housecat—scrambled to its feet, its glowing eyes wide with curiosity. Within moments, the youngling was running alongside its mother, mimicking her every move.

"Incredible," Emma murmured, her eyes fixed on the screen. "Look at how it mirrors her movements. Every step, every pause—it's like it's instinctive."

"That's because it is," Rick said, his voice steady. "Ferals don't have the luxury of learning by trial and error. They're born into a world that's out to get them, and their instincts reflect that. From the moment they're born, they're wired to survive."

Emma nodded, rewinding the footage to watch the youngling again. "What's even more fascinating is how quickly they adapt. Watch this—when the mother pauses to sniff the air, the youngling does the same. It's not just following her—it's learning from her."

Rick leaned over to get a better look, his brow furrowing slightly. "And they're not just mimicking. Look at the way the youngling adjusts its footing when the mother moves. It's anticipating her movements, not just reacting to them."

Emma made a note on her tablet, her excitement growing. "That level of coordination and learning is remarkable. It's not something you see in any other species—not even in vampires. It's like they're born with a blueprint for survival, and they start filling in the details the moment they're exposed to the world."

Kyle wandered over, his curiosity piqued by their conversation. "What are you two geeking out over now?"

Emma turned the tablet toward him, replaying the footage. "Watch this. This youngling is less than a day old, and it's already running alongside its mother. Look at the coordination, the awareness. It's lightyears ahead of anything you'd see in human or vampire infants."

Kyle's eyes widened as he watched the video. "That's... insane. I mean, I knew ferals were fast learners, but this? It's like they skip the entire baby stage."

"They do," Emma said. "It's a survival mechanism. In the wild, a slow-developing youngling wouldn't stand a chance. Ferals have evolved to grow up as quickly as possible because their environment demands it."

Kyle scratched his head, his brow furrowed. "But wouldn't that kind of rapid development come with downsides? I mean, humans and vampires develop slowly for a reason—it gives their brains and bodies time to grow properly."

"Exactly," Emma said, her tone growing more serious. "That's the trade-off. Ferals develop quickly, but it comes at a cost. Their lifespans are shorter, and their bodies are under constant stress to maintain that level of performance. And then there's the psychological toll—imagine being born into a world where you have to fight for your life from day one. That kind of pressure leaves scars."

Rick's expression darkened slightly. "It's why they're so aggressive. They don't know anything else. Trust, safety, comfort—those aren't part of their world."

Kyle glanced back at the younglings in the enclosure, his gaze softening. "But these girls... they're different, right? I mean, they're here, not out there. They're getting a chance to grow up in a safer environment."

Emma smiled faintly. "They are. And that's what makes this so important. If we can show them that survival doesn't have to mean constant fear and aggression, maybe we can start to bridge the gap. Maybe they can learn to trust."

Rick nodded, his gaze fixed on Raven as she nudged Luna gently with her claw. "It's a long shot, but it's worth trying. These girls are smart—they're survivors. If anyone can make it work, it's them."

As the evening wore on, the team continued their work, occasionally glancing toward the observation enclosure where the younglings rested. Raven, ever the leader, lay sprawled at the entrance to their makeshift den, her sharp eyes still glowing faintly in the dim light. Skye and Willow chirped softly to one another, while Luna nestled close to Raven, her small form trembling slightly with each sound from the lab beyond the glass.

Rick sipped his coffee, leaning against the counter, his gaze fixed on the group. His expression was thoughtful, but there was a faint tension in his posture—a hint of the memories stirring in the back of his mind.

"You know," he began, his voice breaking the silence, "it's a miracle these four are even alive."

Kyle glanced up from his notes, frowning slightly. "What do you mean? Because they lost their mother?"

Rick shook his head slowly. "That's part of it, yeah. But it's more than that. Out there, it's not just the environment they have to survive. It's each other. Adult ferals don't exactly have a reputation for being... gentle with younglings, especially ones that don't belong to their group."

Emma set down her tablet, her expression growing serious. "He's right. Ferals are fiercely territorial, and that doesn't change just because there are children involved. If anything, it makes them even more dangerous."

Kyle frowned, leaning forward slightly. "So... what? They'd kill kids just because they're from a different group?"

"It happens all the time," Rick replied, his tone grim. "To them, younglings from another group aren't kids—they're competition. They eat the same food, take up the same resources, and weaken the group as a whole. And ferals don't do competition. They eliminate it."

Emma nodded, her brow furrowing. "There's no sentimentality in their world. If a youngling is a liability, it's either abandoned or killed outright. And if it belongs to another group? The best-case scenario is that it gets chased off. Worst-case? It's food."

Kyle paled slightly, setting his clipboard down as he processed the information. "They eat kids?"

Rick's gaze didn't waver. "It's not common, but it happens. When resources are scarce, ferals do whatever they have to do to survive. That includes cannibalism."

Kyle rubbed the back of his neck, his unease clear. "That's... brutal."

"It is," Emma agreed. "But that's their reality. It's a world where the weak don't survive, and the strong only survive because they're willing to do whatever it takes. It's why these girls are so unique—they've managed to survive without becoming as vicious as the adults out there."

Rick crossed his arms, his gaze drifting back to the girls. "And then there's the kidnapping."

Kyle raised an eyebrow. "Kidnapping?"

Emma sighed, her tone growing heavier. "It's more common than you'd think. An adult feral might take a youngling from another group, either to raise it as part of their own or to use it for other purposes—like bait for hunting."

"Bait?" Kyle asked, his voice barely above a whisper.

Emma nodded grimly. "Ferals are incredibly resourceful. They'll use a youngling to lure in prey, distract predators, or even as a bargaining chip in territorial disputes. But most of the time, the youngling doesn't survive. The stress alone is enough to kill it."

Kyle frowned. "Stress?"

"It's not just psychological," Emma explained, pulling up a detailed diagram on her tablet. The screen displayed an intricate map of neural pathways and stress response systems. "The separation from their mother or siblings triggers an intense physiological reaction in feral younglings. Their bodies flood with cortisol and adrenaline—stress hormones designed for survival in the short term but catastrophic in the long term. Their immune systems shut down, growth halts, and even their organs can begin to fail. The trauma alone is often fatal."

Rick's jaw tightened as he observed the younglings through the glass. They were huddled in their den, their soft chirps and growls now muffled by the heavy weight of his thoughts. "And the ones that do survive?" His voice was low, edged with a bitterness that betrayed the memories lurking beneath. "They're broken. Whatever trust they might've had? Gone."

Emma nodded, her expression grim. "Survival becomes their only priority. They don't know safety, only fear. That fear turns into aggression, violence—it's all they have left to protect themselves."

Rick's gaze lingered on the younglings, his voice barely audible. "And that's why we can't let that happen to them. Not again."

Kyle leaned against the counter, his expression a mix of awe and unease. "So… these girls. They're lucky?"

"Lucky doesn't even begin to cover it," Emma replied. "The odds were stacked against them from the moment they were born. Losing their mother was a death sentence for most younglings. The fact that these four managed to survive long enough for us to find them is nothing short of miraculous."

Rick nodded, his tone softening slightly. "And that's why this matters. If we can show them that survival doesn't have to mean violence, that trust and cooperation can work… maybe we can break the cycle."

Kyle glanced back at the enclosure, where the girls were beginning to stir. "But can you really undo that? I mean, it sounds like everything about them is built for survival at all costs. Can you really change that?"

Emma folded her arms, her gaze steady. "It's not about changing who they are. It's about giving them an alternative. Right now, ferals don't see any other way to survive. But if we can show them another path—if we can help them understand that there's more to life than just fighting to stay alive—they might take it."

"And if they don't?" Kyle asked.

Rick smirked faintly. "Then at least we tried."

The younglings were fully awake now, chirping softly to one another as they moved about the enclosure. Skye darted toward the water feature, splashing excitedly, while Willow followed with more measured steps. Luna lingered near the den, her glowing eyes darting between her sisters and Raven, who remained at the entrance, her gaze sharp and watchful.

"They're survivors," Emma said quietly, watching as Raven let out a low chirp, calling Luna closer. "But they're also kids. And that's something we can't forget. For all their strength, for all their instincts—they're still just kids."

Rick nodded, his expression thoughtful. "Kids who've already seen more of the world's cruelty than most adults ever will. And that's why we can't fail them."

Kyle glanced at the enclosure one last time, his gaze softening. "No pressure, right?"

Rick chuckled softly, though there was no humor in the sound. "Pressure's what we signed up for, kid.

Late into the evening, the lab was quiet save for the soft hum of the equipment and the occasional scratch of Rick's pen against paper. Emma had stepped out for a moment to retrieve more files, leaving Rick and Kyle alone in the observation area. Kyle, still fidgety from the day's revelations, was scribbling notes while stealing glances at the younglings in the enclosure.

The girls had been restless since their last meal. Raven sat near the glass, her sharp claws clicking faintly against the smooth floor as she watched Rick with an intensity that was almost unnerving. Behind her, Skye paced back and forth, occasionally chirping to her sisters. Willow sat calmly, her glowing eyes fixed on the cards displayed near the feeding slot. Luna peeked out from their den, her small frame trembling slightly as she observed from a safe distance.

It was Raven who moved first. Rising to her full height, she padded over to the glass, her glowing eyes scanning the array of cards Emma had left on the table outside the enclosure. She tilted her head slightly, letting out a low chirp before reaching out with one clawed hand to tap the glass near the picture of food.

Kyle blinked, sitting up straighter. "Uh… Rick? Did she just—"

"She did," Rick replied, smirking faintly. He set down his pen and leaned back in his chair, watching as Raven tapped the glass again, this time more deliberately.

The sound of her claw against the glass drew the attention of her sisters. Skye bounded over, chirping loudly as she nudged Raven out of the way and began tapping the glass with both hands, her movements rapid and chaotic. Willow followed at a slower pace, her gaze calm but curious as she watched her sisters' antics.

"Looks like they're hungry," Kyle said, chuckling softly.

"They're testing us," Rick corrected, his tone amused. "They know what they want, and they're not afraid to ask for it."

Skye, impatient as ever, began tapping the glass more insistently, her claws clicking in a steady rhythm that grew louder with each passing second. She let out a sharp chirp, glancing back at Raven as if expecting her to join in. Raven, ever the leader, responded with a low growl before tapping the food card on the glass herself, her movements deliberate and precise.

"They're ganging up on us," Kyle said, his voice filled with mock concern. "What do we do?"

Rick chuckled, shaking his head. "We wait."

The girls, however, were not deterred. Skye pressed her face against the glass, her glowing eyes wide with determination as she tapped the card again and again. Willow nudged her out of the way, her clawed hand brushing the card with a calculated precision that seemed to echo Raven's leadership. Even Luna, hesitant as ever, crept closer to the glass, her small claws barely brushing the card as she let out a soft chirp.

"It's like they're working together," Kyle observed, his tone filled with awe. "Raven leads, Skye causes a scene, Willow cleans up after them, and Luna... well, Luna tries."

Rick smirked. "That's about right."

The tapping continued for several more minutes, growing louder and more insistent. Skye added a series of chirps to the mix, her high-pitched noises echoing through the lab as she clawed at the glass with increasing fervor. Willow, ever the methodical one, took over, tapping the card with slow, deliberate movements as if trying to show her sisters how it was done.

Meanwhile, Raven sat back, watching the chaos unfold with an air of amused patience. She let out a low chirp, prompting the others to pause and glance in her direction. With a single motion, she stepped forward and tapped the card one final time, her sharp claws clicking against the glass with a decisive sound.

"Alright," Rick said, standing up and stretching. "I guess they've earned it."

Kyle raised an eyebrow. "You're really going to reward them for that?"

Rick smirked as he approached the feeding slot. "They're learning, Kyle. This isn't just about food—it's about communication. And they're getting better at it."

He prepared a small portion of meat, placing it in the slot with practiced ease. The younglings immediately perked up, their chirps turning to excited trills as they crowded around the slot. Skye was the first to grab a piece, chirping triumphantly as she darted back to their den. Willow followed, her movements calm and deliberate as she took her share. Luna hesitated, glancing nervously at her sisters before Raven nudged her forward with a gentle growl. With Raven's encouragement, Luna retrieved her piece, letting out a soft chirp of gratitude.

Raven was the last to eat, taking her portion and retreating to the den to watch over her sisters as they devoured their meal. Her glowing eyes met Rick's through the glass, and for a brief moment, there was a flicker of understanding—a silent acknowledgment of the unspoken bond forming between them.

Kyle leaned back in his chair, shaking his head in disbelief. "You know, it's kind of adorable when they're not trying to kill us."

Rick chuckled, returning to his seat. "Don't let them fool you. They're still ferals. But… yeah. It's a start."

Emma returned just as the girls finished eating, raising an eyebrow as she noticed the empty feeding slot. "Let me guess—they talked you into another snack?"

"They earned it," Rick replied, his smirk faint but genuine.

Emma glanced at the girls, who were now chirping softly to one another as they curled up in their den. Raven stretched out at the entrance, her glowing eyes half-closed as she kept watch. "They're getting smarter," Emma said quietly. "And they're starting to trust us."

Rick nodded, his gaze steady. "One step at a time."

CHAPTER 21

A few minutes later, Emma entered the lab, balancing a tray with practiced ease. On it were neatly arranged portions of prepared food: small bowls of meat cut into manageable pieces and a bag of synthetic blood specially formulated for vampires. The faint hum of the lab's machinery provided a backdrop as she casually sipped from her own blood drink, the straw held delicately between her fingers.

The girls immediately perked up, their glowing eyes locking onto her. Raven was the first to move, stepping forward with deliberate confidence. Her claws clicked softly against the glass as she approached, her gaze fixed on the tray. Behind her, Skye darted out from their makeshift den, chirping excitedly as she pressed her face against the glass. Willow followed at a calmer pace, her movements precise as always, while Luna peeked out cautiously from the back, her wide eyes flicking between Emma and her sisters.

"They know what you've got," Rick remarked from his spot at the counter, smirking faintly as he watched the scene unfold.

"They're not subtle about it, either," Emma replied, her tone amused. She nodded toward the cards the girls had begun pressing against the glass—specifically the one with the image of food. Skye had grabbed it first, slapping it against the surface with an impatient chirp, while Raven let out a low growl of approval. Willow nudged the card into a better position, her calm demeanor in stark contrast to her sisters' excitement.

Emma set the tray down on a nearby table, sipping again from her blood drink. "Alright, alright, I see you. No need to rush me."

The girls didn't let up. Skye chirped louder, tapping the card against the glass with both hands now. Raven remained silent but watchful, her sharp eyes flicking between Emma and the food on the tray. Willow stayed back, her glowing eyes calm but intent. Even Luna had crept closer, her small claws resting lightly on the glass as she let out a soft, hesitant chirp.

"You've got an audience," Kyle muttered, glancing up from his notes.

Emma chuckled, grabbing a bowl of meat from the tray. "They're nothing if not persistent." She walked over to the feeding slot, holding the bowl just out of reach for a moment. "Alright, who's first?"

Raven immediately stepped forward, her commanding presence clear as she nudged her sisters aside. Skye let out a protesting chirp but backed off, while Willow moved without complaint. Luna lingered at the edge, her eyes darting nervously between Raven and the food.

Emma slid the bowl into the slot, watching as Raven retrieved it with practiced ease. She let out a low growl, carrying the bowl back to the den and setting it down. Her sisters chirped softly, gathering around her as she distributed the food with a series of deliberate nudges and growls.

"They're organized," Kyle observed, scribbling a note. "Even with food, Raven's in charge."

"Of course she is," Rick replied, his tone matter-of-fact. "She's the leader. She makes sure everyone gets their share—and that no one steps out of line."

As the girls ate, Emma took another sip of her blood drink, leaning against the counter beside Rick. "It's interesting, isn't it?" she said, her tone thoughtful. "They don't just grab and hoard. Even Skye, for all her impatience, knows to follow Raven's lead."

Rick nodded, his gaze steady. "It's survival. They know that working together gives them a better chance. Even at this age, they get it."

Kyle frowned slightly, watching as Luna hesitated before taking her share. "What about Luna? She always seems... unsure."

"She's the youngest," Emma explained. "And in feral dynamics, the youngest is often the most vulnerable. But she's lucky—Raven looks out for her. If she didn't..." She trailed off, letting the implication hang in the air.

Kyle shifted uncomfortably, glancing at the younglings again. "Do you think that's why they're so attached to each other? Because they've had to rely on each other for everything?"

Emma nodded. "Absolutely. They've been through more in a few short years than most of us will face in a lifetime. That kind of bond doesn't break easily."

Once the food was gone, the girls began pressing the card against the glass again, their chirps growing more insistent. Skye was the most vocal, her high-pitched noises echoing through the lab as she tapped the card repeatedly. Raven let out a low growl, silencing her for a moment before taking the card herself and pressing it against the glass with deliberate force.

"They're not shy about asking for seconds," Emma said with a smirk.

"They're testing boundaries," Rick replied, his tone calm. "They're seeing how far they can push."

Emma grabbed another bowl from the tray, sliding it into the slot. "Well, let's see how far they go."

This time, Raven didn't move immediately. She nudged the bowl toward Skye, allowing her sister to take the first share. Skye chirped happily, dragging the bowl back toward the den. Willow followed, her movements measured, while Luna hesitated at the edge of the group. Raven chirped softly, her tone almost reassuring, and Luna finally stepped forward, taking her piece with trembling hands.

Rick watched the interaction closely, his expression thoughtful. "They're learning," he said quietly. "Not just how to communicate, but how to trust."

Emma nodded, her gaze softening as she watched Luna retreat to the den with her food. "And they're teaching us, too. About them, about each other... maybe even about ourselves."

Kyle scribbled another note, glancing between the younglings and the team. "You know, for ferals, they're... kind of adorable."

Rick smirked faintly. "Don't let them fool you, kid. They're still ferals. But... yeah. They've got their moments."

Emma chuckled, raising her blood drink in a mock toast. "To their moments, then. May they keep surprising us."

As the girls finished their second round of food, the lab settled into a brief moment of quiet—brief being the key word. Skye, ever the ball of energy, decided she wasn't quite done making noise. She chirped loudly, dragging the now-empty bowl toward the glass with a series of sharp, scraping sounds that made Kyle wince.

"Does she ever stop?" Kyle asked, rubbing his temples.

"She's got the energy of a toddler hyped up on sugar," Rick replied dryly, leaning back in his chair. "And the persistence of a door-to-door salesman."

Emma chuckled as she returned from the other side of the lab, carrying a small box of toys. "Speaking of energy, I thought they might like these. Something to keep them busy."

Skye immediately perked up as Emma approached the feeding slot, her glowing eyes fixed on the box. Raven growled softly, stepping in front of her sister to investigate first. She chirped once, tilting her head as Emma slid the box into the enclosure.

"What's in there?" Kyle asked, craning his neck to see.

"Nothing fancy," Emma said, smirking. "Just some indestructible balls and a few puzzle toys. Let's see what they do with them."

Raven was the first to approach the box, her claws clicking against the floor as she sniffed it cautiously. Skye, impatient as ever, darted forward and shoved her nose into the box, earning an annoyed growl from Raven. Willow observed from a distance, her calm demeanor unshaken, while Luna hovered near the den, watching with wide eyes.

The first item out of the box was a bright orange ball, which Skye immediately grabbed with her teeth and began to shake like a dog with a new toy. The ball didn't give an inch, much to her frustration. She dropped it and let out a series of high-pitched chirps, batting it across the enclosure with her claws.

"Looks like someone's found her favorite," Rick remarked, watching as Skye chased the ball in circles, her movements a chaotic blur of energy.

Willow finally stepped forward, picking up one of the puzzle toys with delicate precision. It was a cube with sliding pieces that revealed hidden compartments. She sniffed it once before using her claws to nudge one of the sliders, her movements careful and deliberate. Within moments, she had opened the first compartment and pulled out the small treat inside.

"Well, there's your brains of the operation," Emma said, nodding toward Willow. "She didn't even hesitate."

"Skye's the brawn, Willow's the brains," Rick added with a smirk. "And Raven's the boss. Poor Luna's just along for the ride."

As if on cue, Luna crept closer to the group, her glowing eyes darting nervously between her sisters and the scattered toys. She paused for a moment, her small frame trembling slightly, before tentatively picking up a small rubber ring from the box. Her claws gripped it tightly as she retreated back to the den, her movements quick and cautious.

"She's still so nervous," Kyle observed, a faint frown tugging at his lips. "Is that normal for the youngest?"

Rick nodded, his tone calm and assured. "Completely. She's looking to Raven for guidance. Once she feels safe enough, she'll start figuring things out on her own."

Raven, meanwhile, had decided the box needed further investigation. She tipped it over with a single swipe of her claw, spilling its contents across the floor. Skye let out a delighted chirp and immediately pounced on another ball, while Willow calmly sorted through the remaining toys with an almost methodical precision.

"Do they ever get tired?" Kyle asked, his voice tinged with disbelief.

"They do," Emma replied, smirking. "Eventually. But trust me, you don't want to be the one trying to outlast them. They'll win every time."

The room erupted into laughter when Skye batted her ball too hard, sending it ricocheting off the glass and straight into Raven. The older sister let out an irritated growl, her glowing eyes narrowing as she turned to glare at Skye. Skye chirped innocently, crouching low and wagging her claws in what could only be described as an attempt to playfully apologize.

"Did she just... try to act cute?" Kyle asked, blinking in disbelief.

"She's smart enough to know when she's in trouble," Rick said, shaking his head. "Even if she's not great at hiding it."

Raven, unimpressed, swatted the ball back at Skye with enough force to send it skidding across the enclosure. Skye chirped happily, apparently taking it as an invitation to keep playing. She darted after the ball, her energy seemingly endless.

Willow, meanwhile, had solved another puzzle, pulling out a treat and nibbling on it quietly. She glanced at Raven, who gave her a single approving chirp before returning to her perch near the den. Luna, still clutching her rubber ring, peeked out from behind Raven, her wide eyes filled with curiosity as she watched her sisters.

"They're like a little circus," Kyle said, shaking his head with a faint smile. "I can't believe how different they all are."

"That's what makes them so fascinating," Emma replied. "Each of them has their own personality, their own way of interacting with the world. And together? They're unstoppable."

As the night wore on, the girls began to wind down, their energy finally ebbing. Raven led them back to the den one by one, chirping softly to guide her sisters. Skye reluctantly abandoned her ball, while Willow carefully placed her puzzle toy near the edge of the den as if saving it for later. Luna crawled in last, her rubber ring still clutched tightly in her claws.

"They're learning," Rick said quietly, his gaze fixed on the den. "And they're starting to trust us. Little by little."

Emma nodded, finishing the last sip of her drink. "It's a long road, but we'll get there."

Kyle leaned back in his chair, watching as the girls curled up together in their den. "You know, for ferals, they're not so scary."

Rick smirked. "Don't let them fool you, kid. They're cute now, but give them a reason, and they'll remind you why they're called ferals."

"Noted," Kyle replied, grinning. "But for now, I'll take the cute."

As the night deepened, the girls' den became a hive of activity again. Skye, apparently having regained all her energy in record time, darted out of the den, chirping excitedly as she batted her favorite orange ball across the enclosure. Willow sighed—yes, sighed—and glanced at her sister with a look that could only be described as exasperated before returning to the puzzle she had abandoned earlier.

Raven, however, wasn't in the mood for chaos. She let out a sharp growl, her glowing eyes narrowing as she stared at Skye. The younger feral froze mid-pounce, ball trapped between her claws, and tilted her head in an unmistakable gesture of defiance.

"Oh boy," Kyle muttered, leaning forward slightly. "Here we go."

Rick smirked, crossing his arms. "Raven's laying down the law. Watch this."

Raven let out another growl, this one louder and more insistent. Skye chirped back, a sharp, high-pitched sound that was almost comical in its audacity. For a moment, it seemed like a standoff was about to break out—but then Raven stood up, her claws clicking ominously against the floor as she approached her sister.

Skye immediately dropped the ball and scurried back to the den, chirping in what sounded suspiciously like an apology. Raven didn't stop until she had nudged the ball back toward the far corner of the enclosure, her movements deliberate and authoritative.

"She's the boss, all right," Kyle said, shaking his head. "No one messes with Raven."

"Not unless they want to regret it," Emma added, chuckling softly.

Meanwhile, Luna had ventured out of the den, clutching her rubber ring in her tiny claws. She chirped softly, glancing around the enclosure as if checking to make sure the coast was clear. Raven, now back at her perch near the den, gave a single approving chirp, and Luna relaxed visibly.

"She's testing the waters," Emma observed. "Trying to see how far she can go."

Rick leaned forward, his gaze thoughtful. "She's getting braver. That's a good sign."

Luna padded over to the water feature, dipping the rubber ring into the shallow pool and tilting her head as she watched the water drip off it. She chirped softly, then dunked the ring again, clearly fascinated by the way it absorbed and released the water. Her sisters, however, had other plans.

Skye, now bored with her self-imposed timeout, bounded over to Luna with an enthusiastic chirp, startling the younger feral. Luna dropped the ring, letting out a soft squeak as she scrambled back toward the den. Skye, undeterred, grabbed the ring and began shaking it wildly, water spraying in all directions.

"Oh, come on," Kyle groaned, throwing his hands up. "She's like a toddler at a pool party."

Emma laughed, setting her clipboard aside. "Skye has two settings: chaos and more chaos."

Willow, who had been quietly working on her puzzle, finally decided enough was enough. She stood up, her movements slow and deliberate, and marched over to Skye. With a single well-placed nudge, she knocked the ring out of her sister's claws and picked it up herself, carrying it back to the den with an air of quiet authority.

Rick chuckled, shaking his head. "Willow's the enforcer. She doesn't make a fuss, but she gets the job done."

"Every group needs one," Emma agreed, still smiling. "And it's probably good for Skye to have someone keeping her in check."

Raven chirped softly from her perch, seemingly satisfied with Willow's intervention. Skye, for her part, chirped back with a tone that could only be described as pouty before plopping down near the water feature and sulking.

"Is she... sulking?" Kyle asked, his voice tinged with disbelief.

"She is," Rick confirmed, smirking. "Don't worry, she'll be back to causing trouble in about five minutes."

True to Rick's prediction, Skye was back on her feet in no time, this time trying to climb the sides of the enclosure. She made it about halfway up before slipping back down with a chirp of surprise, her claws scraping against the glass as she landed on her feet.

"That's new," Emma remarked, raising an eyebrow. "She's testing the limits."

Rick nodded, his expression serious despite the humor of the situation. "They always do. It's part of their nature."

Raven let out a sharp growl, cutting Skye's antics short. The younger feral chirped softly, retreating back to the den without further protest. Willow and Luna huddled closer to Raven, the three of them forming a protective circle that radiated quiet strength.

"They really do look out for each other," Kyle said, his tone thoughtful. "Even when they're being little terrors."

"That's what makes them special," Emma replied. "They've been through so much, but they still have that bond. It's what's going to help us reach them."

Rick leaned back in his chair, a faint smile tugging at the corners of his mouth. "And it's what's going to keep us on our toes. They're smart, they're stubborn, and they're relentless. But they're also a team. And that's something we can work with."

As the night wore on, the girls finally began to settle down, their energy fading as they curled up together in their den. Skye let out a soft chirp before tucking herself into the pile, her earlier chaos forgotten. Willow nudged Luna gently, her calm demeanor reassuring the youngest feral as she drifted off to sleep. Raven remained awake for a while longer, her glowing eyes fixed on the humans outside the glass.

"She's watching us," Kyle said quietly, his gaze meeting Raven's.

"She always does," Rick replied. "That's how she protects them. But one day, maybe, she'll realize we're here to protect them too."

CHAPTER 22

A few days later, Emma sat at her workstation, quietly observing the younglings through the glass. The lab was calm, the hum of equipment providing a gentle backdrop to the girls' antics. They had been playing with their cards for a while now, pressing familiar ones like "food" or "water" against the glass whenever they wanted something. But today was different. Today, they seemed to be experimenting.

Raven, as always, took the lead. She had carefully selected several cards from their collection, spreading them out on the floor of the enclosure with deliberate precision. Her glowing eyes scanned the symbols intently, her expression focused and calculating. After a moment, she let out a sharp chirp, summoning her sisters.

Skye was the first to respond, bounding over with her trademark enthusiasm, her claws clicking against the floor as she skidded to a stop beside Raven. Willow followed more cautiously, her steady movements a stark contrast to Skye's chaotic energy. She settled beside Raven, her calm presence grounding the group. Luna, however, lingered near the den, her small frame half-hidden as she watched the others from a distance, her glowing eyes flickering with hesitation.

"They're up to something," Emma murmured to herself, a small smile tugging at her lips.

Raven picked up the "food" card first, tapping it against the glass as she usually did. Emma raised an eyebrow, glancing at the feeding slot. "Sorry, Raven, you've already had your meal," she called out, her tone light.

Raven tilted her head, seemingly unbothered by Emma's lack of response. She chirped softly, then picked up another card—this one showing "water." She pressed it against the glass next to "food," chirping louder this time.

Emma chuckled, leaning forward. "Oh, so you think adding 'water' will change my mind? Nice try."

Skye, growing impatient, grabbed the "play" card and slammed it against the glass with both hands, chirping excitedly. The noise startled Luna, who let out a soft squeak and scurried further back into the den. Raven growled softly, nudging Skye aside as if to say, *Let me handle this.*

Willow, ever the methodical one, picked up the "open" card and placed it next to "food" and "water." She nudged the cards together with her claws, her movements slow and deliberate, before looking up at Emma with a curious chirp.

Emma raised an eyebrow, her smile widening. "Are you trying to tell me something, Willow? Open what? Open food? Open water? You've got to give me more than that."

Raven, clearly dissatisfied with Emma's response, began rearranging the cards herself. She added the "sleep" card to the lineup, followed by "play." The resulting combination made no real sense, but the girls didn't seem to care. They chirped and growled among themselves, as if debating the effectiveness of their chosen words.

After a few minutes of trial and error, Skye seemed to lose patience. She grabbed as many cards as she could and began slapping them against the glass at random, her chirps growing louder and more frantic.

"Alright, alright, calm down," Emma said, laughing. "Skye, you're not even trying anymore."

Raven growled sharply, silencing her younger sister with a single commanding look. Skye chirped softly in apology, dropping the cards and retreating a few steps. Willow picked up where Skye left off, rearranging the discarded cards into a new combination: "food," "open," and "play."

Emma tilted her head, pretending to consider the message. "Hmm. Open food and play? Is that what you're saying?"

Raven let out an impatient growl, picking up the "now" card and slamming it against the glass with enough force to make Emma laugh.

"Well, that's clear enough," Emma said, leaning back in her chair. "You want it, and you want it now. Got it."

Luna finally crept out from the den, her tiny claws clicking softly against the floor. She picked up the "sleep" card and tapped it gently against the glass, looking up at Emma with wide, innocent eyes.

"Oh, Luna," Emma said, her tone softening. "Are you tired? Or are you just trying to see what I'll do?"

Raven let out a low growl, nudging Luna back toward the den. But Luna resisted, chirping softly as she pressed the card against the glass again.

"She's testing boundaries," Rick said from the doorway, startling Emma. He crossed his arms, smirking faintly as he watched the scene unfold. "Even the quiet ones have their moments."

"They're all testing boundaries," Emma replied, gesturing toward the scattered cards. "They don't fully understand what the words mean, but they're starting to figure out that combinations get reactions. It's trial and error."

Rick nodded, his gaze fixed on Raven as she rearranged the cards once more. "Smart. They're experimenting. Seeing what works, what doesn't."

"And they're doing it together," Emma added. "Even Luna's getting involved, which is a big step for her."

Raven finally settled on a new combination: "food," "play," and "now." She tapped the cards against the glass, her movements deliberate and insistent. Skye chirped excitedly, bouncing on her claws as if cheering her sister on.

Emma sighed, shaking her head. "You're relentless, aren't you?" She stood up and grabbed a small treat from the counter. "Alright, you win this round."

She placed the treat in the feeding slot, watching as Raven retrieved it with a triumphant chirp. The leader shared it with her sisters, distributing the pieces evenly before retreating to the den. Even Luna got a small share, thanks to Raven's watchful eye.

"They're learning faster than I expected," Emma said, her tone thoughtful. "It's like they're not just trying to communicate—they're trying to understand us."

Rick smirked, his gaze steady. "They're ferals. Survival is what they do. And right now, learning how to talk to us is part of their survival."

Emma nodded, a small smile tugging at her lips. "Let's see how far they take it."

Later that evening, the girls had taken their experiments to a whole new level. Raven was now fully in charge of the cards, sorting through them with sharp, deliberate movements while her sisters hovered around her. Skye chirped loudly every few seconds, clearly impatient to see what would happen next, while Willow sat calmly, observing every motion. Luna lingered at the back, peeking out from the den with wide, curious eyes.

"They're persistent," Kyle remarked, sitting at the counter with a cup of coffee in hand. "Do they ever give up?"

Rick smirked, leaning against the wall with his arms crossed. "Not when they think there's a reward involved. Ferals are relentless when it comes to getting what they want."

Emma glanced up from her notes, her lips quirking into a faint smile. "And what they want is for us to keep responding. They're testing how far they can push."

Raven placed a new combination against the glass: "play," "open," and "food." She tapped the cards in sequence, her glowing eyes flicking between the humans and her sisters as if gauging their reaction.

Emma tilted her head, her expression amused. "That doesn't even make sense, Raven. You want us to play with open food?"

Skye chirped loudly, slapping her claws against the glass as if trying to emphasize the point. Raven growled softly, swatting at her sister to quiet her before rearranging the cards again.

This time, she added the "now" card to the mix, her movements precise and insistent. Willow joined in, nudging the cards into a neat line while chirping softly in agreement.

"They're collaborating," Emma said, her tone thoughtful. "It's not just trial and error anymore—they're working together to build a message."

Kyle raised an eyebrow. "But do they even know what they're saying?"

"Not fully," Rick replied, his gaze steady. "But they know that certain words get certain reactions. They're starting to piece it together."

Luna finally ventured out of the den, her tiny claws clicking softly against the floor. She chirped hesitantly, glancing at her sisters before picking up the "food" card. Raven growled low, stepping aside to let her younger sister place the card on the glass.

"She's trying to help," Emma said softly, watching as Luna pressed the card next to the others. "Raven's letting her take the lead for once."

"It's a good sign," Rick added. "She's starting to feel more comfortable."

Luna chirped again, looking up at Emma with wide, expectant eyes. The youngest feral's timid movements and soft sounds were enough to melt even Rick's stoic demeanor.

"You're lucky you're cute," Emma said with a chuckle, standing up to grab a small treat from the counter. She placed it in the feeding slot, watching as Luna darted forward to retrieve it.

Skye let out an excited chirp, bounding after her sister, but Raven stepped in, growling sharply to keep her in line. Luna retreated to the den with her treat, her small frame trembling slightly as she nibbled on it under Raven's watchful eye.

As the girls settled down, Emma turned to Rick and Kyle, her expression contemplative. "You know, they're showing more intelligence than I expected. It's not just instinct—they're problem-solving."

Rick nodded, his gaze fixed on the enclosure. "That's what makes them dangerous. But it's also what gives them potential. If they can learn this much on their own, imagine what they could do with the right guidance."

Kyle leaned forward, his tone curious. "Do you really think they can be rehabilitated? Like, fully integrated into society?"

"It's too early to tell," Emma replied. "But what they're doing now—communicating, cooperating, even teaching each other—that's a foundation we can build on."

Rick smirked faintly, his arms still crossed. "If anyone can prove it's possible, it's these four. They're survivors. And survivors adapt."

The girls continued to experiment with their cards well into the evening, their chirps and growls filling the lab with an odd, almost musical rhythm. Raven remained the leader, directing her sisters with quiet authority, while Skye provided the energy and enthusiasm. Willow's methodical approach balanced the group's chaos, and Luna, though timid, was starting to find her place.

"They're like a little team," Kyle observed, his voice tinged with wonder. "Each of them has a role."

"And they're figuring out how to work together," Emma added, smiling softly. "It's fascinating to watch."

Rick nodded, his gaze unwavering. "They're more than a team. They're a family. And that's what's going to make all the difference."

Over the next few days, the younglings began to master the use of their cards, their attempts becoming increasingly precise and deliberate. Raven, ever the leader, spearheaded the efforts, meticulously experimenting with different combinations. She observed the humans' reactions with sharp, calculating eyes, each response reinforcing her growing understanding.

Her sisters quickly followed suit, their natural instincts merging with an emerging awareness of cause and effect. Skye's boundless energy made her the most enthusiastic participant, her chirps of excitement filling the enclosure as she tested new card pairings. Willow's calm and measured approach brought balance to the chaos, while Luna, still hesitant, watched closely from the sidelines before tentatively joining in.

It was during one of these sessions that Emma noticed something new.

"They're... negotiating," she said aloud, her tone filled with both surprise and amusement.

Rick glanced up from his paperwork, raising an eyebrow. "Negotiating?"

Emma pointed toward the enclosure, where Skye had gathered a small collection of toys near the glass. The energetic feral chirped loudly, pressing a card for "play" against the surface. When no immediate response came, she added the "now" card, tapping it insistently.

Raven, perched nearby, let out a low growl, her glowing eyes narrowing at her younger sister. With a single swipe, she nudged Skye aside and took control of the cards, arranging "play" and "now" in a neat line. Then, in an unexpected twist, she added the "food" card to the mix.

"They're offering something in exchange," Emma explained, leaning closer to observe. "Raven's trying to trade."

Rick chuckled, shaking his head. "Smart. She's figured out that adding more cards gets a better reaction."

Kyle, who had been silently observing, frowned slightly. "But what exactly are they offering? They don't have food to trade."

"They're not offering food," Emma replied, smirking. "They're asking for it. But by including 'play,' they're suggesting an exchange. Like, 'We'll play with the toys if you give us food.'"

As if on cue, Raven nudged one of the toys toward the glass with her clawed hand, chirping softly as she pressed the cards again. Her sisters watched intently, their glowing eyes fixed on Emma.

"Well," Emma said, standing up and grabbing a small treat from the counter, "let's see how far this goes."

She placed the treat in the feeding slot, watching as Raven retrieved it with calm precision. The leader shared it with her sisters, dividing it equally before returning to the glass. This time, she grabbed the "play" card alone and tapped it once, then pointed to the pile of toys.

"She's testing limits now," Rick observed, smirking. "Seeing what she can get without overcomplicating it."

Skye, ever the opportunist, darted forward and grabbed one of the toys—a small ball she had claimed as her favorite. She chirped loudly, slamming it against the glass with her usual chaotic energy. When this didn't produce immediate results, she added the "food" card to her pile, chirping even louder.

"Subtle," Kyle muttered, shaking his head. "She's like a kid throwing everything at the wall to see what sticks."

Raven growled sharply, silencing Skye with a single commanding sound. The younger feral chirped softly, backing off with the ball still clutched in her claws.

Willow, meanwhile, had taken a different approach. She picked up the "water" card and placed it next to the "open" card, her movements slow and deliberate. Then she nudged the combination toward the glass, her calm gaze meeting Emma's.

"She's asking for water," Emma said, nodding approvingly. She grabbed a small bowl and filled it, sliding it into the enclosure.

Willow retrieved the bowl with care, chirping softly in thanks before carrying it back to the den. Raven watched her go, her glowing eyes thoughtful, before turning her attention back to Emma.

The breakthrough came later that evening, when Luna—timid but observant—took her turn at the cards. She had been watching her sisters closely, learning from their successes and failures. Now, with tentative movements, she arranged "food" and "play" together, then added the "thanks" card at the end.

Emma blinked, a grin spreading across her face. "She's saying thank you. That's new."

"Not bad for the shy one," Rick said, his tone impressed. "She's figuring it out."

Emma placed a small treat in the slot, watching as Luna chirped softly and retrieved it. The youngest feral hesitated for a moment, then nudged the treat toward Skye, who chirped in delight before sharing it with Raven.

"They're starting to think beyond themselves," Emma remarked, her voice thoughtful. "It's not just about survival anymore. They're learning the value of cooperation—and now, trading."

Rick nodded, his gaze steady. "It's a small step, but it's a big one. If they can understand this, it opens up a whole new world for them."

By the end of the week, the girls had turned their trading into an art form. Raven, ever the strategist, had begun combining cards to create more complex requests. Skye experimented constantly, her chaotic energy resulting in a mix of successes and failures. Willow refined her methodical approach, learning which combinations worked best. And Luna, though still hesitant, grew bolder with each passing day.

"They're teaching each other," Emma said, watching as Raven demonstrated a new combination for Luna. "Raven figures something out, and the others follow her lead."

"It's how they've survived," Rick replied. "And now it's how they're learning to thrive."

Kyle, still fascinated by the process, couldn't help but smile as he watched the girls work. "You know, for ferals, they're starting to seem... kind of civilized."

Rick smirked, crossing his arms. "Don't get ahead of yourself, kid. They've got a long way to go. But yeah... they're getting there."

CHAPTER 23

Over the next few days, the girls became increasingly skilled at using their cards, refining their techniques with a blend of instinct and trial and error. Each attempt seemed more deliberate, and their growing proficiency revealed just how quickly they were learning.

Raven, of course, was at the forefront of the efforts. She no longer merely tapped the cards against the glass but began arranging them on the floor in clear combinations before presenting them. Her movements were measured, her glowing eyes scanning the humans for any sign of reaction. Skye, on the other hand, relied on brute force and enthusiasm, slapping as many cards as she could find against the glass in rapid succession. Willow continued her methodical approach, testing small changes in her combinations and observing the results. Even Luna, timid as ever, began experimenting, often mimicking her sisters' successful strategies.

"Look at that," Emma said, gesturing toward the enclosure with a mixture of awe and amusement. "They're working together now. Even Luna's starting to hold her own."

Rick leaned back in his chair, his arms crossed as he watched Raven rearrange a set of cards. "They're not just working together—they're competing. Each of them wants to be the one who gets it right."

On this particular morning, Raven had set up a sequence of four cards: "food," "play," "open," and "now." She tapped the glass lightly after arranging them, her gaze fixed on Emma.

When Emma didn't respond immediately, Raven growled softly, glancing over her shoulder at her sisters. Skye chirped impatiently, darting forward to rearrange the cards herself.

"That's not going to end well," Kyle muttered, watching as Skye's chaotic rearrangement earned her a sharp growl from Raven.

Sure enough, Raven swatted Skye aside with a single swipe of her claws, her expression one of unmistakable annoyance. Skye chirped in protest, but Willow intervened, nudging both of them apart before calmly resetting the cards.

"Willow, the peacekeeper," Emma remarked with a smile. "She's the only one who can keep those two in line."

Willow's combination was simple but effective: "food" and "now." With deliberate precision, she pressed the cards gently against the glass, her calm demeanor a striking contrast to her sisters' more intense energy. Emma, quick to respond, placed a small treat into the feeding slot.

The moment the treat appeared, Raven let out a soft growl of approval, her sharp gaze flicking toward Willow. In an uncharacteristic display, she nudged her sister gently—a gesture that seemed almost like gratitude. Skye, unable to contain her excitement, chirped loudly and darted toward the treat, but Raven intercepted her with swift precision. The young leader carefully distributed the pieces, ensuring each of her sisters received a share.

"They're learning to take turns," Kyle observed, his voice tinged with admiration. "Even Skye's starting to get it... sort of."

Rick smirked. "Give her time. She'll get there."

The girls' trading experiments grew more complex as the day went on. Skye, still determined to make her mark, tried combining "food," "play," and "thanks" in a haphazard arrangement. When this failed to elicit a response, she chirped loudly and added "water" to the mix, slamming the cards against the glass with her usual chaotic energy.

"Skye, you're trying too hard," Emma said, laughing softly. "It's not about quantity—it's about quality."

Raven growled again, stepping in to rearrange the cards in her usual meticulous fashion. This time, she added the "rest" card, her movements deliberate and precise.

"That's interesting," Rick said, leaning forward. "She's trying to expand the request."

Emma nodded, watching closely as Raven presented the new combination. "Food, rest, play… She's testing what else she can get."

Emma rewarded the effort with another small treat, sliding it into the feeding slot. Raven retrieved it with a satisfied chirp, once again ensuring each of her sisters got a share.

By the afternoon, even Luna was joining in the trading experiments. The youngest feral carefully selected the "play" card and paired it with "now," tapping them against the glass with hesitant chirps. When Emma responded by sliding a small rubber ball into the enclosure, Luna's eyes widened with delight. She picked up the ball and retreated to the den, her quiet joy evident as she chirped softly to herself.

"She's starting to figure it out," Emma said, her tone warm. "She's still shy, but she's getting bolder."

"She's got Raven backing her up," Rick replied. "That makes all the difference."

The breakthrough came later that evening when Skye, after countless failed attempts, managed to create a successful trade entirely on her own. She placed "water" and "play" together, chirping loudly as she pressed them against the glass. Emma, curious to see what would happen, slid a small bowl of water and a toy into the enclosure.

Skye's chirps turned triumphant as she darted forward to claim her prize. For once, she didn't rush to hoard it. Instead, she brought the toy back to the den and nudged it toward Luna, chirping softly as if offering a gift.

"They're not just learning to trade," Kyle said, his voice filled with awe. "They're learning to share."

Rick's smirk softened into a faint smile. "That's the key. If they can work together, if they can learn to trust... they've got a real shot."

As the day wound down, the girls continued their trading experiments, their chirps and growls filling the lab with a lively rhythm. Raven remained the leader, guiding her sisters with quiet authority, while Skye provided the energy and enthusiasm. Willow's methodical approach kept things on track, and Luna's growing confidence added a new layer to their dynamic.

"They're getting better every day," Emma remarked, watching as Raven set up another combination. "At this rate, they'll have us wrapped around their little claws in no time."

Rick chuckled, his gaze steady. "They already do."

By the end of the week, it became clear that the girls weren't just experimenting with their cards for general requests—they had a specific target in mind. Blood.

Raven had started it. She'd observed Emma drinking her daily blood packs during their sessions in the lab, and something about the crimson liquid clearly fascinated her. Over time, her focus shifted, and she began integrating the "blood" card into her trades, pairing it with different combinations to see what worked.

"She's fixated on it," Emma said, watching as Raven tapped the glass with the card yet again. This time, it was paired with "food" and "now."

"They know it's important," Rick replied, leaning against the counter. "Blood is survival for vampires, and ferals are no different. But they've also learned it's something *we* value."

Emma smirked. "Are you saying they're trying to bribe us with their own trades? That's... actually brilliant."

The first real trade attempt came from Skye. She chirped loudly, dragging a ball toward the glass and dropping it dramatically at Raven's feet. Raven gave her an unimpressed look but allowed the younger feral to continue. Skye then tapped the "play" and "blood" cards together, her chirps growing more insistent.

Kyle raised an eyebrow as he watched. "Is she trying to trade a ball for blood? That's... optimistic."

"She's learning the art of negotiation," Emma replied with a laugh. "Even if her terms are a little one-sided."

Raven, clearly unimpressed with Skye's approach, took over. She added the "food" card to the mix, arranging the cards in a neat line before tapping the glass with calculated precision.

"That's more sophisticated," Rick observed. "She's combining things she knows we respond to."

Emma leaned forward, her gaze thoughtful. "They're testing us. Seeing what works and what doesn't. It's trial and error—but with a purpose."

The experimentation continued throughout the day. Willow, ever the methodical one, tried a new approach by presenting the "blood" card on its own, then chirping softly as she pointed toward Emma's drink.

Emma raised an eyebrow. "You want what I'm having, huh?" She held up her blood drink, watching as Willow's chirps grew more insistent.

Raven growled softly, stepping in to nudge Willow aside. She arranged the "blood" and "food" cards together, then added "now" for emphasis. Her movements were calm but firm, her glowing eyes locking onto Emma's.

"They're getting bolder," Kyle remarked. "And more specific."

Rick smirked. "It's impressive. They're not just asking—they're negotiating. They've figured out that offering something in return increases their chances."

Later that evening, Luna surprised everyone by making her first attempt at a trade. The youngest feral, usually hesitant to step forward, crept out of the den with a small toy clutched in her claws. She chirped softly, glancing nervously at her sisters before placing the toy near the glass. Then, with trembling hands, she picked up the "blood" card and tapped it gently against the surface.

Emma's heart melted at the sight. "Oh, Luna," she said, her tone soft. "You're too cute for your own good."

"Don't fall for it," Rick said with a smirk. "She knows exactly what she's doing."

Emma chuckled, sliding a small treat into the feeding slot instead of blood. Luna chirped softly, retrieving the treat and retreating to the den with her prize. Raven let out a low growl, clearly annoyed that Luna hadn't secured the blood they wanted, but she didn't intervene.

"They're persistent, I'll give them that," Kyle said, shaking his head. "But are we ever going to give them what they're asking for?"

"Not yet," Emma replied. "They need to understand that blood isn't just another reward. It's different—it's special."

By the next day, the girls had refined their tactics even further. Raven, ever the leader, arranged the cards into increasingly complex combinations. At one point, she used "blood," "food," and "thanks" together, tapping them with deliberate force before gesturing toward the feeding slot.

"They're trying gratitude now," Rick observed, smirking. "Smart move."

Emma nodded. "They're figuring out what gets a positive response. And they're not giving up."

Skye, meanwhile, was trying her usual chaotic approach, dragging multiple toys to the glass and slapping the "blood" card on top of them. Her chirps were loud and insistent, but Raven growled sharply, silencing her.

"She's reigning them in," Emma said, her tone impressed. "Raven knows this has to be a group effort."

The breakthrough came that afternoon, when Raven tried a completely new strategy. Instead of using just the cards, she brought one of the puzzle toys to the glass and tapped the "blood" card alongside it. Then, she chirped softly, nudging the toy toward the humans as if offering it in exchange.

"They're offering something tangible now," Emma said, her eyes widening. "That's… a big step."

Rick nodded, his expression serious. "They've figured out that actions speak louder than cards. They're showing us they're willing to give something up to get what they want."

Emma hesitated for a moment, then grabbed a small, diluted sample of synthetic blood from the counter. She placed it in the feeding slot, watching closely as Raven retrieved it. The leader sniffed the sample cautiously before chirping softly, her tone almost approving. She distributed it among her sisters, ensuring each of them got a share.

"They earned that one," Emma said with a smile. "Let's see what they do next."

Hours later, the girls were at it again, their makeshift den temporarily abandoned in favor of experimenting with their growing collection of cards. Raven led the charge, as always, her glowing eyes scanning the options laid out before her. She picked up the "food" card first, tapping it lightly against the glass, as if testing whether the humans would react to a single, simple request.

Rick glanced up from his desk, his gaze briefly meeting Raven's. When he didn't move, she growled softly and added another card—"now." Still, there was no response. Her growl deepened, and she added a third card: "open."

"She's trying to figure out the minimum effort required," Emma observed from across the lab, a smirk tugging at her lips. She jotted a quick note on her clipboard before stepping closer to the glass. "Sorry, Raven. That combo's not going to work this time."

Raven chirped in irritation, her claws clicking against the floor as she rearranged the cards. Skye, watching nearby, grew impatient with the slow progress. With a loud chirp, she grabbed as many cards as she could and began slapping them against the glass in rapid succession.

"Food! Play! Water! Open! Now!" Kyle called out, laughing as he mimicked Skye's chaotic energy. "She's just throwing everything at the wall."

Rick smirked, shaking his head. "That's her strategy—overwhelm us until we give in."

Despite Skye's efforts, Raven reclaimed control, swatting her sister aside with a low growl. She rearranged the cards with careful precision, this time combining "thanks" with "food" and "now." When Emma still didn't respond, Raven let out an irritated chirp and added "play" to the mix.

Emma tilted her head, pretending to consider the combination. "You're close, Raven, but not quite there." She stepped away from the glass, leaving the girls to their experimentation.

Willow, ever the calm observer, took her turn next. She approached the cards slowly, her movements deliberate as she added "water" to the lineup Raven had created. She then tapped the cards gently against the glass, her glowing eyes fixed on Emma with an almost pleading expression.

Emma raised an eyebrow, intrigued. "Oh, Willow. You're definitely the smartest of the bunch." She grabbed a small treat and placed it in the feeding slot. Raven retrieved it immediately, distributing the pieces evenly among her sisters, though not without a stern glance at Skye to ensure she didn't try to take more than her share.

The girls' experimentation continued into the evening, their combinations growing more elaborate as they learned what worked and what didn't. At one point, Luna surprised everyone by stepping forward with her own attempt. The youngest feral, still timid but increasingly curious, picked up the "food" and "thanks" cards, tapping them softly against the glass.

Emma's heart melted at the sight. "She's learning so quickly," she said, her voice filled with warmth. She rewarded Luna with a small treat, watching as the youngling scurried back to the den with her prize.

"She's more observant than we give her credit for," Rick remarked, his tone thoughtful. "She watches what the others do and adapts it for herself."

"And she's careful," Emma added. "She doesn't take risks the way Skye does. It's like she knows she can't compete on brute force, so she relies on subtlety."

By the time the lab lights dimmed for the evening, the girls had turned their experiments into a coordinated effort. Raven directed her sisters with quiet authority, dividing the cards among them and guiding their attempts. Skye, though still prone to chaotic bursts of energy, followed Raven's lead with surprising focus. Willow remained the steady, methodical one, testing small changes to combinations and recording the results in her own way. And Luna, though hesitant, began contributing more frequently, her chirps soft but determined.

"They're like a little research team," Kyle said, shaking his head in amazement. "They're figuring this out faster than I expected."

Rick nodded, his gaze fixed on the younglings. "They're survivors. And survivors adapt."

Emma leaned against the counter, her arms crossed as she watched Raven rearrange the cards once more. "The real question is how far they can take this. If they're already this smart, what's next?"

The session ended with one final attempt from Raven. She combined "food," "thanks," and "play" in a neat line, tapping the cards with deliberate force. Emma, unable to resist rewarding the effort, placed a small treat in the slot. Raven retrieved it calmly, chirping softly in approval before sharing it with her sisters.

"They're learning more than just communication," Emma said quietly. "They're learning how to negotiate. To work together."

"And that's exactly what we need them to do," Rick replied. "If they can master this, there's hope for them yet."

CHAPTER 24

The lab hummed with quiet activity as the girls explored the new cards they'd been given. Skye was predictably the most enthusiastic, chirping and slapping the cards against the glass in random combinations, while Raven carefully observed, rearranging the discarded cards into more methodical groupings. Willow studied the symbols with her usual focus, nudging Luna closer to the pile whenever the youngest feral hesitated to participate.

Rick leaned back in his chair, arms crossed, watching the scene unfold with quiet amusement. Emma was nearby, jotting down notes on the girls' behavior, her lips curving into a faint smile as Luna tentatively picked up a card and added it to Raven's grouping.

The lab door opened with a soft hiss, and Rick's posture straightened instinctively. The room seemed to grow colder as a tall figure stepped inside, her presence commanding and almost otherworldly. The Boss of Spearhead—an ancient vampire and the last of her kind—swept her gaze across the room, her sharp eyes immediately zeroing in on the enclosure.

Emma glanced up, her smile faltering slightly. "Boss," she greeted, her tone neutral but respectful. "Wasn't expecting you today."

The Boss didn't respond immediately, her attention locked on the younglings. The girls had noticed her arrival, but instead of retreating or cowering as most ferals would, they continued their activity. Skye chirped loudly, holding up a card as if presenting it to the imposing figure on the other side of the glass. Raven growled softly, nudging her sister back but not showing any signs of fear herself.

"They're not afraid of me," the Boss said, her voice low and smooth, carrying a faint edge of surprise.

Rick stood and approached, his expression calm but curious. "Is that unusual?"

The Boss shifted her gaze to him, her lips curving into a faint smile that didn't quite reach her eyes. "You know it is. Ferals instinctively recognize what I am—what I represent. Most are terrified the moment they sense me."

Emma stepped closer, her clipboard tucked against her chest. "It's interesting, though, isn't it? These four... they're different. Maybe it's because they've been here long enough to feel safe. Or maybe it's something else."

The Boss returned her attention to the enclosure, watching as Raven picked up the "blood" card and tapped it against the glass with deliberate movements. "She's their leader," the Boss remarked. "Her confidence sets the tone for the others."

"Raven's definitely the alpha," Rick agreed. "But even alphas usually react to you."

The Boss's smile widened slightly, a glimmer of intrigue in her gaze. "Perhaps they don't see me as a threat. Or perhaps they're testing me, the same way they're testing those cards."

Skye, undeterred by Raven's growls, picked up the "play" and "thanks" cards, slamming them against the glass with enthusiastic chirps. The sound echoed in the quiet lab, drawing the Boss's attention. For a moment, she simply stared at the youngling, her expression unreadable.

Then, to everyone's surprise, Skye chirped again and pointed at the Boss, her glowing eyes filled with curiosity rather than fear.

"Well, that's new," Emma said, raising an eyebrow. "I think she likes you."

The Boss chuckled softly, a sound that sent a shiver down Kyle's spine as he lingered near the back of the room. "Bold little one," she murmured. "But boldness can be dangerous."

"She's not reckless," Rick said, stepping closer to the glass. "She's just... curious. They all are. It's what's kept them alive this long."

The Boss tilted her head, her gaze lingering on Raven as the leader growled softly, her claws clicking against the floor. "They have potential," she said finally, her tone thoughtful. "But potential means nothing without direction."

Emma nodded, her expression serious. "That's what we're working on. They're already learning faster than we expected, but there's still a long way to go."

The Boss's eyes narrowed slightly, her focus sharpening. "And do you believe they can be integrated? Truly?"

Rick didn't hesitate. "I think they can. It won't be easy, and it won't happen overnight, but these four are special. They've already proven that."

The Boss regarded him silently for a moment before turning her attention back to the girls. "If anyone can prove it, it will be these four," she said. "But remember, they're still ferals. Never forget what they're capable of."

"We don't," Emma said firmly. "But we also won't underestimate what they're capable of becoming."

The Boss stepped closer to the glass, her gaze fixed on Raven. For a brief moment, the leader of the younglings locked eyes with the ancient vampire, her glowing pupils narrowing in what could only be described as defiance.

"She's not afraid of me," the Boss said again, this time with a note of amusement. "Interesting."

Raven growled softly, holding her ground as her sisters chirped and shuffled around her. The tension in the room was palpable, but neither the Boss nor the youngling looked away.

Finally, the Boss straightened, her expression unreadable. "You have your work cut out for you," she said, addressing Rick and Emma. "But I'll admit—I'm intrigued."

With that, she turned and left the lab, her presence lingering like a shadow long after the door hissed shut.

"That went... better than I expected," Kyle said, exhaling a breath he hadn't realized he'd been holding.

"She's intrigued," Emma said, a faint smile returning to her face. "That's a good thing. It means she'll let us keep going."

Rick watched the girls for a moment longer, his gaze thoughtful. "They're not afraid of her," he said quietly. "Maybe that's what makes them different. They don't see the world the way other ferals do."

"Let's hope that difference is enough," Emma replied. "Because we're going to need it."

As the door slid shut behind the Boss, Kyle let out a shaky breath, leaning heavily against the counter. "Man, she's intense," he muttered, his voice low, as if worried she could somehow still hear him.

Rick, on the other hand, casually leaned against the glass enclosure, arms crossed and a smirk tugging at his lips. "Intense? That's putting it mildly, kid. You looked like you were about to pass out."

Kyle shot him a glare, though the effect was diminished by the nervous twitch in his hands. "Hey, she's terrifying, alright? Don't pretend like you don't feel it too."

"Terrifying?" Rick raised an eyebrow, his smirk growing. "Sure, she's got that whole 'ancient vampire, might snap your neck without blinking' vibe, but you've got to learn to roll with it. She's not going to bite your head off. Probably."

"Probably?" Kyle squeaked, his face pale.

Emma, still scribbling notes, chuckled under her breath. "Rick's been working under her for years, Kyle. Trust me, if she hasn't fired him yet, you're probably safe."

Kyle frowned, glancing between them. "Wait, she hasn't fired him yet? What's that supposed to mean?"

Rick shrugged, his smirk never faltering. "Let's just say I don't exactly follow all the rules. Boss knows it, and yet, here I am. Still standing. Guess I'm too good at what I do."

"Or she's just waiting for the right moment to throw you out," Emma added, her tone playful.

"Please." Rick waved a hand dismissively. "She loves me. Deep down, she knows I'm the best shot she's got at making this crazy experiment work."

Kyle shook his head, incredulous. "I don't get how you're so calm around her. She looked at me once, and I felt like my soul was about to leave my body."

Rick snorted. "That's your problem, kid. You're too easy to rattle. The trick is to act like you don't care. She hates that."

Emma rolled her eyes. "He's not wrong, but don't take that advice too seriously, Kyle. Rick's playing with fire half the time. The only reason she hasn't fired him is because he delivers results."

"And because I'm charming as hell," Rick added with a wink.

Kyle groaned, burying his face in his hands. "I don't know how you do it. I swear she's got some kind of supernatural aura that just makes people freeze up."

Rick laughed, clapping him on the shoulder. "Supernatural aura or not, she's still just a person. Well, mostly. Look, kid, you stick around long enough, and you'll learn how to handle her. Or you'll keep hiding behind Emma and me. Either way works."

As the girls chirped and shuffled behind the glass, Raven tapped a card against the surface, drawing their attention back to the enclosure. Emma smiled, gesturing toward the younglings. "Looks like they're getting restless again. Should we see what they want?"

Rick pushed off the glass, still grinning. "Sure. Anything to give Kyle a break from his existential crisis."

"Thanks for the support," Kyle muttered, his sarcasm earning a laugh from both Rick and Emma.

Kyle huffed as he glanced at the glass enclosure, doing his best to redirect his focus from Rick's teasing. The girls had gathered near the front, Raven holding up a card that read "play." Her glowing eyes shifted between Rick and Emma, chirping softly as she waited for a response.

"She's been getting a lot more deliberate," Emma remarked, stepping closer to observe. "Notice how she's not just slamming the card anymore? She's holding it up, like she's asking."

Rick leaned on the counter, his smirk softening into something more thoughtful. "Yeah, she's watching us. Testing the waters. You can practically see the wheels turning in her head."

Raven growled softly, tapping the card against the glass with a touch more urgency. Skye chirped behind her, darting around with restless energy, while Willow nudged Luna forward, encouraging her to join the group.

Kyle straightened up, his clipboard momentarily forgotten. "What do you think they want to play with this time? Another ball? More puzzles?"

"Only one way to find out," Emma replied, pulling a small container of items from a nearby shelf. She sifted through it, holding up a few options. "We've got stacking blocks, the shape puzzle, and… oh, this one's new." She pulled out a simple maze toy, its clear casing containing a small ball that had to be guided through twists and turns to reach the end.

Rick raised an eyebrow. "Think they're ready for that? It's a bit more complicated than their usual stuff."

"That's the point," Emma said with a grin. "Let's see how far they've come."

She placed the toy in the feeding slot, sliding it into the enclosure. The girls immediately crowded around it, their chirps and growls blending into a chaotic symphony of curiosity.

Raven, as expected, claimed the toy first, her claws tapping lightly against its surface as she examined it. She tilted her head, her glowing eyes narrowing as she traced the ball's path with surprising precision. Skye, however, had no patience for Raven's methodical approach. She chirped loudly, grabbing at the toy with her usual enthusiasm.

"Here we go," Rick muttered, shaking his head. "She's about to ruin it."

Raven let out a sharp growl, holding the toy firmly in her claws. Skye chirped indignantly, but one look from her older sister was enough to make her back off—albeit with a sulky chirp of protest.

Willow and Luna stayed at the edges, observing quietly as Raven began to work. She tilted the maze carefully, her claws surprisingly delicate as she guided the ball through its first few turns. When she hit a dead end, she growled softly, turning the toy in her hands until she found the correct path.

Kyle leaned closer, his expression a mix of fascination and disbelief. "She's actually figuring it out."

"They're smarter than people give them credit for," Rick said, his tone quiet. "This isn't just instinct—it's problem-solving."

It didn't take long for Skye's impatience to get the better of her. With a loud chirp, she darted forward and swatted at the toy, knocking it from Raven's grasp. The ball skittered out of position, and Raven growled furiously, swiping at her sister with enough force to send her scrambling back.

"Skye really needs to learn to wait her turn," Emma said, laughing softly. "But at least they're not outright fighting."

"They've got a system," Rick said. "Raven keeps them in line. Without her, this would be chaos."

Raven picked up the toy again, a low growl rumbling in her throat as she focused on the intricate puzzle. Her sharp claws gripped the edges firmly, tilting the maze with careful deliberation. Willow, ever the composed observer, stepped closer, her glowing eyes fixed on Raven's progress. She let out a soft chirp, her head tilting slightly, as though offering silent advice.

Raven paused mid-motion, her sharp gaze flicking toward Willow. For a moment, the two sisters locked eyes in a wordless exchange. Then, with measured precision, Raven adjusted the maze, tilting it in the direction Willow seemed to suggest.

"She's accepting help," Emma noted. "That's new."

"Shows she's learning," Rick replied. "Raven knows when to take charge and when to listen. That's why she's the leader."

Luna, meanwhile, stayed near the back, her small frame half-hidden behind a stack of blankets. She watched her sisters with wide eyes, chirping softly as if cheering them on. When Raven finally completed the maze, Luna let out an excited chirp, darting forward to join the others as they examined the toy.

"They're not just solving problems," Kyle said, his voice filled with wonder. "They're celebrating their wins together. That's... kind of amazing."

Rick smirked. "Told you they're more than just ferals. There's a lot more going on up here." He tapped his temple. "It's just a matter of bringing it out."

Emma nodded, watching as the girls began to experiment with the maze again, this time taking turns under Raven's watchful eye. "They're learning faster than I expected. If they keep this up, who knows what they'll be capable of?"

"Hopefully something good," Rick replied, his gaze thoughtful. "Because if we can't prove they're worth saving... no one else will."

The room fell quiet for a moment, the weight of Rick's words settling over the group as they watched the girls work. Even Kyle, usually quick to crack a joke, said nothing, his eyes fixed on the younglings with a newfound respect.

CHAPTER 25

While Rick was in the meeting with the Boss, Emma decided to try something she'd been thinking about for days. She stood near the glass enclosure, her hand hovering over the control panel that operated the door. The girls were inside, busy with their cards and toys, their chirps and growls creating a lively atmosphere.

"Alright, girls," Emma murmured to herself, tapping the control to slide the door open. A soft hiss echoed as the barrier retracted, revealing an unobstructed path to the rest of the lab.

The girls froze.

Raven was the first to notice, her glowing eyes snapping to the now-open door. She tilted her head, her claws clicking lightly against the floor as she straightened. A low growl rumbled in her throat, her gaze darting between Emma and the unfamiliar space beyond the enclosure.

Skye chirped loudly, darting toward the edge of the doorframe, but stopped short when Raven growled sharply. Willow and Luna hung back, their movements cautious as they peered around their leader.

Emma knelt a few feet away, her body language calm and non-threatening. "It's okay," she said softly, knowing they couldn't understand the words but hoping the tone would reach them. She placed a small treat on the floor just beyond the door, then leaned back on her heels, watching.

Skye was the first to move, her curiosity getting the better of her.

She chirped again, glancing at Raven before taking a cautious step forward. When Raven didn't stop her, Skye darted out of the enclosure, snatching the treat with quick, jerky movements.

"That's it," Emma encouraged, her voice steady. "You're safe."

Raven growled softly but stepped closer to the threshold, her eyes scanning the room with sharp precision. Willow followed hesitantly, her movements slow and deliberate, while Luna remained in the back, her small frame half-hidden behind the den.

Skye, emboldened by her brief venture, chirped excitedly and began exploring the lab in earnest. She darted toward a nearby table, sniffing at the legs and clawing at the edges before climbing up onto a chair. Her chaotic energy filled the room, and Emma couldn't help but smile.

"You're always the brave one, huh?" she said, shaking her head as Skye knocked over a small stack of papers.

Raven stepped fully out of the enclosure, her movements fluid and deliberate, exuding a quiet authority. A soft growl rumbled in her throat as she glanced back at Willow and Luna, her glowing eyes sharp and expectant. The gesture was unmistakable—an unspoken command for her sisters to follow.

Willow hesitated, her claws resting just at the edge of the enclosure. She tilted her head, considering Raven's stance before cautiously stepping out, the faint click of her claws against the lab floor breaking the silence.

Luna chirped nervously from the back of the enclosure, her glowing eyes darting between her sisters and Emma. She took a hesitant step forward, then stopped, her body language tense.

"It's okay, Luna," Emma said softly, holding out her hand. "You're safe here."

It took a few minutes, but eventually, Luna crept out of the enclosure, her movements small and uncertain. She stayed close to the wall, her eyes wide as she took in the unfamiliar space. When she reached Raven, her older sister growled softly, nudging her gently with her nose. The reassurance seemed to help; Luna chirped quietly and relaxed, if only slightly.

The girls began to explore the lab in earnest under Emma's watchful eye. Skye climbed onto every available surface, knocking over tools and papers in her relentless pursuit of discovery. Willow, by contrast, focused on examining the objects within her reach, her movements slow and deliberate as she sniffed and clawed at various items. Raven maintained her usual composure, staying close to Luna and keeping a watchful eye on the room.

Emma stayed nearby, observing their behavior with a mixture of amusement and fascination. She made no sudden movements, letting them adjust to the new environment at their own pace.

At one point, Raven stepped forward, her glowing eyes locking onto Emma with an intensity that froze the room. The feral leader's movements were slow, deliberate, and cautious as she crept closer, her low growl rumbling softly in the still air. Her nose twitched as she sniffed, testing the air between them, every step measured and calculated.

Emma didn't move, her posture calm and non-threatening, though her heart thudded in her chest. "That's it," she murmured, her voice steady and soothing. "You're curious, aren't you? Trying to figure me out. Wondering if I'm safe."

Raven's growl softened, her sharp claws clicking lightly against the floor as she paused just out of reach, her predatory gaze never wavering. Emma held her ground, her expression warm but neutral, letting Raven make the next move.

After a moment of tense stillness, Raven leaned in and sniffed Emma's outstretched hand. Her glowing eyes studied the human with a cautious intensity before she let out a soft chirp and backed away, retreating to Luna's side.

Emma let out a breath she hadn't realized she was holding. "Progress," she murmured to herself. "Slow, but it's happening."

By the time Rick returned from his meeting, the lab was in mild disarray. Papers were scattered across the floor, a few tools had been knocked over, and Skye was perched on a stool, chirping triumphantly as she swiped at a hanging light fixture.

Rick froze in the doorway, his eyebrows shooting up. "What the hell happened here?"

Emma grinned, gesturing toward the open enclosure door. "Science."

"Science?" Rick repeated, his tone incredulous. "This looks like a feral hurricane."

"They're exploring," Emma said defensively. "And it's going well. They've been cautious, no major incidents, and Raven even came up to me."

Rick crossed his arms, his expression skeptical but amused. "And what's your plan when they figure out how to take over the lab?"

"They won't," Emma replied confidently. "Because we're showing them they don't need to. This is about trust."

Rick glanced at the girls, who were now gathering near the enclosure again, chirping and growling softly to one another. Raven growled sharply, herding Skye back inside as the others followed.

"They put themselves back?" Rick asked, his eyebrows raising in surprise.

"They're learning boundaries," Emma said with a smirk. "You could learn a thing or two from them."

Rick chuckled, shaking his head. "Let's just hope your experiment doesn't backfire."

The lab was quiet, save for the soft chirps and growls of the younglings as they settled back into their den. Emma and Rick stood nearby, keeping a watchful eye on them while discussing the progress they'd made that day.

"They're getting bolder," Emma said, leaning against the counter. "Even Luna's starting to come out of her shell."

Rick nodded, his arms crossed as he watched Raven organize the remaining cards. "It's a good sign. They're starting to trust us—and each other more."

The peaceful moment shattered abruptly as the distant sound of yelling reached their ears. Both Rick and Emma straightened immediately, their instincts on high alert. The shouting grew louder, accompanied by the unmistakable thudding of heavy boots against the floor.

"What the hell—" Rick began, but he was cut off by a deafening crash as the door to the lab burst open.

A feral, fully grown and wild-eyed, charged into the room. Its claws scraped against the polished floor, and its snarling, guttural growls echoed in the confined space. The creature's matted hair and gaunt frame spoke of desperation, and its glowing eyes darted frantically around the room.

"Get back!" Rick barked, stepping forward instinctively.

Emma, wide-eyed but composed, backed up toward the enclosure, positioning herself between the feral and the younglings. The girls had huddled together at first, chirping nervously, but as the feral's gaze landed on them, their demeanor shifted.

Raven was the first to react. She stepped forward, her claws clicking against the floor as she rose onto her hind legs, her glowing eyes narrowing in defiance. Her lips curled back to reveal her sharp fangs, and a low, menacing hiss escaped her throat. Skye, Willow, and even Luna followed suit, each of them standing tall, their growls blending into a unified warning.

Emma's breath caught in her throat as she watched them. The younglings, who typically preferred the safety of all fours, were now standing like warriors, their small but fierce forms radiating a protective energy that sent a chill down her spine.

The feral lunged toward the girls, its claws outstretched in a vicious arc, but Rick was faster. In a blur of motion, he intercepted the creature mid-leap, his body colliding with it in a controlled tackle that sent them both crashing to the ground. The impact rattled the nearby equipment, a sharp clang echoing through the lab.

Pinned beneath him, the feral writhed and snarled, its glowing eyes wild with fury. Its skeletal frame belied its immense strength, every muscle coiling and straining against Rick's hold as it thrashed violently, claws scraping against the reinforced floor.

"Get your asses in here!" Rick roared, his voice echoing through the lab as he struggled to pin the feral down. "Where the hell are the guards?"

The feral thrashed wildly, its claws swiping dangerously close to Rick's face. He gritted his teeth, using every ounce of his strength to keep it subdued. Blood dripped from a shallow cut on his forearm where the creature had managed to graze him, but he didn't falter.

Emma, still shielding the younglings, glanced back at the girls. They hadn't retreated to the back of the enclosure as she'd expected. Instead, they stood their ground, their hisses growing louder and more aggressive. Even Luna, usually the most timid of the group, was baring her fangs, her small frame trembling with a mix of fear and determination.

"Emma!" Rick's voice snapped her out of her thoughts. "Stay

back! Don't let them get involved!"

"I'm trying!" she called back, though she knew full well she wouldn't be able to stop the younglings if they decided to act.

Raven took another step forward, her claws flexing as she let out a guttural growl. Her sisters mirrored her movements, their glowing eyes locked on the feral. There was no fear in their stances—only anger and defiance. They were protecting their territory, their home, and each other.

The lab door burst open again, and two guards stormed in, their weapons drawn. One carried a tranquilizer gun, while the other wielded a containment pole, its loop designed to secure the feral's neck. They hesitated for a split second, taking in the chaotic scene.

"Don't just stand there!" Rick barked. "Get this thing under control!"

The guard with the pole moved first, expertly looping the containment device around the feral's neck and pulling it taut. The creature thrashed violently, its snarls growing more desperate, but the tranquilizer dart that followed quickly began to take effect. Within moments, the feral's movements slowed, its growls fading into a low whine before it finally went limp.

Rick let out a breath, wiping the sweat from his brow as he stood. "About damn time," he muttered, glaring at the guards. "What the hell happened? How did it get loose?"

"We're not sure," one of the guards stammered. "It slipped through the containment bay. We think it—"

"Save it," Rick snapped, his voice sharp. "Just get it out of here."

The guards quickly complied, lifting the unconscious feral onto a stretcher and wheeling it out of the lab. Rick watched them go, his jaw tight, before turning back to Emma and the younglings.

Emma was still standing near the enclosure, her hands raised slightly as if to keep the girls from making a move. They hadn't retreated, their fierce postures unwavering even as the danger passed. Raven was the last to lower herself back onto all fours, her growl lingering as she watched the door where the feral had been taken.

"They... didn't back down," Emma said, her voice tinged with awe. "They stood their ground."

Rick stepped closer, his gaze softening as he looked at the younglings. "They're tougher than we thought," he said quietly. "Even Luna."

Emma nodded, her eyes fixed on Raven. "She was protecting them. They all were."

Rick crouched near the glass, his tone calm and steady. "Raven," he said softly, his gaze meeting hers. "It's over. You're safe."

Raven growled once more before finally relaxing, her glowing eyes scanning the room one last time. She nudged Luna gently, guiding her back toward the den. The others followed, their movements slow but deliberate.

"They're not just survivors," Emma said, her voice filled with quiet admiration. "They're protectors."

Rick straightened, a faint smile tugging at his lips. "And they're starting to trust us. That's the biggest win of all."

As the lab settled back into an uneasy calm, Emma couldn't help but glance at the younglings again. They had proven themselves in a way no one could have predicted, and the implications were both thrilling and terrifying.

"Let's hope they never have to do that again," she said quietly.

Rick nodded. "Agreed. But if they do... at least we know they can handle it."

CHAPTER 26

Later that night, the lab was quiet. The hum of the overhead lights was the only sound as Rick sat alone at his desk, staring at the small stack of files spread out before him. The day's events played on a loop in his mind—the girls standing their ground, their protective instincts kicking in against the loose feral. It had been an unexpected moment of clarity, one that raised more questions than answers.

Rick leaned back in his chair, running a hand over his face. He glanced over at the glass enclosure. The younglings were curled up together in their makeshift den, their soft chirps and occasional twitches filling the silence. Even Raven, always the watchful leader, had let herself relax, her head resting protectively over Luna's smaller frame.

"They've come so far," Rick muttered to himself, his voice barely above a whisper. He couldn't help but feel a swell of pride at how much progress they'd made. These weren't just ferals anymore—they were something more.

But what did that mean for their future?

The thought gnawed at him as he poured over the files. Integration into society had always been the long-term goal of Spearhead's research, but the idea often felt more like an idealistic fantasy than a practical reality. Ferals were dangerous, unpredictable, and widely feared by humans and vampires alike. The sanctuary was the closest thing to a compromise—a place where ferals could exist without endangering others.

Yet the girls were different. They'd shown an intelligence and adaptability that went beyond what anyone expected. They were learning to communicate, to negotiate, even to protect. If these younglings could grow and evolve beyond their feral instincts, what else might be possible?

Rick tapped a pen against the edge of his desk, his thoughts swirling. Could the girls one day live in the normal world? Could they walk among humans and vampires, not as threats but as something… more?

It was a dangerous question, one that bordered on hope—a luxury he hadn't allowed himself in years.

And then there was the other possibility—the one that both intrigued and unsettled him in equal measure. If the girls could learn, adapt, and grow in such extraordinary ways, could their potential stretch even further? Could they be trained, not just to coexist in the normal world, but to contribute to it? To play an active role in Spearhead's mission? The thought lingered, a tantalizing question that straddled the line between ambition and uncertainty.

The idea wasn't entirely without precedent. Spearhead had long used specialized teams to track, capture, and contain ferals, but the work was grueling and dangerous, even for the most experienced agents. The girls, with their unique abilities and instincts, could potentially bridge the gap between ferals and humans in a way no one else could.

He thought back to the moment earlier that day when Raven had stood tall, hissing and baring her fangs at the intruding feral. She had been fearless, protective, and deliberate in her actions. It wasn't just instinct—there had been purpose behind it.

"They could help," Rick murmured, leaning forward in his chair. "Not just survive… but help."

The more he considered it, the more sense it made. The girls understood feral behavior in a way no human or vampire ever could. They shared the same instincts, the same primal drives, but they were learning to temper those instincts with intelligence and trust. With the right training, they could do what no Spearhead agent had ever done—connect with ferals on their own terms.

But there were risks, and Rick knew them all too well. The girls were still young, still unpredictable. Pushing them too far, too fast, could undo everything they'd accomplished. And then there was the question of how society would react. Would humans and vampires ever accept ferals, even ones as unique as these girls?

Rick sighed, his fingers drumming against the desk. He couldn't deny the potential he saw in them, but it was a long road ahead, filled with uncertainty. Still, for the first time in a long while, he felt a flicker of hope—not just for the girls, but for the future of Spearhead's mission.

He glanced back at the enclosure. Raven stirred slightly, her glowing eyes opening just enough to meet his gaze. She chirped softly, a low, questioning sound, before resting her head back down.

Rick smiled faintly, shaking his head. "You're going to change everything, aren't you?" he said quietly. "I just hope the world's ready for it."

Emma's voice broke through his thoughts, soft but curious. "Burning the midnight oil again?"

Rick looked up to see her leaning against the doorway, a cup of coffee in her hand. She walked over, setting the mug down on his desk before pulling up a chair.

"Thinking about the girls?" she asked, nodding toward the enclosure.

"Always," Rick admitted. He tapped the files in front of him. "They've got something, Emma. Something no one else has. I can't help but wonder... could they do more than just survive?"

Emma raised an eyebrow. "You mean... integrate?"

Rick nodded. "Not just that. What if they could help? What if they could be the ones out there, tracking and capturing other ferals? They'd understand them better than anyone."

Emma considered this, her gaze thoughtful. "It's a bold idea. And it's not impossible. But you know how people are going to react to it. Hell, even Spearhead might push back."

"I know," Rick said, his tone serious. "But think about what it could mean. If these girls can prove there's another way—if they can show that ferals aren't just mindless monsters—it could change everything."

Emma smiled faintly. "You've always been an idealist, Rick."

He chuckled softly. "Yeah, well, someone's got to be."

The two of them sat in silence for a moment, watching the girls as they slept. The possibilities stretched out before them, uncertain but undeniably compelling. Rick knew there was still a long way to go, but for the first time in years, he felt like they were moving in the right direction.

And for now, that was enough.

Emma leaned back in her chair, her coffee in hand, and glanced at the enclosure. The girls stirred faintly, their quiet chirps and the soft rustling of blankets the only sounds from within. "You know," she began, her tone light, "when you first got assigned to this, I thought you were going to bolt."

Rick raised an eyebrow. "Bolt? Really?"

She smirked. "Come on, Rick. You've got a reputation for pushing boundaries, not taking orders. Babysitting four feral kids doesn't exactly scream 'Rick's kind of gig.'"

Rick chuckled, leaning forward to rest his elbows on the desk.

"Fair. But you know me—if something's got a challenge, I'm all in."

Emma sipped her coffee, her expression thoughtful. "This isn't just about the challenge, though, is it? It's about something deeper."

Rick didn't respond immediately. He let the silence stretch, his gaze drifting back to the girls. Raven shifted slightly in her sleep, pulling Luna closer to her side. The sight made him smile faintly.

"They remind me of what's possible," he said finally. "What we're doing here—it's not just about them. It's about everything they represent."

Emma tilted her head, intrigued. "And what do they represent to you?"

"Change," Rick said simply. "For too long, we've just been containing ferals, shoving them into sanctuaries and pretending that's the solution. But it's not. It's just a way to keep the problem out of sight."

Emma set her cup down, nodding slowly. "You're right. Containment isn't a solution. It's... maintenance."

Rick's jaw tightened as he leaned back in his chair. "These girls—if they can prove that ferals aren't just lost causes, that they can be more—they could change the way the world sees them. Maybe even change how we see ourselves."

Emma smiled, her eyes sparkling with a mix of admiration and curiosity. "You really believe they could be the key to all that?"

"I have to believe it," Rick said, his tone resolute. "Because if I don't, who will?"

She studied him for a moment, her expression softening. "You're a good man, Rick. Rough around the edges, sure, but your heart's always in the right place."

"Don't get all mushy on me," Rick teased, though his smirk softened the words. "You're going to ruin my reputation."

Emma laughed quietly. "Fair enough. But seriously, I think you're onto something. These girls... they're special. Even if it's just the four of them, it's worth trying."

Rick nodded. "Yeah, but it's not going to be easy. People don't like change, especially when it challenges what they think they know. And let's be honest—most people think ferals are nothing more than dangerous animals."

Emma sighed, running a hand through her hair. "It's going to take time. A lot of it. But we've got time, and we've got determination. That's got to count for something."

Rick smirked, lifting his coffee mug in a mock toast. "Here's to stubbornness."

Emma clinked her mug against his, grinning. "And to proving the world wrong."

They fell into a comfortable silence, the weight of their shared mission settling over them like a quiet, steady presence. Outside the enclosure, the lab lights dimmed slightly, signaling the late hour. Inside, the girls remained asleep, their small forms huddled together in a way that seemed impossibly peaceful, a stark contrast to their feral instincts.

After a moment, Emma broke the silence, her voice softer this time, almost reflective. "Do you ever think about it? What it might look like... if they succeed?"

Rick tilted his head. "What do you mean?"

"I mean... if they could live in the world, really live in it. What would that even look like? Would people ever accept them? Would they even want to?"

Rick's expression grew serious. "I think it depends. Not just on them, but on us. On how we handle this, how we prove they're more than what everyone thinks."

"And if we fail?" Emma asked, her voice barely above a whisper.

Rick's gaze didn't waver. "Then we fail. But at least we'll know we tried."

Emma smiled faintly, nodding. "I guess that's all we can do."

Rick glanced at the girls one last time, watching as Raven stretched slightly in her sleep before settling back down. "They're worth it," he said quietly. "Every risk, every fight—they're worth it."

Emma reached over and patted his arm gently. "We'll figure it out. One step at a time."

Rick nodded, his expression resolute. "Yeah. One step at a time."

As Rick poured himself a fresh cup of coffee, the girls pressed themselves against the glass, their glowing eyes tracking his every movement. Raven chirped softly, her claws clicking against the floor as she nudged Skye aside for a better view. Luna stayed close to Willow, her small frame half-hidden but her eyes just as curious.

"They're watching your every move," Emma said, amused as she sipped her coffee. "It's like you're the most interesting thing they've ever seen."

Rick glanced over his shoulder at the girls, smirking. "Can you blame them? I'm a captivating guy."

Emma rolled her eyes. "Or they're just hoping you'll bring them food."

Before Rick could respond, the sound of the lab door opening drew their attention. The Boss stepped in, her presence as commanding as ever, though she looked less composed than usual. Her shirt was slightly unbuttoned, her tie hanging loosely around her neck, and her normally pristine hair was tousled, as if she'd just come from a particularly grueling meeting—or a fight.

Rick raised an eyebrow, setting his coffee down. "Rough night?" he asked, his tone casual.

The Boss gave him a sharp look, though there was no real heat behind it. "You could say that," she replied, her voice low and smooth. She crossed the room, her movements as graceful and deliberate as ever, and leaned against the counter.

Rick grabbed another mug and poured her a cup without asking. "Cream and sugar, right?" he asked, already reaching for the container.

She nodded, a faint smile tugging at the corner of her lips. "You know me too well, Rick."

Emma watched the exchange with a mix of curiosity and amusement. "You're awfully comfortable around her," she remarked to Rick, keeping her tone light.

Rick shrugged as he stirred the coffee. "She's just a person. A very old, very intimidating person, sure, but still a person." He handed the mug to the Boss, who accepted it with a quiet word of thanks.

"Most people don't see me that way," the Boss said, her gaze drifting briefly to the enclosure where the girls were still watching intently. "They see a threat, a relic, or worse."

Rick leaned against the counter, his arms crossed. "Well, most people are idiots."

The Boss raised an eyebrow, taking a slow sip of her coffee. "Careful, Rick. You're dangerously close to sounding like you actually respect me."

He smirked. "Don't let it go to your head."

Emma laughed softly, shaking her head. "You two are something else."

The Boss turned her attention to the girls, her sharp gaze softening slightly as she observed them. "They're still not afraid of me," she murmured, more to herself than anyone else. "It's... unusual."

"They're curious," Rick said, following her gaze. "They don't see you as a threat. Maybe because you're not acting like one."

"Or maybe they're smarter than we think," Emma added. "They've already shown they can read people, figure out who's safe and who's not."

The Boss tilted her head, her expression thoughtful. "It's possible. They're certainly unique."

Raven chirped loudly, tapping the glass with her claws as if trying to get their attention. Skye joined in, her movements more chaotic as she clawed at the edge of the enclosure. Even Willow and Luna seemed more animated, their eyes darting between the humans and the coffee pot.

"They want coffee now?" Emma joked, her lips quirking into a smile.

Rick chuckled, shaking his head. "Not a chance. They're hyper enough as it is."

The Boss set her mug down, her gaze lingering on the girls. "They're growing bolder. That's good... but it's also dangerous. Confidence can lead to recklessness."

"We're keeping an eye on that," Emma assured her. "Raven's a good leader—she keeps the others in line."

"For now," the Boss said, her tone cautious. "But they're still young. And young minds are unpredictable."

Rick nodded, his expression serious. "We're ready for that. We know this isn't going to be easy."

The Boss met his gaze, her sharp eyes narrowing slightly. "Just make sure you're ready for what happens if you're wrong."

The room fell quiet for a moment, the weight of her words hanging in the air. The girls, oblivious to the tension, continued their curious chirps and growls, their focus shifting back to their cards and toys.

Finally, the Boss picked up her coffee, her expression softening slightly. "You're doing good work here," she said, her tone quieter. "Don't lose sight of that."

Rick inclined his head, a faint smile tugging at his lips. "We won't."

The Boss turned to leave, her steps measured and deliberate. As the door closed behind her, Emma let out a breath she hadn't realized she'd been holding.

"She always knows how to make an exit," Emma said, shaking her head.

Rick picked up his coffee, his smirk returning. "Keeps things interesting."

Emma laughed softly. "You've got a weird definition of interesting."

"Hey, I'm still here, aren't I?" Rick quipped, raising his mug in a mock toast. "Cheers to surviving another day."

Emma clinked her mug against his, a smile tugging at her lips. "Cheers."

CHAPTER 27

As the quiet returned to the lab, Rick drained the last of his coffee and set the mug down with a satisfied sigh. He rolled his shoulders, his muscles still tense from the earlier commotion. "Alright," he muttered, pushing off the counter. "Guess I should make myself useful."

Emma arched an eyebrow, watching as he walked over to the refrigerated unit along the wall. "What are you up to now?"

Rick glanced back at her, a playful smirk tugging at his lips. "You think I'm going to let those girls turn in without their bedtime snack?"

Emma laughed softly, shaking her head. "You've gone soft, you know that?"

"Soft?" Rick pulled open the unit, the cool air brushing against his face as he grabbed a blood bag. He held it up for emphasis. "This is called building trust, Emma. You should try it sometime."

"I do plenty of that," Emma shot back, her grin widening. "But sure, you're the hero of the hour."

Rick gave her a mock salute, the blood bag swinging lightly in his grip as he made his way toward the enclosure. Inside, the girls perked up immediately, their glowing eyes zeroing in on the prize. Raven, as always, was the first to react. She rose onto her hind legs, her sharp claws clicking against the glass as she chirped loudly to get his attention.

Rick knelt in front of the enclosure, holding up the bag. "Alright, ladies, you know the drill. Play nice, and there's enough for everyone."

He slid the blood bag through the slot, watching as Raven seized it with practiced efficiency. She let out a sharp chirp, a clear command that brought the others scurrying to her side. Their happy noises blended into an excitable symphony, each sound brimming with anticipation.

Skye was the most exuberant, chirping loudly and bouncing on her claws as she eagerly waited her turn. Willow approached more cautiously, sniffing at the bag before delicately taking her share. Luna, smallest of the group, stayed pressed close to Raven, her small frame leaning against her older sister for reassurance as she timidly nibbled her portion.

Emma walked over, her arms crossed as she observed. "You know, if you keep spoiling them like this, they're going to expect it every night."

"Good," Rick replied, leaning back on his heels. "That means they trust us. Trust is the first step to everything else."

Emma smiled faintly, her gaze softening as she watched the girls. "I suppose you're right. They're a lot calmer now than they were a few weeks ago."

"Progress," Rick said, standing up and brushing his hands against his pants. "Slow and steady."

He turned and headed toward the couch in the corner of the lab, collapsing onto it with a dramatic sigh. "Now, if you'll excuse me, I'm going to get a few minutes of shut-eye before something else goes sideways."

Emma chuckled, returning to her desk. "You're lucky I'm the one finishing all the paperwork."

"Lucky? No, no. I call that good delegation," Rick teased, closing his eyes. "Wake me if the world ends."

"Don't tempt me," Emma muttered, her tone laced with amusement.

The lab settled into a peaceful rhythm, the soft hum of the lights and the occasional chirps from the girls filling the space. Emma worked quietly at her desk, the scratch of her pen on paper a steady backdrop. Despite the long day, there was a sense of calm, a rare moment of stillness in their otherwise chaotic world.

Rick, stretched out on the couch, let his mind drift. The weight of the day lingered, but so did the satisfaction of small victories —the girls' progress, their growing trust, and the moments that proved this was all worth it.

As the minutes passed, the younglings finished their meal and returned to their den. Raven settled at the center, her glowing eyes scanning the room one last time before she curled up with her sisters. Even Luna, who had once been so timid, chirped softly as she nestled close, her small frame finally at ease.

Emma glanced over, her gaze lingering on the girls. "They're doing better," she said quietly, more to herself than anyone else.

Rick opened one eye, his voice low but steady. "Yeah. They are."

For a moment, neither of them spoke. The night stretched on, calm and unbroken, as the younglings drifted into sleep. And in that quiet, Rick and Emma allowed themselves a rare moment of hope—for the girls, for their mission, and for the future they were building, one small step at a time.

Rick stretched out on the couch, his body sinking into the worn cushions with a satisfied groan. "Alright, Emma, I'm officially clocking out," he said, closing his eyes. "Wake me if the girls learn how to open the door—or if the building catches fire. Anything less, handle it yourself."

Emma snorted softly from her desk, her pen scratching against the last of the paperwork. "I'm not your babysitter, Rick."

"Could've fooled me," he muttered, smirking faintly as he folded his arms behind his head. "Goodnight, Emma."

"It's not even midnight," she replied, shaking her head. But her voice held no malice, just the familiar rhythm of their banter.

Rick didn't respond, his breathing already evening out as sleep claimed him. Emma glanced over at him, his usually tense features relaxed for once, and smiled to herself. She quietly returned to her work, the sounds of the lab settling into their usual nocturnal rhythm.

The girls had quieted as well, huddled together in their den. Raven, ever the protector, rested at the center, her sharp eyes half-closed but still watchful. Skye twitched occasionally in her sleep, her restless energy persisting even in dreams. Willow had nestled beside her, her calm presence a steadying force. Luna, small and timid, clung to Raven's side, her breathing soft and steady.

Emma paused in her work to watch them, the sight tugging at something deep within her. "You're going to change everything," she murmured softly, echoing Rick's earlier sentiment. She shook her head, a faint smile on her lips, and turned back to her papers.

It was close to dawn when Emma finally finished the last of the day's work. She stretched, her spine cracking softly, and let out a contented sigh. The lab was silent, save for the soft hum of the lights and the occasional chirp from the younglings as they shifted in their sleep.

She stood and crossed the room, glancing one last time at the enclosure. The girls were deep in slumber, their small forms curled together in a way that spoke of safety and trust. It wasn't perfect—there was still so much to do, so much to prove—but it was a start.

Emma grabbed a blanket from a nearby shelf and walked over to the couch where Rick lay. He hadn't moved, his breathing slow and steady. She draped the blanket over him, her movements careful, and sat down in the chair beside him.

For a moment, Emma allowed herself to relax, leaning back and closing her eyes. The weight of the day lingered, but there was a quiet satisfaction in knowing they'd made progress—small, perhaps, but undeniable. The girls were learning, adapting, and proving that they were more than just ferals. They were something new, something that could change everything.

As the first faint light of dawn seeped through the reinforced windows, Emma finally allowed herself to drift off, her head leaning gently against the back of the chair. The lab was still, the hum of machinery blending with the distant, muffled sounds of the outside world. For now, the peace held, fragile but undeniable.

The future loomed ahead—uncertain, daunting, and filled with challenges. Yet, amidst the uncertainty, there was hope. Rick, Emma, and the younglings had carved out a fragile foundation, a growing spark of something better, something worth fighting for.

And for this quiet moment, as the lab rested and the world seemed to pause, that spark was enough.

To Be Continued

Acknowledgments and Creative Contributions
The core ideas, plot, and concepts presented in this book are entirely original to the author. I extend my heartfelt gratitude to OpenAI's ChatGPT for its significant support in brainstorming,

structuring, and refining narrative elements such as dialogue, descriptions, and other creative components throughout the writing process. Its contributions were invaluable in shaping the final work.

Disclaimer

This is a work of fiction. All names, characters, places, and incidents are either products of the author's imagination or used fictitiously. Any resemblance to actual persons, living or deceased, or real events is purely coincidental.

Made in the USA
Coppell, TX
13 February 2026

71114855R00173